FORGOTTEN VISIONS

THE DIVINITIES, BOOK ONE

LIA DAVIS

Forgotten Visions

The Divinities, book 1

© copyright 2016 Lia Davis

Published by Davis Raynes Publishing Group, LLC

PO Box 224 | Middleburg, Fl. 32050

Digital ISBN: 978-1-944060-14-5

Print ISBN: 978-1-944060-15-2

Cover by and Formatting by Glowing Moon Designs

www.AuthorLiaDavis.com

Forgotten Visions

Childhood sweethearts reunite to search for a killer but find themselves in the middle of an ancient war between witches and demons.

Kalissa Bradenton isn't your average coffee shop owner. Born to an elite witch bloodline with a rare genetic mutation, she's a Divinity on a mission. Her investigation into the deaths of her parents sends her straight into the middle of an ancient war between witches and demons. After a near-fatal accident, a childhood friend, Ayden Daniels, comes to her aid and triggers visions of a past she doesn't remember, sparking an old flame and new desires. With their history slowly becoming clearer, Kalissa eagerly sets her sights on mending Ayden's heart and gaining his trust —until a ghost from her past returns to claim her as his demonic mate.

While investigating a series of Divinity murders, Ayden, the new sheriff of Maxville and grandson of the oldest living Divinity, comes face-to-face with the one woman he hopes to have little to no contact with. Old pain rises instantly and is quickly followed by anger and resentment. Through his rare power of adaptability, however, he learns that things from his past may not be what they seem. Hope fills his broken heart, and determination pushes him to do whatever it takes to win Kalissa once more before he loses her forever.

Together, they must find the strength to mend their

tattered souls and learn to love again, while fighting an evil out to destroy the world.

CHAPTER ONE

A cool sensation passed over Kalissa Bradenton's subconscious as she entered her bedroom. She shivered and suddenly found it hard to breathe. A feeling of abandonment rose from deep inside and coiled around her like a cold current. Panic and fear raced through her veins, increasing her heart rate in alarm. The faces of her parents flashed in her mind.

No.

She rushed to her dresser, picked up her phone with shaky hands, and dialed her mother's cell. No answer. With blurred sight and a lump in her throat, she tried her father's. It went straight to voicemail. Kalissa's dread cut through her soul, and the bitter taste of fear rose in her throat as hot tears slid down her cheeks.

Gods no! She dialed again and again. Still nothing. It wasn't like them to not pick up.

Her parents had driven into Jacksonville for dinner to celebrate their fiftieth wedding anniversary. They should've been on their way home.

Kalissa staggered back a few steps as her Divinity gift of visions transported her to the event. One minute she was in her bedroom, and the next, she stood on the side of the highway. A royal blue Mercedes barreled past her and repeatedly flipped across the median and into oncoming traffic on Interstate 10. The sound of crunching metal cut through the stillness of the night, and broken glass littered the ground, trailing to where the car had slammed into a large oak tree.

The heavy, sulfur scent of dark magic flowed on the breeze.

When the vision cut off, tightness gripped her chest, and a lump stuck in her throat.

Pocketing her cell, Kalissa ran from her bedroom to her twin sister's room on the other side of the second floor of their family home. She charged into Khloe's room without knocking. "We have to go. Grab a jacket."

Kalissa ran down the stairs and grabbed her car keys off the small table next to the door. She turned and met Khloe's watery teal eyes. They didn't need to speak out loud because magical twins shared a psychic bond. The words they could hear each other think lingered between them. *Mom and Dad had an accident.* The tears threatening to spill from Khloe's eyes said she already knew. Instant loss and painful sorrow passed between them. Their Divinity link with their parents cut off like someone had flipped a switch, leaving behind a cold and empty space in their hearts.

A blast of frigid air slapped Kalissa in the face as she stepped out into the frozen January night. She ignored the bite of cold wind against her skin and rushed to her car parked a few feet from the front door.

They climbed into the Audi, pulled out of their driveway, and sped down their street toward the highway at speeds sure to get her a healthy ticket if she were caught. A mile down the Interstate, her heart sank at the scene in front of her. Their parents' car sat half wrapped around a tree off the side of the road. It was two in the morning, and the few cars on the road were stopped along the shoulder. Beams of headlights cut through the darkness. Concerned citizens stood, observing the scene in amazement and horror.

Kalissa parked her car on the shoulder, pressed her forehead to the steering wheel, and closed her eyes. With deep, ragged breaths she called to her Divinity gift of visions once more. Images of the accident replayed in her mind, this time with more detail.

A man steps out onto the dark highway, illuminated by the headlights of the Mercedes. The wind blows his long black hair behind him and wraps the hem of his long trench coat around his legs. Startled, Troy hits the brakes hard, but they don't work. He jerks the car to the left and hits an icy patch on the road at the edge of the grassy median, sending the car into a spin. Panic assails him, and he overcorrects. The car slides through the median, hits a dip in the grass, and repeatedly flips into oncoming traffic until it lands in the woods, wrapping around a large oak tree. Troy, and Connie, his wife, die on impact.

Kalissa couldn't hold back the tears as the vision faded. She let the fat, heavy drops fall from her eyes. She allowed herself to break down. To get it out of the way so she could face the authorities.

After a few minutes, she wiped her eyes, took a deep breath, and opened the door. When she stepped out of the car, the wailing of sirens cut through the whispering voices of the bystanders. Red and blue lights flashed wildly as the emergency vehicles advanced toward the accident.

She met Khloe at the front of the car. Kalissa glanced at her sister and asked, "Are you staying here or coming with me?"

"No…yes."

"Me neither," Kalissa grumbled in reply to her sister's indecisive answer. She didn't want to see her parents' lifeless bodies trapped inside the mangled car. Curiosity pulled at her to investigate, see for herself what had killed two powerful, hard to kill witches. She was sure it was a spell that had killed them, her vision told her as much. Still she wanted to see for herself.

Kalissa held out her hand. "Come on." They tried not to draw too much attention to themselves in public with their telepathy. It disturbed those who didn't understand. Although, humans knew about witches and other *magickin*, they held prejudiced views of the supernatural.

Fifteen minutes later, Kalissa stood with her arms crossed over her chest, scowling at the several policemen from the Jacksonville Sheriff's Office as they took statements from witnesses. None of which saw a damn thing except her parents' car lose control.

The slam of a car door drew her attention to the new arrival. Maxville Sheriff's Deputy, Zach Manus, emerged from his unmarked 2011 Chevy Camaro and stalked toward them, deep sorrow and anger laced across his handsome features. His light brown hair was standing a little more on ends than usual. He stopped in front of them, his frown deepening and his golden brown eyes darkening.

Zach, along with most his family, was empathic. Kalissa didn't need to tell him how she felt. A flicker of grief laced his features, then disappeared in a flash. He inhaled deeply, facial features blanked, devoid of emotions. *He put up his shields that block others' emotions*, she mused. Why hadn't he slammed them in place before getting out of the car?

He was testing our mood, she thought sourly to Khloe.

"Don't do that twin thing with me." Zach gave a forced smile.

"What twin thing?" she and Khloe asked at the same time, trying to look innocent. But it was next to impossible while they stood there wrapped in grief.

His dark brows dipped downward as he shifted to look at Fire Rescue working to get the flattened top of the Benz open. Turning his head back in Kalissa's direction, eyes narrowed, he said, "You've been arguing with them?"

She flicked her attention to him. Yeah, she'd argued. JSO had the most irritating and pigheaded officers. The chief detective hadn't wanted any insight from her. Prejudiced bastard.

Zach was like a brother to them, and Kalissa trusted him fully. Sometimes, it was hard to remember that he had a serious, responsible side. Around family, he was playful and sarcastic. But tonight, there were no sheepish smiles or factitious remarks.

"They won't talk to me. I tried to tell them this wasn't

an accident, but they dismissed me like I was nobody." She hugged her waist, staring back at the crushed car. It had been pulled away from the tree and loaded onto a wrecker. "They shouldn't have died," she whispered. What kind of power could kill two immortals like that? Who was that man in her vision? Was he a man at all?

Zach reached out to Kalissa, rubbed her arm with one hand, and took Khloe's hand in his other to draw her into a comforting brotherly hug. "I know. There is a presence of dark magic," he said, making Kalissa look into his golden brown eyes. "I'll handle it," he told her. "Do not investigate this on your own. I mean it, Kalissa. If you find something or have more visions, let me know. I don't need you to suffer the same fate."

He knows something.

Agreeing with Khloe's telepathic acknowledgement, Kalissa traded glances with her sister. She pushed it aside —for now—and scanned the scene one last time before she climbed back into her car.

A man standing behind the growing crowd of onlookers a few feet away caught her attention. He wore a ball cap pulled down low, hiding his face. There was something about him. Something familiar. She narrowed her eyes. He lifted his head in a sudden movement and looked directly at her as if he felt her stare. Their gazes locked.

A scene from her earlier vision popped into her mind. *The man steps out in front of her parents' car.* She concentrated on that scene, stilling it as though she'd pushed the pause button on a TV remote. The eyes of the man in her vision and the eyes of the man looking back at her now were similar. Kalissa stalked toward him without any idea what she was going to do when she got there. Was this the same guy? And if so, why had he caused the accident that had taken her parents away? By damn, she wanted some answers. And Mr. Ball Cap looked guilty of something.

The man moved out of Kalissa's sight, ducking behind the crowd. She increased her pace. When she arrived at the spot where he'd stood moments before, he was gone.

Had she imagined the whole thing?

CHAPTER TWO

Kalissa needed answers. Eighteen months was long enough to sit by and wait for the authorities. The building frustration said it was time to take matters into her own hands.

After much debate and hours of heated discussion, she'd finally convinced her twin to go into the attic to search through their parents' things in hopes of finding clues about their deaths.

On her way up the stairs of the mansion-sized farmhouse, the familiar country vibe their mother loved swirled around Kalissa. She and Khloe shared the same love of their home, and couldn't imagine living anywhere else. That's why, at thirty-two, they still lived there. It was almost customary. Witches lived in covens; communities where *magickin*—witches, fae, and other magic-born beings—lived away from human judgment and prejudices. *Magickin* lived together for most of their lives.

The fact that she and her twin were Divinities was all the more reason to stay close to the coven. There were things lurking in the shadows that wanted possession of the god-like powers running in their blood.

In the attic, she cast a longing glance around the room and the boxes that held their parents' lives. Converted to a home office a month after her parents had moved in, it looked like the rest of the rooms throughout the house. Walls painted white with honey maple wood trim. Their mother's personal touches were scattered throughout the office, lavender and sage curtains hanging from the single small window. Family photos from all stages of life littered the shelves and walls. Kalissa didn't have the heart to take any of them down.

That would be too much of a goodbye. So they would remain as a positive reminder of the loving family they'd once been.

She took a deep, shaky breath and pushed on. It was hard to part with their parents' belongings, but they couldn't hold on to everything. Kalissa's heart ached for the loss of the two people she'd wrapped her life around.

"Hey, Lo, look at this," she said as she pulled a sheet of paper out of a box. The drawing had two big stick people with two little stick people. There was no hair, no hands, and no feet. In the left-hand corner, was a round purple object. Kalissa looked at the drawing more closely. Little Ws in the sky represented birds flying, and the white, puffy clouds told her it was daytime. It was just like her mother to keep their drawings from when they were children. Kalissa inhaled deeply to keep from bursting into sobs.

"Oh, my gods! That is so funny." Her sister leaned over to take the drawing from her. She had a smile on her angelic face that Kalissa hasn't seen much of since the deaths. Khloe turned it over. "Mama wrote on the back. *'Khloe, age four.'*"

"This whole box is full of them. We could make scrapbooks of them by age." Kalissa closed the flaps on the box and moved it to the 'keep' pile. She stood from her chair and stretched, arms straight up over her head with fingers laced.

With a heavy heart, Kalissa moved to the desk and picked up the pile of books that were going to the children's hospital in Jacksonville. Their mother had read those books to them when they were little. Sorrow enveloped her at the thought of parting with them, but she knew the kids at Wolfson's would enjoy them as much as she and Khloe had.

"What's this?" Khloe held out a star-shaped, wooden box.

Kalissa glanced curiously at the hand-carved oak container. After placing the books inside an empty box, she took the five-pointed star from her sister. At closer inspection, there was no visible opening. Puzzlement twirled in her mind, quickly replaced by a nosey need to figure the thing out. *What is it?* She silently repeated Khloe's question.

It looked like one of her mother's trinket boxes at a glance. But it was different. Magical essence coated the wood and made it warm to the touch. The wood felt almost alive, enchanted.

"It could be spelled," Khloe chimed in.

"Where did you get it?"

"In here." Khloe looked inside the box that she was

going through. A piece of her pink-streaked blond hair escaped her ponytail and fell on her face. Their hair and eyes were the only way to tell them apart. Khloe had teal eyes and had cast a glamour spell over her hair so it was a light blond with pink streaks on either side of her slightly oval face.

Kalissa never cared for glamour, never wanted to bring any kind of attention to herself. Her very vivid violet eyes did that enough.

"Ah!" Khloe extracted another, larger wooden box and opened it. "There are ritual items in here. Salt, chalk..." She lifted a piece of parchment paper and carefully unfolded it.

"What is it?" Kalissa moved closer.

"Instructions," Khloe stated in a matter-of-fact tone. Kalissa rolled her eyes as her sister read through the directions.

"Set the star in a circle. Touch each point, and recite the corresponding element counterclockwise, starting with south."

"What?"

Khloe laughed out loud, and Kalissa couldn't hold back her own smile. Picking up the glass jar of salt, Khloe made a perfect circle on the hardwood floor, big enough for the star-shaped box. She took the box from Kalissa and set it inside the circle. Slowly, she touched the left bottom star point. "Fire." She moved to the point to the right, "Air," and continued around speaking the remaining elements of each point: earth, spirit, and water.

When she was done, she raised her hand above the pentacle and said, "I will thee to open. So shall it be."

The top of the star clicked and unlocked.

Kalissa raised her eyes to meet her twin's. Khloe gave a shrug and motioned to open it. A whiff of her mother's perfume hit Kalissa as soon as the lid was removed. Tears stung the backs of her eyes as she lifted the box to her nose and inhaled. A blend of tuberose and vanilla oils invaded her senses, wrapping around her like the hug she longed for. Her mother's face instantly came to mind. Her beautiful smile. The twinkle in her eyes when she looked at her family. Then Kalissa held the star out to Khloe and watched her vivid teal eyes fill with tears as she took in their mother's scent.

Blinking back the tears, Kalissa pulled a single sheet of paper out of the container. It was a letter from their mother.

Hello, my angels,

If you are reading this, then I am not with you. That thought deeply saddens me. I had hoped to explain things to you before my passing. I wish I could be there to help you on your journey. I regret not sharing what I'm about to reveal to you before now. For that, I am so sorry. I had only meant to protect you. The demons are looking for the Sinew, the Divinity power source. It is now up to you to recover the Sinew and find others like you. You will know each other through your birthmarks. Remember what I taught you about your special gifts. Follow the clues I left at the address inside the pentacle, rebuild the Divinities, and protect the Sinew from evil.

Love always, Mom.

Other Divinities? The only others Kalissa knew of were their mother, Noah Daniels—the Maxville Coven elder—and Ayden Daniels—Noah's grandson and the new sheriff. As far as she knew, there weren't many Divinities left. They were born to rare and ancient witch bloodlines. Each bore a unique birthmark, a vivid red rose with a lush green stem and leaves etched on the inside of their left forearm. *Magickin* lore claimed that they were gifts from the gods to help protect them from evil with their Divine gifts and god-like powers.

So what was she to do? Go around searching witches' arms for the Divine Rose?

Kalissa peered back into the pentacle case for the rest of the contents. Sure enough, a second slip of paper that held only a street address rested inside.

Khloe shifted to the laptop they'd brought with them and did a Google search. The address came back as a small law office in Charlotte, North Carolina.

They looked at each other knowingly. A spark of hope rose in Kalissa's aching chest. This had to be the lead they were waiting on. Of course, the address could prove to be nothing, but it was more than they'd had moments before.

"I guess you're going to Charlotte?"

Kalissa frowned at her sister's soft-spoken tone. The longing to investigate together lingered between them. She wanted Khloe to come too but knew a certain deputy would put a halt to all travel plans. "You have to stay here and cover for me. You know what Zach said at the accident site." And several times during the last year and a half.

Khloe smirked. "I know. He's going to be so mad at us."

Kalissa rolled her eyes. He had told her not to follow

leads on her own, but she had to search this out. No way was she telling Zach Manus, deputy and acting sheriff until Ayden arrived, about the letter and that she was doing her own investigating. He would wrap up this morsel in so much red tape it wouldn't see the light of day. He would say it was a matter of police business. But he would be wrong. It was Divinity business, and as a Divinity herself, Kalissa had every right to explore the one clue left by her mother.

After discovering the address, they sat down to collaborate on a story to tell Zach. It would be the first time either of them had ever lied to him. Since he was empathic, could they even pull it off?

THE FOLLOWING MORNING, Kalissa hopped into her Mercedes and headed to Charlotte.

Guilt crept up inside her for leaving Khloe home. Feelings of shutting her out played heavily on Kalissa's mind. But they did have two businesses to run. Even though the Coffee Café did well enough and had a very dependable staff, she still worried about leaving town.

Bradenton Design, on the other hand, was Khloe's domain, and she had a deadline to meet.

One of them had to stay behind. Since Khloe had threatened bodily harm if Kalissa ever got near her computer graphics business, Kalissa had made the trip to check on the address.

Five hours into the trip, her phone rang, like it did every hour. She pressed a button on her steering wheel that allowed her to talk hands-free—thanks to Bluetooth technology and Khloe's know-how to install it.

"Hi, Lo."

"Are we there yet?" Khloe giggled.

Kalissa laughed. "Almost. Tom Tom says it's another thirty minutes away."

"Oh, good. Because I am exhausted."

Kalissa rolled her eyes, only realizing her sister wasn't there to see it. "You're not the one driving."

"Yeah, but all this anxiety has done a number on my nerves." The smile had left Khloe's voice.

Kalissa sighed. They hated to be apart from each other. The only other time they'd spent more than twenty-four hours away from one another was when Khloe had stayed the night in the hospital after taking cold medicine. They'd found out the hard way that night that she was highly sensitive to medications and alcohol.

"So, what time are you going to the...conference in the morning?"

She smiled. Zach was there, and Khloe didn't want to give anything away. They'd told him Kalissa was going to a restaurant seminar just outside Charlotte. Kalissa had every intention of attending the seminar. Zach thought it was a weekend-long conference and trade show. It was actually a lunch-and-learn event. The attendees were to meet at the conference room in the hotel Kalissa was staying at around noon, have a catered lunch, and then listen to a couple of CEOs from some of the largest restaurant chains in the United States talk about management and leadership skills. It was going to be a very boring afternoon. If all went well, Zach would never know her real reason for going to North Carolina.

Zach, Khloe, and Kalissa had grown up together and treated each other like family. He was the protective older brother they'd never had, and he would blow a gasket if he knew what Kalissa was up to. He'd told her that he would handle it and that she was to trust him to get to the bottom of her parents' deaths. Eighteen months later, Zach was no closer than he was the first day.

She doubted the new sheriff would be any better. Even if he was Zach's cousin.

"I'll be there as soon as the doors open," she answered. Khloe fell silent. "I'll let you go and call you in the morning."

Khloe released a heavy sigh. "Okay. Call when you get up before you do anything else."

A soft laugh escaped Kalissa's lips. She could almost see the pout on her sister's face. "I promise. Love you."

"Love you."

She pushed the button on the steering wheel to end the call. A yawn took hold of her, and she wished she'd stopped off at the last rest area. Her eyes burned, and she repeatedly blinked to try and relieve some of the sting from driving fatigue, while the urge to rub them strongly tugged at her. Relief washed over her at the sight of the Charlotte exit sign indicating her turn was next.

A few minutes later, a car sped by and jumped over into her lane. She gasped, heart dropping to her abdomen as she jerked the steering wheel to the right to avoid hitting the car. It was too late. Metal scraped metal as the vehicles collided.

The impact pushed her car off the road. Everything happened so fast, she couldn't concentrate or grasp on to reality. Her heart pounded furiously behind her ribcage as a rushed panic assailed her. Kalissa hit the gas instead of the brake. The Benz barreled off into the woods and slammed into something hard. The airbag deployed into her face, slamming her head into the driver's-side window. A sharp pain shot through her skull. A blaring horn was the last thing she heard before falling into the dark void of unconsciousness.

AYDEN DANIELS HAD ONLY BEEN in Charlotte an hour before his cousin, Zach, called with a favor. No. Not quite a favor. A request that sounded more like a plea.

"You're shittin' me."

"I'm afraid not. Charlotte PD said it was a hit and run."

Right. "Please tell me she's…"

"She's alive. A bump on the head, but she'll be okay." Zach hesitated before continuing. "I know how you feel about her, but you'll have to go get her."

A muttered curse slipped from his lips at the same time his heart lodged in his throat. "Fine." The word came out in an irritated huff. Ayden hung up and wished he had never answered the damn phone. No, that wasn't completely true. He would never forgive himself if something had happened to Kalissa that he could've prevented.

She was the one person he'd hoped to avoid as much as possible once he'd taken his place as sheriff of Maxville. It wasn't that he disliked her. That was the problem. Despite his better judgment, he still cared too damn much for the woman. He was a glutton for punishment.

The mere mention of her name made his pulse race with excitement. His body responded to just the thought of seeing her again after fifteen years. But his mind screamed to walk away. To let her be. She was trouble, and a hazard to his heart. She'd broken it once; tore it right out of his chest at the age of seventeen.

A human friend had laughed at the mention of their young age and Ayden's claim that she was the only one for him. A mistake on his part to confide in a human and expect him to understand *magickin* way of life. *Magickin* children developed at a faster rate. At the age of seventeen, he was as mature as most twenty-five-year-old humans, and fully aware that he had met his eternal companion.

They were life partners, magical mates destined to spend their immortal lives together. And to find one at such a young age was a gift.

A gift she'd stolen from him.

It was unclear whether a Divinity could have more than one life partner. As far as he knew, she was the only one for him. At least, that's what his heart said. He'd tried to search for another. To put the past behind him and mend his broken heart, but no other could fill the void.

Taking a deep, long breath and then exhaling slowly, he picked up his keys from the nightstand and moved toward the door. Putting it off was not going to make it less painful.

Ten minutes later, he parked in the half-empty hospital emergency room parking lot, climbed out of his Jeep Wrangler, and walked toward the entrance. Dread, excitement, and anger filled him, making his head pound, and his heart ache. What would he say to her? How would she react to him?

He entered the double glass doors and walked up to the security desk. Pulling out his badge, he introduced himself. "Sheriff Ayden Daniels, here for Kalissa Bradenton."

The woman behind the desk wore a blue security uniform, her salt and pepper hair pulled back in a tight bun on the top of her head. She appeared to be in her early fifties. Humans looked their age. Witches and other magical beings, once they'd reached maturity, aged slower and often lived to be about two hundred years of age. They never showed the signs of aging until the last seventy-five years of life. Divinities, however, were immortal; they didn't die of natural causes, or ever age past thirty-five.

The security woman looked at his badge and then back up to his face. "You're a little out of your jurisdiction, Sheriff." She spoke with a thick southern drawl.

He smiled at her. "Yes. I'm a family friend and in the area on personal business. Her sister asked me to come."

The woman frowned, looking down at her computer screen. She clicked on the keyboard with her two-inch-long fingernails. "Go through those doors." She pointed to the double doors to Ayden's left. "She's down the hall in room 127."

He thanked the woman and walked towards Kalissa's room. A policeman stood outside her door, talking to a nurse. The young officer smiled widely and seemed to enjoy the conversation a little too much for it to be business-related. However, waves of discomfort came from the nurse. She shifted nervously and glanced at her watch several times in the short while it took Ayden to reach them. When he approached, relief flooded the woman, and she took his appearance as her chance to escape the officer's attentions, excusing herself with a shy smile before darting off to the nurses' station.

Ayden read the nametag on other man's uniform shirt. "Evening, Officer Meyers. I'm Ayden Daniels."

Officer Meyers nodded. "Yes, Chief Wells said you were on your way." He turned to look at Kalissa's closed door and frowned. Meyers looked back at Ayden. "She'll need a ride, too. The car's totaled. It was sandwiched between two trees. If it weren't for the airbags…" Meyers paused, shook his head, and after a second, continued. "Anyway, when she came to, she said she was clipped in the front by another car. Typical hit and run."

Ayden clenched his jaw, forming a tic in his temple. There was nothing typical about a hit and run, especially when it involved a Divinity. He was following leads that comprised similar 'hit and runs.' Too much evidence pointed to a serial killer. The victims were all Divinities.

"Meyers." The officer turned his gaze back to Ayden. "Go see if Miss Bradenton is ready for discharge while I speak with her."

Meyers drew his dark eyebrows together until they looked like a unibrow. He hesitated for another second before he dropped his shoulders and walked to the nurses' station a few feet away.

Rookie. Ayden released a soft chuckle. Officer Meyers was probably still in his first year on the force. The smile dissipated as Ayden squared his shoulders and turned toward Kalissa's door.

CHAPTER THREE

Kalissa sat on the edge of the hospital bed and swung her legs back and forth in frustration. Anger swarmed inside her like pissed off bees trapped inside a hive. Her beloved car was impounded and possibly totaled. If she hadn't been knocked unconscious, the driver of the other car would have faced her... her what? Would she have beaten him with visions? The All-Seeing Eye?

Whatever. Who was she fooling? Yes, she took self-defense classes and sparred with her sister on a regular basis, but she was as tame as a lamb. She could never intentionally hurt anyone.

The clock on the wall said she'd been awake for forty-five minutes. She was still unsure how long she'd been out of it.

She hated medical facilities. The heavy stench of anti-septic turned her stomach.

Where was that freaking nurse with her discharge papers?

Why did it always take ten times longer than it should to get in and out of the ER?

It was unusually and eerily quiet for an emergency room. The only sounds were the beeping of the monitors at the nurses' station, footsteps outside her room, and muffled voices. Her closed door did nothing to calm her rattled nerves, or soothe her irritation.

Her legs stilled as a new set of footsteps halted outside her door. A familiar magical signature floated through the air. She listened, but couldn't make out the hushed voices through the wood.

After a few minutes of muffled conversation, the door slowly opened. A man walked in and closed the door behind him.

At first, confusion clouded her mind. A dull headache crept into her temples, and a hint of panic rose in her chest. The man that stood inside her hospital room looked familiar and put off a magical energy that called to her. He had golden brown hair and the most vivid baby blue eyes she'd ever seen. And a body that belonged on the front cover of Men's Health magazine. Her gaze roamed over his broad shoulders and down his chest.

Shifting her eyes back to his face before she really embarrassed herself, realization hit her. This was Zach's cousin from California. The new sheriff of Maxville.

"Ayden?" she asked with a smile. "I hardly recognized you." Now she remembered. He'd visited the coven during the summers and had hung out with them when they were kids. But this was a big change from the Ayden she knew fifteen years ago.

Her gaze drifted over him again. The t-shirt he wore

left nothing to the imagination. It clung to him, showing off those hard muscles and tight abs perfectly. Kalissa had a sudden urge to run her hands down his chest.

Did he feel as good as he looked?

She forced her gaze away to look down at the floor in front of her as heat rose in her cheeks.

Get a grip, Kalissa, she scolded herself. "Did Zach send you?" she asked, trying not to ogle him like a tiger would a piece of raw meat. But she couldn't look away for long. As soon as he moved, her eyes flicked up and found his.

He narrowed his eyes as he stalked toward her, looking less than thrilled to be there. But there was a hint of something else in his gaze. Something that looked vaguely like pain, or sadness.

Several seconds passed before he spoke, and when he did, Kalissa's heart skipped a beat. Her body warmed, reacting in a way it never had before. "Your sister's worried."

The statement confused her. It caught her off guard. She opened her mouth to reply, but he spoke first. "She's the emergency contact on your driver's license."

She looked down to her linked fingers in her lap and asked, "Why are you here?" The silence made her look back up to see a pained expression passing across his face. "I didn't mean it like it sounded. I meant…"

"I know what you meant," he harshly cut off her statement.

She blanched at his tone and looked back down and picked nervously at her fingernails. Ayden's words felt too close to rejection. Her chest tightened, and she didn't understand why.

His hand came out and captured her by the chin. She froze, finding it hard to breathe as he gently raised her face to meet his gaze. His expression softened, but he still looked at her in irritation.

She hadn't recalled doing anything to warrant such a reaction from him. Squaring her shoulders, she pushed the anxiety aside. "If it's such a bother to come here, then leave. I'll catch a cab to my hotel."

He knitted his brows, and after a moment, he relaxed. Not saying a word or explaining, he reached up to move her hair away from her temple to look at her injury. She wanted to smack his hand away, but an electrifying current swept through her when the tips of his fingers touched her skin. Desire and heat swirled inside her, threatening to erupt into an inferno. And it scared the hell out of her.

The sensation left as soon as he lowered his hand, allowing the hair to fall back in place. But returned when he touched her cheek with the backs of his fingers. "I was in the neighborhood." His tone was gentler. She gave him a conflicted look. *Was he bipolar?* One minute, he acted like he didn't want to be there, and the next, he was okay with it. What was his problem?

He smiled at her and said, "I was in town on personal business. Zach called and asked me to check on you."

"Oh." It was all she was able to say. She'd completely lost herself in Ayden's baby blue eyes and the weird, erotic feelings he raised in her. Maybe his mood swings were contagious.

She was so captivated by the swirls of silver that

danced around his pupils that she didn't notice when Ayden shifted forward to stand between her legs. His hand cupped her cheek as he lowered his head to hers. Just before their lips touched, a light knock sounded on the door. Ayden dropped his hand and backed away from her a second before the nurse walked into the room.

Damn nurse. She resisted the urge to kick the woman out.

"You're free to go, Ms. Bradenton," the nurse said with a chipper voice as she walked over and handed the discharge papers to her. "Are you sure you don't need a prescription?"

It took her a couple of seconds to form a coherent thought. "Yes, I'm sure. Thanks." Like all *magickin*, she had a high tolerance for pain. Plus, most human pain medications messed with their nervous systems. She shared the same unusual sensitivity to meds and alcohol as Khloe. Though her sensitivity wasn't as severe. She could drink wine in moderation without an adverse effect. Her twin, on the other hand, was drunk as a skunk after only a couple of sips. It was very easy for them to accidently overdose, so they had to be careful what they took. Kalissa had lucked out that the ER doctor had treated witches before and was fully aware of what medications they could take.

The nurse gave one last bob of the head and left the room.

Kalissa had never felt more relieved to leave a place than she did at that moment. She hopped off the bed, only to have her balance thrown off. A wave of dizziness overtook her, and her knees refused to hold her weight.

Ayden reached out with one of his large arms and wrapped it around her waist to help her regain her balance. "You'll stay with me," he commanded.

Kalissa shook her head. "I have a reservation."

"Where are you staying?" he asked.

She told him, and he laughed out loud. When she shot him a peeved looked, he shook his head and said, "I'm sorry. That's where I'm staying. I'm sure they'll understand."

CONCERN SURGED through him at her dizzy spell when she hopped off the hospital bed. After making sure she was strong enough to walk on her own, he led her to his Jeep and drove to the hotel in silence.

They entered the hotel lobby and went straight to the front desk. The same perky young redhead that had checked him in over an hour ago greeted them with a smile. "Can I help you, Mr. Daniels?" The bright, warm smile diminished slightly when her peridot eyes shifted to Kalissa standing next to him. Envy swirled off the hotel clerk. *Women.*

"I hope so," he said, giving her a mildly seductive smile when she looked back at him. "I would like to upgrade my room to a suite. Miss Bradenton had a reservation, which she would like to cancel since she will be staying with me." He reached down and took Kalissa's hand in his as a warning for her not to protest. She was about to. The shift in her mood told him that. Stubbornness rolled off her, wanting to reject his proposal.

The desk clerk frowned, but quickly recovered, glancing to the computer screen. A few seconds later, she swiped a set of keys and handed them to him. "There is a cancellation fee…"

Her sentence cut off when he took her hand that held the key cards and stroked his pinky over her wrist. "Can it be waived?" He leaned into her a half an inch.

Her cheeks colored, and she pulled her hand back. He let it go, taking the keys from her.

"Let me…see what I can do."

Moments later, Kalissa and Ayden were on the elevator. Ayden laughed at Kalissa's narrowed-eyed gaze. She hadn't said anything, but she didn't need to. "You would have done the same thing."

She lifted her head in a stubborn, proud pose. "I thought only women used their looks to get what they wanted."

"If you got it, use it."

She didn't respond. She was jealous. He'd picked up on the emotion at the front desk, when he'd flirted with the clerk. That amused and confused him.

Her reaction to him at the hospital was that of an old friend seeing him for the first time in fifteen years. Buried pain resurfaced. But he couldn't resist touching her. It had gone downhill from there.

She was the same Kalissa he'd fallen in love with over fifteen years ago, but she didn't remember him. Ayden, like the rest of his family, was empathic. Being a Divinity only amplified the empathy, and, combined with his very rare power of adaptability, gave him the ability to pick up on others' feeling and thoughts. He'd grasped on to Kalissa's gift of visions and had used it with his empathy to see into her mind. And into the past. There was a hole in her memory. His anger dissolved into confusion. Hope sparked into a tiny flame. That flame grew with every minute they were together. Who would erase her memory? Better yet, why erase her love for him but not all of him from her memories? How in the hell was that even possible?

The main reason for invading her memories, besides being a selfish bastard, was to find out why she'd dumped him for someone else so many years ago. He hadn't expected her memory to be altered.

Is this my second chance? Can I trust her with my heart again?

It was wishful thinking. There wasn't a second chance. He wouldn't allow it, couldn't allow it. Because if she never returned those feelings...

He cut that thought right off and opened the door to their suite. Ayden held the door for Kalissa. She muttered, "Thank you," and continued on to the bedroom, closing the door behind her.

CHAPTER FOUR

When Kalissa woke up the next morning, Ayden was gone. His duffel bag still sat on top of the small dresser, but the sofa bed he'd slept on was folded up. She still couldn't get over the way he'd manipulated the young woman at the front desk to upgrade his room to a one-bedroom suite for the two of them. He'd used a sexy smile and his good looks to get the clerk to cancel Kalissa's reservation and waive the cancellation fees.

Hell, the way he had smiled and spoken in a low husky voice, Kalissa would have given him anything he asked.

How would that voice sound whispered in her ear? A heat wave of desire rolled through her as it had in the hospital room. He had been about to kiss her before they were rudely interrupted. And she would have let him. Even just the thought of his mouth on hers weakened her knees. And brought on the tang of panic she'd fought for years to control.

They'd been friends when in their teens. They'd hung out at the coven with the rest of the youth. She didn't remember having feelings like that toward him. But she wondered how it would have felt to be kissed by Ayden Daniels. What would he taste like?

She started to wonder if the attraction to him was in her head, a result of the bump she'd gotten from the accident. Men like Ayden didn't look at her like that. Not many men gave her more than a glance. That was fine by her. After the relationship she'd had with Liam Loomis, she wasn't interested in another.

Of course, she didn't help in that department either. She never wore makeup, and most times, her long, dark blond waves were piled on top of her head in a messy bun. Simplicity was her calling card. Leave the dramatics to her sister.

She and Liam had dated in high school, and the relationship continued through college until he'd collapsed with heart failure during football practice. Liam had anger and aggression issues, which had caused many heated fights between them. She'd been relieved to finally be out from under his control, but saddened because she'd been the reason for his sudden heart condition.

Then she'd gotten the painful news six months later that his mother had killed herself. It had sent a wave of grief over Kalissa. She had loved his mom. Barbra was the sweetest, most loving woman.

Her cell phone rang, bringing Kalissa back to the present. She picked up the phone from the nightstand and glanced at the caller ID. Khloe. With a smile, she answered. "*Hola.*"

"Hi. How's your head?"

"Feels better. I'm heading out in a few," she said while

she stood, and then sat back down on the edge of the bed, shoulders hunched. "Oh, no."

"What?" Khloe had a hint of panic in her voice.

"I don't have my bag." The only clothes she had were the ones she'd worn the day before and Ayden's shirt that fit her like a nightgown.

"Just conjure up some clothes, Kalissa. We're Divinities. With god-like powers."

She wasn't sure she liked her twin's tone. There was an eye roll in there. But she was right. Kalissa, Khloe, and others like them had the power to conjure things they desired. Within reason. The three-fold law wasn't a myth, and Karma was more than happy to let it be known.

The truth was, Kalissa didn't fully trust her magic. It had failed her on many accounts, but mostly, her visions brought her too much pain. Physical and emotional. "I guess I could try."

Taking a deep breath, she closed her eyes and visualized the articles of clothing that she wanted from her room. Every detail was important, especially where the garments came from. She didn't want to take someone else's clothes off their back. That would be embarrassing for both parties involved.

She held her hands out in front of her and imagined standing in front of her dresser at home. Carefully, she chose a pair of panties, a t-shirt, and a pair of jeans from her drawers. Then willed them into her hands where she sat on the hotel bed. She opened her eyes and smiled.

"I did it. No pain."

Khloe's soft laugh came over the phone. "See. You're not defective."

Normally, she'd argue with her sister, but today, Kalissa wasn't in the mood. She had to get out of the hotel without Ayden seeing her.

"So...what did you sleep in?" The wickedness in Khloe's voice made her heart flutter. Images of Ayden popped into her mind.

His baby blue eyes lit with desire and need. His soft lips crushed against hers. Kalissa shuddered and shoved all those steamy visuals to the back of her mind. That was all they could be, visuals and fantasies. Thanks to Liam, she couldn't get that close to another man.

"Ayden lent me a shirt. And before you say it, I slept in the bed, and he was on the sofa."

"I wasn't going to say a word." Khloe fell silent, and after a few moments, said, "Have you talked to him? Has he said anything unusual?"

"No. Should he?"

"I don't know. Men can be weird."

It was an odd thing to ask. Then again, Khloe could be purposely cryptic at times. So Kalissa dismissed it. "I better get going."

"Oh, all right. Love you."

"Love you, too."

She hung up the phone, grabbed her tote, and entered the living room. When she passed the small table, she saw the hotel notepad positioned near the edge with writing on it. Curiously, she stopped and peered down to read it.

Meet me downstairs for breakfast. Ayd.

Great. He probably had a front-row view of the elevators, waiting for her.

~

"I CAN'T BELIEVE you didn't tell me," Ayden growled into the phone.

Zach released a heavy sigh. "I wasn't sure. I asked Papa once if it was possible to take a Divinity's memory. He said it was, but he also said it's a dark spell and only the warlocks are brave enough to try it. I didn't give it a second thought until you mentioned it."

The knowledge that his cousin had information and didn't share it irritated him. Zach knew how the breakup had killed him. Why hadn't he told him?

"How long have you known?" he asked, trying to sound calm.

"Not long. I first suspected it after her parents died. I'm sure Lo knew longer than that, but she never said anything to me." Uncertainty flowed through Zach's words.

Ayden pushed it away, for now. "Someone took her memories," he said through clenched teeth. What pissed him off was that someone had wanted them split up enough that they would alter Kalissa's mind. She was not the cause of his broken heart. Not directly. "What about that guy she started dating?"

"Liam?" Zach said with disgust in his voice. "He was human…and is no longer a problem."

Ayden wasn't sure if he wanted to ask about the last part of that statement. He looked up to see Kalissa emerge from the elevator and resented his body for reacting. Her blond hair hung loosely, cascading around her shoulders to stop over her breast. She turned toward him, and violet eyes met his. For a moment, he lost all coherent thought. Clenching the phone tighter, he broke from the dangerous thoughts of possessing the only woman he'd ever loved and ended his call with Zach. "Well, keep hunting. Someone wanted me out of her life, and I want to know who."

His cousin agreed, and they hung up. Ayden sighed. He'd have to win Kalissa's heart all over again. First, he would get to the bottom of her missing memories. This time around was going to be different. The pull to do something he should have been done years ago was too strong. Undeniably so. She was his life partner. She belonged to him. He was going to see to it that she became his bonded eternal companion, even if it killed him.

Ayden stood and pulled out a chair when she reached the table. "Morning."

"Morning," she replied softly, not meeting his eyes. She sat down and scooted her chair in before Ayden could do it.

He took his seat next to her. "I thought we could go get your things from impound after we eat." She tensed. But it was so subtle he would have missed it if his shields were up that blocked others' emotions. He'd lowered those mental shields when she got off the elevator. That way, he could read and monitor her emotions.

She was in Charlotte for a reason. He had a hunch it was the same reason he'd come.

The waiter came by to take their orders and pour their coffee. After he'd left, Ayden added, "I have to make a stop first. My father left me a package at his lawyer's office before he died." He watched her take a nervous sip of her coffee and set the cup down in front of her gently, almost too calculated. She was very good at remaining calm and controlled. But the empath in him sensed the uneasiness that hung around when someone was hiding something. "That's why you're here," he accused, not taking his eyes off her.

She snapped her eyes to his, shocked. He smiled. She narrowed her eyes. "You're empathic." He nodded. Her shoulders dropped in defeat.

"The Divinities that died left a package of some sort for their surviving children." He paused when the waiter came with their breakfast. He waited until they were alone before speaking again. "I've been investigating the cases. Papa provided me with as much information as he could. There seems to be a trail of clues. Papa said your mother knew where the Sinew is hidden."

Eyes wide, she peered at him. Curiosity rolled off her in waves, and he could almost see the wheels turning in her head as the questions piled in. "What cases? How is my mother involved?"

Her questions stopped when he placed a hand on top of hers. "There've been others who've had accidents."

"Besides our parents?"

He gave her a nod in answer and wasn't surprised that she knew his parents had died from a plane crash. She'd probably heard the news from Zach.

"How many?" she asked.

"Five. Two are missing, the other three are dead." He looked into her violet eyes and wanted to take her back to Maxville where she belonged, far from harm's way. "Two of the Divinities killed are from Canada and out of my jurisdiction. Their coven isn't sharing. Plus, I'm not sure if their deaths are even related. The other, Caleb, was the husband of one of the missing Divinities."

"Angelica," Kalissa whispered.

Ayden nodded. "You knew them?"

Kalissa shook her head. "No, but my mom talked about them. They had two children. I think they are about ten years older than us."

"I was hoping to run into them. If Angelica is still alive, then they'll be looking for her." Ayden took the last bite of his pancakes and chewed before speaking again. "We'll have to get our packages and move on."

"We?"

"Yes. I'm not letting you out of my sight."

"I don't need a babysitter," she replied with a hint of anger.

"You were run off the road last night and almost killed," Ayden shot back, barely controlling the anger bubbling inside him.

"That was just an accident..." She broke off and looked back at him with realization in her gaze. Those beautiful violet eyes darkened as she glared. "Okay, let's pretend it was a deliberate attack on my life. What good would it do to kill me?"

"You are investigating your parents' deaths and pose a threat."

She folded her arms over her chest and hardened her stare. "What about you? You're investigating all of the deaths."

The corner of his mouth lifted in a sideways smirk. "I've had my run-ins."

"And?"

"My Divine gift allows me to use others' abilities. Papa calls it the power of adaptability. I can adapt others' powers as my own. It apparently works with demons, too." Ayden tried not to be amused with her annoyance but failed. He liked the way her violet eyes changed with her moods. They became a deep, almost royal purple when she was angry or sad and lightened with swirls of lavender when she was happy or excited.

Without thinking, he reached over to move her dark blond hair aside to look at the wound on her forehead. And to feel the silken strands against his fingers. She flinched slightly when he touched her face. He brought his eyebrows together in a frown. "Does it still hurt?"

"No." It came out in an almost nervous squeak. She took his hand in hers to set it back on the table. Their hands never made it to the table. Instead, he brought hers to his lips. A sudden intake of breath escaped her as soon as his lips touched the backs of her fingers. His rose birthmark tingled as if awakened. He was sure Kalissa's did the same when her desire reached out to him like a lover's caress.

They were true magical mates.

She snatched her hand out of his grasp. "What did you just do?" she asked, moving her arm out of sight under the table.

"Nothing," he said with a smirk. "Come on. I want to show you something before we leave."

CHAPTER FIVE

Silence encircled Kalissa and Ayden inside the elevator as it glided toward their floor. She didn't know what to say to him. He was like a stranger, but surges of familiarity seeped into her subconscious. When she tried to recall memories of him from her childhood, sharp pain shot through her temples. The headache became almost crippling when she used her gift of visions to see into the past. A reminder of why she'd locked them down after Liam died.

That only happened once. She wasn't into self-inflicted pain.

Ayden noticed, too. He looked at her with concern etched on his face and reached out to her. She waved him off, unsure what his touch might do.

What the hell had happened at the table before getting on the elevator? The second his lips had touched her skin, powerful, warm, electric energy coated her fingers and spread down her wrist to her rose birthmark on the inside of her left forearm. Rivers of roaring pleasure sailed through her, and her Divine Rose pulsated like it was alive, a breathing organism.

It had been strangely arousing, and frightening.

Once inside their room, she sat down on the sofa and waited for him to gather his things. A few minutes later, he came out of the bedroom and handed her a file folder before sitting next to her. She took it with a frown, opened the folder, and gasped. Tears sprang to her eyes as a lump formed in her throat. It was her parents' case file. She closed it and shoved it at him.

"I…can't." She moved to stand up, but his hand on her arm stopped her.

"I'm sorry. I didn't…" He trailed off with a muttered curse. He opened the folder, pulled out a single photo, and handed it to her.

Kalissa hesitantly peered at the picture. When she saw the man in the photo, her mouth fell open. It was the same man she had seen in her vision of the accident and again at the scene. "Who is he?" she said, darting her eyes to Ayden's face.

"You recognize him?"

"He caused the accident." Kalissa pushed the photo back to him. "Who is he?" she asked again.

"His name is Demetrius. He was spotted at the other accidents, too. I believe he also had something to do with my parents' deaths. That's all I know right now, other than that he's a demon General for Khan." Ayden put the photo back inside the folder. "Zach's looking for more information. Papa gave him access to the archives."

Kalissa didn't try to keep the anger out of her voice.

"How come it took so long? I mean, it's been eighteen months."

"Because none of us knew until I found my father's note," Ayden said soothingly. She glared at him in suspicion. What did he know? Was he keeping something from her? "My father left me clues. They led to a note he'd written, explaining what he'd found out and telling me to pick up my final package from his lawyer's office," he explained.

His father's note sounded similar to the one her mother had left; only hers wasn't so informative. "And Todd knew about Demetrius?" No doubt Zach knew, too. And she'd wasted her guilt on lying to him about this trip.

Ayden dropped his shoulders and nodded. "My father and your mother were actively investigating the disappearances of Angelica and Kristof Rayners, and the death of Caleb."

Kalissa frowned. "I didn't know." He took her hand in his, and she looked back at him.

"We need to pick up our packages and find out where the next destination is." He stood up and offered his hand to her.

She took it, but only because she needed the support. The new information twirled dizzyingly inside her mind. She'd stepped in the middle of something that was way over her head.

TEN MINUTES LATER, they pulled into the parking lot of The Law Offices of Sindee Donnelly. The office building was much smaller than Kalissa had initially pictured. Most law offices in Jacksonville were large, expensive buildings. The modest building in front of her was a house turned into a business. Multi-colored brick covered the exterior, with white trim around the windows and doors. The front porch stretched across the front of the home with two white columns—one on either side of the steps.

She and Ayden entered the law office into a large open room that must have been a living room. They crossed the bamboo floors to the receptionist's desk located in the center of the room. The dark-haired woman behind the desk had eyes only a *magickin* possessed, midnight blue with flecks of gold. She smiled in greeting. "Sindee will be right with you."

Kalissa smiled back and let Ayden place his hand on the small of her back and gently direct her to a light brown leather loveseat against the wall. "Watch what you think. The receptionist is telepathic," he whispered, his lips inches from her ear.

She tensed, but managed to whisper back, "That's good to know." That explained how the receptionist knew they were there to see Sindee. It wasn't unusual for witches to be telepathic or have other gifts if they were from one of the Divinity bloodlines.

They didn't wait long before the receptionist called out, "Sindee will see you now."

Kalissa stood and followed him down the hall without direction from the receptionist. "You've been here before?"

"I helped my father with a few things," he answered, not looking at her.

Stepping inside Sindee's office, Kalissa's questioning stare shifted from Ayden's back to glance around the room. It was large, elegantly furnished with a leather loveseat and two matching recliners on one side. On the other side was a large, cherry-stained oak desk. A woman dressed in a cream-colored pantsuit and wearing a warm, welcoming smile stood up to walk from behind the desk. Her strawberry-blond hair hung loosely, cascading to her waist. She went straight to Ayden and pulled him into a tight hug. He returned it with a brief hug of his own and then reached around his back to take her hands in his. "Sin, this is Kalissa." His smile was uneasy, almost forced.

He was uncomfortable. Kalissa sensed it as the emotion brushed against her aura. That was strange. Kalissa wasn't empathic, yet she clearly felt his tension.

Sin, as Ayden had addressed her, turned to look at Kalissa. She let go of Ayden's hands and smiled. "You look just like your mother." She gathered Kalissa into a hug, only to pull back with concern in her eyes a moment later. "You must keep your third eye open at all times," she whispered in Kalissa's ear, then released her and walked back to her desk.

The third eye was a witch's psychic intuition. To Kalissa, it was the source of her visions. It was something she had locked down several years ago. How did Sindee know that?

Ayden gestured for Kalissa to take a seat. Together, they sat down in the chairs across the desk from the beautiful lawyer. She pulled out two FedEx envelopes from one of her drawers and handed one to each of them. "Jacen and

Lydia Rayners have already retrieved theirs. I tried to hold them off, but that Lydia is very persistent."

Ayden let out a sigh. "How long ago?"

"Two days ago."

Ayden muttered a curse. "I'm sorry…"

Sindee held up her hand and shook her head. "No need to be sorry. You didn't come here on a social call." She smiled and stood. Ayden and Kalissa stood as well and followed her out of the office to the receptionist's area. Sindee turned to them. "The two of you will have to visit when things settle down."

Kalissa thought it was an odd thing to say. Did she actually think they were a couple? Ayden took her arm, pulling her out of her thoughts to guide her out the door and across the parking lot. She waved to Sindee as she got into the Jeep and put her seatbelt on with a click. "That was a little strange. She felt like a Divinity, but different."

Ayden sighed. Kalissa snapped him a narrow-eyed look. Bad news always followed a sigh like that. "What?"

"Sindee is what Papa calls a Dark Divine."

Kalissa almost hated to ask, but curiosity got the better of her. "What are they?"

"They're the demons' version of the Divinity. They only started to make an appearance about a century ago. Most are as dark as the demons. Some, like Sindee, were raised by witches and stay loyal to our side of the war." He fell silent, and she thought about it for a few seconds.

"And the others side with the demons." It wasn't a question. She needed to hear it out loud. They were fighting demons and the Dark Divine. "These dark counterparts of ours, are they equal to our powers, or stronger?"

"Equal. As far as we know. Sindee is the only one we have had contact with," Ayden answered as he pulled out of the parking lot and onto the road.

After a long silence, Kalissa finally spoke. "What about the envelopes?"

He glanced at her from the driver's seat and then looked back to the road. "Open yours first."

She tore open the cardboard FedEx envelope, peered inside, and pulled out two sheets of paper. One look at the writing made her frown. "It's not in English," she muttered, shifting the pages so he could see.

Ayden glanced over at the papers. "It looks like Latin," he acknowledged and looked back to the road.

"Can you read them?" Kalissa asked hopefully.

Ayden shook his head. "No. Do you think Khloe can translate them for us?"

"She might. At least, she'll know of some computer software that could translate them." Kalissa opened the envelope for Ayden. Inside was a single piece of paper. His message was in English, but it didn't make any sense to her.

Travel south to the state of peachiness, and then turn west toward the gold. Meet the others at The Wheel.

Kalissa read it three times to herself before reading it out loud. "I hate riddles. I was never good at them."

"After we get your things from impound and the car taken care of, we'll stop for lunch. Then we'll figure out where to go from there."

Kalissa nodded and rested her head against the seat. Although he was trying to soothe her nerves, her stomach wasn't so easily convinced.

CHAPTER SIX

Ayden reached over to cover Kalissa's hand that rested on the console between them and gave it a gentle, comforting squeeze. Her uneasiness drifted from her tense form. "What's wrong?"

Kalissa gave a little shrug. "I have a weird feeling."

"What kind of feeling?" he asked, wondering if it was the same old sensation he'd picked up on.

She shook her head. "I don't know. It's like I'm being watched, or followed. Maybe I'm being paranoid."

Ayden released her hand to pull into the driveway of the impound yard. She wasn't being paranoid. The presence hadn't shown up until he'd picked her up, and it worried him that she could be right about being followed. Although, that's all he'd picked up on—a feeling. Whoever or whatever it was, did a good job of masking itself.

They walked into the single-story, slightly rundown building and crossed the white linoleum floor to the chest-high counter. A young girl with brown pigtails and large brown eyes greeted them with a warm-hearted smile. "How can I help you?"

Ayden relaxed as Kalissa's mood softened. "I'm Kalissa Bradenton. I'm here about the royal blue Mercedes."

The girl bobbed her head up and down and went to the computer. With a few clicks on the keyboard, she printed out some paperwork and brought it to Kalissa to sign. Ayden took the paperwork from her and sensed her irritated glare on him. "What are you doing?" Kalissa hissed through her teeth.

Ayden smirked. "Just checking everything."

"And does everything look okay, Sheriff?" Kalissa asked with a hint of teasing.

"Yes. Everything's in order," he answered after reading over the report. He smiled widely at her and passed it back.

With a dramatic sigh, she took the papers from him, signed her name, and handed them back to the girl, along with her credit card to pay the fees.

After the payment had been processed and the papers stamped, the girl met Kalissa's stare. "Do you have things to remove from the vehicle?"

"Yes. My suitcase from the trunk." Kalissa dug through her purse for the keys.

The teen walked to the side of the counter, unlocked the half door, and advanced toward them. "I have to walk you out to the car."

Ayden followed them out to the yard and didn't miss that Kalissa had tensed up again. Something she seemed to do when he got close to her. Her emotions screamed out to him, even though he'd tried to block them since breakfast. Conflict rolled off her in waves. She was nervous one minute, turned on the next, and then annoyed with him in between. He was starting to get seasick riding the emotional tidal wave.

But it was the hint of fear he picked up on that worried him.

Noticing her curiosity as she looked around at the wrecked vehicles lined up in rows and landing her gaze on the back of the lot where a row of new cars were parked, Ayden whispered into her ear, "Drug busts." He smiled as the heat of desire rolled off her when his breath touched her ear and neck. Okay. So he liked some of her mood swings.

When they arrived at her car, Kalissa gasped and covered her mouth with her hands. Anger bubbled up in him. How in the hell was she walking after that? The front of the car was smashed in on both sides all the way up to the doors. The driver door and the roof of the car were peeled back like a sardine can. It was obvious that they'd used the Jaws of Life to get her out.

The girl cleared her throat. "I could lose my job for saying anything, but I heard about the accident. They said it was a hit and run, right?" Kalissa nodded. "My dad owns a garage in town, and he had a white Beemer come in with royal blue paint on the passenger rear quarter panel this morning. I may be able to get the license plate number for you."

"That would be great. And no one will ever know where it came from," Ayden said. He'd take any lead he could get. The plate wouldn't do the humans any good except to lead them to the owner of the car, whom they would charge and throw in jail for thirty days. But for him, if that owner was a demon—and he was certain it was—it'd be one more piece to the puzzle. If it turned out to be just a drunken human, then he'd just turn the information over to the Charlotte police as an anonymous tip. But if it *was* a demon....

Ayden pulled out a business card and handed it to the girl. "Just text the tag number to my cell."

The girl beamed. "I sure will. I hope that guy gets what's coming to him. It's not good to run from an accident."

THEY STOPPED at a diner not far from the highway. Kalissa and Ayden chose a booth tucked in the back corner so they had less chance of being overheard. Her mouth watered at the wonderful smells drifting in the air, even though she'd eaten breakfast just a few hours ago.

Around eleven in the morning and not quite lunchtime, the diner was near empty. The experience of owning a café told Kalissa that the few customers that were scattered around the small restaurant were regulars.

An elderly gentleman a few tables away flirted with the waitress like they were old friends. A smile tugged at Kalissa's lips, and a pang of homesickness crept in.

With a sigh, Kalissa pulled out her phone and dialed Khloe. She so hoped that her techno-geek sister would be able to help them.

Khloe answered on the second ring. "Hey!"

"Hi," Kalissa said with a smile. Her sister was her life, especially since their parents had died. Hearing her chipper voice was like a soothing melody. She filled her sister in on the messages. "Do you know what the Wheel could be?"

"Not right off." Kalissa could hear the clicking of the keyboard; Khloe had already started searching the internet.

After a few seconds, Khloe said, "Found it. The Wheel is a family-run diner on Highway 60, right outside Dahlonega. I emailed you the address. Hey, that's an hour away from the cabin."

"It sure is." Kalissa quickly explained what Ayden had said about their mother being in charge of hiding the Sinew. "Do you think Mom hid it somewhere around there?"

"I wouldn't put it past her," Khloe answered.

"There are two more messages written in Latin."

"Not a problem. Unlike you, I paid attention in class," Khloe teased.

"Good. I'll call you when we get to the cabin and fax them to you," Kalissa said, ignoring her sister's teasing.

"Hey, um…"

Kalissa smiled. She knew her sister all too well. "I'll call when we get there, and then you can teleport over." It used a lot of magical energy to teleport. And, other magical beings, demons included, could trace their magical signature. That was why Kalissa had driven to Charlotte. No need to take unnecessary risks. She also assumed that was why Ayden had driven, as well. It was safer that way. They could still be followed, but teleporting made it easier for the demons to know where they were going and possibly be there, waiting for them. They had suspected the demons were involved in their parents' deaths. Now, Kalissa knew, without a doubt, they were the cause.

"You sure that's safe? I could drive up now and meet you there." Khloe had a mix of worry and excitement in her voice.

"It'll be all right. I'll call you from the cabin," Kalissa said. What she didn't tell her sister was that she had a feeling they were being followed already. There was no way she wanted her sister to drive up by herself. "I'll talk to you soon. Love ya."

"Love you, too. Be safe," Khloe said and hung up.

Kalissa opened her email from her smartphone and wrote the address down on the back of Ayden's riddle. She looked across the table at his smiling face. "What?"

He shook his head. "I was just wondering if Lo is still as spoiled as she was when we were kids."

Kalissa laughed. "Oh, yeah. She's gotten worse with age."

"Of course, she has. She is the baby," Ayden teased.

"Only by five minutes." Kalissa rolled her eyes. She wouldn't change anything about her sister. She loved her just the way she was. "Everyone spoils her."

"That's because everyone loves her."

Kalissa looked into Ayden's baby blue eyes that seemed to dance when he smiled. He was right. All the Divinities were treated special, but Khloe ate up every ounce of affection that was shown to her.

Kalissa hated to be the center of attention, and abso-lutely refused to be treated any differently than the rest of *magickin*. She let Khloe suck up all the extra interest with grace and ease.

"So, what about you?" Ayden asked just as the waitress came with their lunch.

"What about me?" Kalissa asked, crinkling up her nose. She hated to talk about herself.

Ayden waited until the waitress had left them alone again before replying. "What have you been doing since high school? I mean, I know you took over your father's cafe, but what else?"

Kalissa shrugged. "I got my degree in Business Management and went to work at the diner as the day shift manager. That's about it."

"You never married?" Kalissa tensed up at the question. She knew he'd picked up on her tension because he asked, "I'm sorry. Did I say something wrong?"

She shook her head and spoke softly. "My fiancé died when we were seniors in college."

"I'm sorry."

She studied Ayden and didn't miss the tic in his jaw. Was he jealous? Of a dead man? "It was a long time ago. Don't be sorry, you didn't kill him."

CHAPTER SEVEN

They reached Dahlonega by 4:00 pm. Ayden drove straight to The Wheel, parked the Jeep, and sat there for a few moments, unsure what to do. Or what to say. His head was still whirling with the knowledge that Kalisssa had been engaged. Jealousy engulfed him but dissolved as it sank in that her fiancé was dead. A mixture of pain and guilt had hung thick in her voice when she'd spoken of it.

Changing the subject to when they were kids, he quickly found out that wasn't any better. Every time he asked a question or brought up a time that involved only the two of them, she got confused or rubbed her temples as if she had a headache. Could the memory loss be the cause of her conflicted and painful expressions?

He filed what he'd learned away for later, eager to get to the cabin so he could call his grandfather. He hoped Noah would have more information to share, as well.

"Should we go in to see if they're in there?" she asked.

Ayden broke from his train of thought and shrugged. "We can go in to check now and maybe come back?"

"Okay. Wanna order dinner? I'm sure there isn't much at the cabin."

He looked at her and smiled. "Sure. We could wait around for a little while to see if they show."

They climbed out of the Jeep and went inside the diner, spotting a wooden booth with red-cushioned seats not far from the door. He scanned the small restaurant before sliding into his seat. There were only two other couples inside the restaurant.

"Do you think they're coming?" Kalissa asked after they'd placed their orders.

"I don't know."

"How long should we wait?"

"Not sure."

"How do we know they will come?"

"I don't know," Ayden said sternly, setting his water glass down on the table hard enough that it made Kalissa jump. Fear jetted off her.

She sat back in the booth and turned to look out the window. Ayden silently cursed himself. Her emotional roller coaster was wearing on him. The more time they spent together, the more in tune with her he became.

Because we're magical partners. It was the natural course that prepared them for bonding.

But the heightened fear that surrounded her now was triggered by his anger. One thing came to mind that caused that type of reaction. If that dead ex-boyfriend was the cause, then Ayden was going to find a necromancer to bring the bastard back to life so he could tear him part, piece by piece.

He stretched his hand across the table, palm up. "I'm sorry. I didn't mean to snap. I'm just…" He trailed off. A part of him was still hurt and angry with her. Why was it so hard for him to just let it go?

"You're just what?" Kalissa asked, still sitting back against the seat as far as she could from his outstretched hand. Fear still leaked out of her, and that worried him.

He would have to probe Zach for more information on the ex-boyfriend.

Ayden dropped his shoulders and sighed. "I'm tired from the drive, frustrated about not getting more information from Papa." It was the truth. That and being around her killed him slowly inside. Not being able to touch her, kiss her sensual lips, and run his fingers through her silky blond hair. It was agonizing. What he wanted to do was drag her to the cabin and have his way with her.

He couldn't do any of those things, because to her, they were never more than friends.

"I truly am sorry," he repeated. She unfolded her arms from around her waist and sat up closer to place her hands on the table. He covered her linked hands with his, and she tensed. Yeah, he would definitely dig more information up on the ex. "I'll call Papa when we get to the cabin and try to get more information about the Rayners," he said in a soft tone.

She nodded. "I'm sorry, too…for asking too many questions."

"Don't be," he said, stroking his thumb over her fingers.

He held her stare for a few seconds before releasing it. The pull toward her was agonizingly strong, growing by the minute. If he didn't find some answers soon, he was going to go mad. He had to find a way to break that damn memory spell. Then maybe they could get on with their lives. Start fresh. Gods, he could only hope.

"ARE YOU READY?" Ayden asked softly, breaking the long silence.

Kalissa took her eyes from the window where she was watching the birds hunt for their dinner in the bushes, to look at Ayden. So absorbed with her thoughts of demons and the Sinew she wasn't sure if she'd heard the question. Realizing what he'd asked, she nodded and said, "Yes."

A few minutes later, they were back in the car, heading west on Highway 60. He offered her the wheel, but she declined. That was a mistake. She sat in the passenger seat, trying to hold down the nausea as he took the twists and turns of the mountain road much too fast.

She looked into her side mirror. The black sedan was still behind them. She was sure it was following them. The past thirty minutes, the Beamer had disappeared and reappeared with each turn. For the last ten, it had tailed them. Closer than the normal safe distance on the winding mountain road.

Before she could ask, Ayden said, "Yes they're following us."

She didn't know whether to be offended or relieved

that he knew what she was going to ask. "Just keep driving toward the cabin."

Ayden shot her a worried look. "But they…"

"They won't get near the place." Kalissa cut off his statement with a smile. She just hoped that she was right. It'd been years since she'd been there.

Another five minutes down the road, and the car was still with them. It wasn't unusual for cars to follow this long. It was the mountains, and there weren't many turnoffs along Highway 60. But the car was obvious. It kept the same speed and never gave any indication it wanted to go around them. In fact, they'd started to inch closer, like the hide and seek game was over.

"They're demons."

Kalissa snapped her head in Ayden's direction, narrowing her eyes. *Why didn't I check for demonic energy?* Turning in her seat, she focused on the two individuals in the BMW. She looked back at Ayden with a frown. "You sure?"

His gave a short nod. "They're masking their aura."

Of course. Ayden and his special abilities. What did she get? Faulty visions that gave her migraines.

"Don't slow down or stop. No matter what happens," Kalissa said. She felt his tension, but he just nodded and tightened his grip on the steering wheel. His features darkened, but he didn't argue.

They passed through an energy wave as they turned the next corner, indicating that they were about a mile away from the cabin's driveway. Kalissa breathed deeply, taking in the energy and then releasing it on an exhale. She was so glad the safeguards were still in place.

"What the fuck was that?" Ayden asked, clearly feeling the wave he'd just driven through.

"Willow's wards," she answered with a relieved laugh. "Keep driving." She unbuckled her seatbelt with a click and shifted to turn around in her seat.

Ayden grabbed her arm. "What are you doing? And who is Willow?" he asked with alarm.

She shook her head and answered Ayden's first question. "I'll be fine as long as you keep the swerving to a minimum."

A rumble sounded to their right. She turned her head in time to see a landslide of rock and dirt come down the incline onto the road, just missing the back of the Jeep. Ayden cursed but kept the Jeep steady. She didn't think the small avalanche would stop the demons. Watching, she knelt on her knees in her seat. The demons' car came out of the dirt and rocks unmarked. *Damn.* The vile creatures had put a circle around the BMW. The landslide hadn't even slowed them down.

A familiar voice drifted on the wind and reached Kalissa's mind. "*Welcome home, Lis.*" The beautiful, childlike voice flowing into Kalissa's mind made her smile.

Kalissa couldn't stop the loving grin from spreading across her face. "*Hello, Willow,*" Kalissa spoke back telepathically. Willow was the woodland nymph that lived on the mountain where the Bradenton cabin was located. For some reason, Willow had bonded with Kalissa's family.

"*Was that your landslide?*" Kalissa sent the thought with a laugh.

Willow huffed. "*That was just a warning shot. Those demons will die for entering my property.*"

"*So, what's the plan?*" Kalissa asked, knowing they didn't have much time left. She didn't want the demons to know where the cabin was. It was well hidden from outsiders, and she wanted to keep it that way.

Willow let out a mischievous laugh that sent a shiver through Kalissa. The nymph could be dangerous when she wanted to be. "*They're going over.*"

Kalissa nodded, understanding what Willow meant. There was an overlook about a half-mile after the cabin's driveway. Willow intended to force the car over the edge. Kalissa just hoped there was no one standing there enjoying the beautiful view.

A loud boom cut through the air, and the Jeep rocked violently. She dropped down into her seat to sit straight. She held on to the comfort that eased through her at Ayden's control. Her heart pounded in her chest. His concerned glance warmed her. Was it his empathic nature that allowed him to read her so plainly? It was like they were connected on a level she'd never known possible.

This wasn't the first time she'd noticed. At the hotel, he'd seemed to be in sync with her thoughts and emotions. A tang of hurt settled in her chest. Was he monitoring her emotions because he didn't trust her? But why would he do that?

Another energy ball flew past the car, drawing Kalissa out of her thoughts. Her heart pounded so hard she thought it would leap out of her chest.

"What the hell was that?" Ayden asked as she shifted to peer over the front seat to the BMW tailing them.

"The demons threw energy balls at us." Ayden let go of the steering wheel to reach out to her. She took his hand, gave a brief squeeze, and pushed it back to the wheel. "Keep driving. Willow is going to handle it."

"Who's Willow?" he asked again.

"She's a forest nymph that lives near the cabin. She's been with my family longer than I've been alive." She continued to watch the demons behind them.

"I thought nymphs were loners."

Kalissa shrugged. "I think my mom made some kind of deal with her. I'm just not sure what." Kalissa hoped the deal would not come back to bite her on the ass, and that her mother had paid her debt before she'd died.

"I'm glad she's on our side," Ayden said with a smirk and motioned with his head to the scene behind them.

Kalissa looked back to see the demons' car being slowed down by a vine that came out of the woods and wrapped itself around the back axel of the Beemer. "Yeah. She doesn't like demons."

"I gathered that," Ayden acknowledged in an amused tone.

Kalissa sat with her back against the door so she could see behind her and look straight at Ayden. She saw Willow swoop in with her knee-length brown hair, wearing a hunter green dress that showed off her graceful and petite figure. The nymph came to a stop in front of the demons' car, hovering in midair. One of the demons threw an energy ball at her. She deflected it into the river that ran alongside the road. Another energy ball flew at her. She tried to deflect it, only to get hit with a second one that she was not prepared for.

Kalissa gasped as Willow took the impact and disappear into the woods on the other side of the road. It became hard for Kalissa to breathe, and her heart pounded so hard it felt like as if it were in her head. What if Willow was hurt? What if she was... No, Kalissa refused to believe that she was dead. She couldn't be.

Ayden reached over and took her hand. The image of Willow being propelled into the woods with an energy ball half her size entered Kalissa's mind. Willow hit the ground hard and slid along the ground farther into the woods. Kalissa let out a sigh of relief when Willow's chest rose and fell in short, labored breaths.

Kalissa broke off from the vision and looked at Ayden. She knew he could use others' gifts, but she hadn't known to what extent until that moment. She wasn't sure if she should be mad at him or relieved. It was technically an invasion of privacy to just pull one's gift out. At the same time, she was glad to know that Willow was alive. "I'm not saying thanks."

Ayden frowned. "I normally don't do that, but you were so worried, almost to the point of panic. I had to make you see because we have bigger issues behind us."

Kalissa nodded. "There is an overlook up ahead."

Ayden gave her a smile as if he knew what she was thinking. *Then again,* she wondered, *he may be able to read my mind.* He was the only Divinity that had the power of adaptability. She started to ask but pushed it to the side for later. Now was not the time. They had to figure out how they were going to get the demons to take a flying leap off the side of the mountain.

Kalissa turned around to sit straight in her seat and pulled the seatbelt over her shoulder to click into place. She looked back in the side mirror to see that the demons'

Beemer was trying to go around them. That gave her an idea. "Don't let them pass until I tell you…and then…"

Ayden gave her a devilish smirk and finished her thought. "Ram them right off the overlook."

She nodded and turned her gaze back to the demons. The demons tried to go around them, but Ayden moved in front of the car every time it tried to pass. After several failed attempts to go around them, the demons decided to ram into the back of the Jeep. The impact jerked Kalissa forward. She put her hands out in front to brace herself on the dash.

"What the fuck? If they can't go around us, they try to go through us?" Kalissa barked out. She looked straight out the windshield. They were getting closer to the cliff. "The overlook is about a hundred yards ahead."

Ayden nodded and reduced speed. "I see it."

The demons tried to pass again. He let them, but increased his speed to match theirs when they came up beside them. When they reached the overlook, he jerked the Jeep, crashed into the side of the Beemer, and slammed on the brakes. She cringed at the nails-on-a-chalk-broad sound of scraping metal as the Jeep slid down the side of the sedan until it reached the bumper. With one last jerk, Ayden sent the car spinning over the edge of the mountain.

"You know they'll teleport before the car hits bottom," Ayden said.

She bobbed her head up and down. "Yeah, at least they're off our tail." She took a deep breath before continuing. "Did you see the spot about a half mile back that looked like a trail?"

"Yeah."

"That was our turn," Kalissa said. When the Jeep didn't move, she added, "It's a hidden drive. You'll see it."

Ayden made a noise but backed up. When he reached the spot she was talking about, he saw it. "Hidden drive," he repeated with amusement. "It's hidden, all right—with a spell," he laughed out, turning onto the driveway and driving up the gravel path toward the cabin.

About a tenth of a mile up the lane, Kalissa asked him to stop. She figured from his puzzled look that he'd forgotten about Willow. When he stopped the Jeep and put it in park, she got out and jogged into the forest. She heard and felt Ayden follow her. It was a little unnerving that she could feel his presence, but right now, she had other worries. Like finding Willow.

She stopped and waited for Ayden to come to stand next to her. Raising her hand for silence, she closed her eyes to take in the sounds around her. Every witch had an element that they were connected to. Kalissa's was air. She could connect with the element and all things that represented it. She listened to the birds chirping happily, and the leaves in the trees rustling in the breeze. She called out to the air spirits to help her locate Willow. Within seconds, Kalissa felt the pull. She cut right through the forest, then left to a small stream where Willow lay on her side with her hand in the water.

"Oh, Willow." Kalissa sat on her knees beside the nymph, hands hovering unsurely over the nymph's petite form.

Willow's pale green gaze met Kalissa's and a wry smile formed on the nymph's pixie-like face. "Hi." She sucked in a breath with a pained expression. She waved off

Kalissa's concern before she had a chance to say anything. "It's just some bruises. They'll heal."

"Come to the cabin with us. I'll make you some tea," Kalissa pleaded. She wanted Willow at the cabin so she could watch over her.

Willow rolled her eyes. She knew Kalissa too well. "Okay, but there will be no cooing over me like some child." She went to sit up but lay back down. "I think I broke something," she laughed out, trying to make light of the situation, but groaned at the pain in her ribs.

Ayden came over and squatted down beside them. "Let me help?" It was a question. Nymphs were temperamental. If he just lifted her in his arms to carry her to the car, she could easily freak out and hurt—possibly kill—him. Kalissa was glad Ayden knew that.

Willow looked at him with her large green eyes and smiled. "Lis, you went and snagged yourself a man, and a damn fine one at that." Kalissa knew she turned every shade of red at Willow's boldness. But before she could deny it, Willow answered Ayden's question. "Yes, you may help."

Kalissa stood and moved to the side to give him room. He carefully lifted Willow off the ground and into his arms. She snuggled into his chest, most likely seeking warmth. Kalissa felt a tiny wave of jealousy run through her that she had no right to feel. She should be grateful for his help. With a mental shake, she led them back to the car.

CHAPTER EIGHT

Ayden let out a frustrated breath and raked his hands through his hair. "Two days?"

"That is a guesstimate, too. They said they had something to look into first. It could be sooner." Zach chuckled into the phone at Ayden's irritated sigh before adding, "This gives you two days alone with Lis. Who knows? Maybe she'll regain her memory."

As good as that sounded, Ayden wouldn't hold his breath. It had been painful enough losing her the first time. He didn't want a repeat.

"It wasn't her fault. If she had her memory, there is no way she would have left you. Especially for someone like Liam." Zach said her ex-boyfriend's name like it was the plague or something.

"I take it you didn't like him," Ayden probed, wanting to find out more about the man she'd left him for fifteen years ago. And the reason for her earlier reaction to his anger.

Zach snorted with disgust. "He was an ass. He

completely controlled her. I don't think there was any physical abuse, but he did a number on her head. It took her years to get over his death."

Ayden wanted to ask more about Liam, but Kalissa's footsteps, followed by the click of the upstairs bedroom door where they'd placed Willow stopped him. Uneasiness had settled over her when the subject had come up at the diner. There was no need to add to her uncertainty. "I gotta go. Talk to you soon."

Zach laughed and muttered something about Ayden being chickenshit because Lis was coming back into the room. Ignoring his cousin, he said a final goodbye and hung up the phone. He slid the cell into his jeans pocket as she descended the spiral staircase in the far corner of the living room.

"How is she?" Ayden asked when Kalissa came off the last step.

Her violet eyes lifted to meet his gaze from across the room. "Resting. I don't think anything's actually broken as she feared."

"That's good." Silence filled the space between them. Nervousness rolled off her and coiled around him. He wanted go to her, wrap her in his arms, and make the storm brewing inside her go away.

A forced smile pulled at her lips as she walked farther into the living room. "She should be back to herself by morning." She stilled in front of the sofa when he moved toward her.

"I thought you hadn't been to the cabin in years."

"It's been about two years."

He motioned for her to sit. After she hesitantly complied, he lowered himself into the seat next to her.

"Willow's half human. My mom raised her. She stays here when no one is around." She answered his unasked question.

The cabin was clean and free of static energy, surprising him since he'd assumed no one had visited it in years. "It must be nice to not have to clean the cobwebs out of the corners."

A soft laugh bubbled out of her sensual lips, warming his heart. "Yes, it is. I'm glad Willow is here to take care of things, especially after…"

"Mom's and Dad's deaths" went unsaid. Her pain was all too familiar to him and cut to the core. He'd also lost his parents, and the grief was still raw.

Her emotions were starting to run rampant again, bouncing from nervousness to desire. He had to reinforce his shields.

She took a deep breath in, like she was gathering strength from the air. "Willow told me that there's been more demon activity recently."

"And you believe they're looking for the Sinew?"

"Yeah. Did you get ahold of Noah?"

"Zach said he was being held captive by his wife." Ayden laughed out loud. "Did you know they're trying to conceive?"

Her violet eyes met his and she smiled. "At their age?"

"Well, they are immortal," he teased. "Cassia will be four in a couple of months. Grams thinks it'd be nice to have another baby in the house."

Her smile widened. "She always said she wanted a houseload of children."

Nodding, he recalled his grandmother saying that but never knew why they'd only had two: Zach's mom, Lynzee, and Ayden's dad, Todd.

"How long have they been trying?" she asked.

"A couple months," he answered and then changed the subject back to her unanswered question, the reason he'd called Noah in the first place. "Zach said Jacen and Lydia called this morning. They are tying up some loose ends and won't be here for another two days."

KALISSA FROZE. For the love of the gods, she was still trying to get used to the idea of spending the night alone with him, but two days? How was she going to keep her distance for two days? Especially since he could pick up on her emotions.

"Lis? Are you okay?" he asked.

"I'm fine," she lied, not caring if he knew she was being untruthful. "What are we going to do until they get here?" she whispered.

He was quiet for a few minutes before answering. "Whatever we do, we need to be on guard just in case the demons are looking for the Sinew. Now that they know we're here."

Oh, great. She was betting he wouldn't let her out of his sight.

"Why don't you call Khloe?" he asked.

"Oh! I almost forgot." What was wrong with her? She

jumped up and went to the bedroom to grab her phone and the FedEx envelope with the messages from their mother. She came back to the living room, sat back down on the sofa, and called Khloe.

"Hey!" Khloe answered after the third ring. She sounded annoyed.

"What's up?" Kalissa asked.

"Charles," Khloe spat out. Kalissa smiled. Charles was Khloe's flavor of the week. Well, he'd been around longer than a week. In fact, the relationship had lasted longer than any of the more recent ones. Khloe was too high-maintenance for human men, or at least that's what she said, but Kalissa knew it was an excuse, a ploy to protect her heart from breaking again.

"What happened?"

"Oh, same shit, different man. 'I'm too exhausting.' Oh! And he had the nerve to say I was too demanding. How am I too demanding?" Khloe was on a roll.

The breakup must have just happened. "You're too good for him anyway." A relieved satisfaction washed through Kalissa. She didn't like the weasel. Every time she was around him, she got an uneasy feeling.

"He was too much of a mama's boy." Zach's voice drifted in from the background.

"And here's the other man that's not too happy with us," Khloe said with sarcasm. "Lis, turn on the video cam."

Kalissa frowned. "You'll have to walk me through it. I'm not sure if I remember how."

Khloe laughed. "It's already set up. Power up the TV, pick up the remote, and push the button that says AUX."

Kalissa did as Khloe said. Within seconds, Khloe and Zach appeared on the TV screen. "Why are we video conferencing? I thought you were going to teleport up."

Khloe released a heavy sigh. "I was, but the studio called an hour ago. They need me to teach a couple of classes."

"Oh," Kalissa said.

"I'm sorry. I can call and cancel."

"No. It's okay." Kalissa tried to keep the disappointment from her voice, but she knew Khloe could sense it anyway. "I'm going to fax the messages to you, then." Kalissa went to the fax machine on the shelf next to the TV. She placed the pages in the tray and punched in their home fax number.

Khloe reached over and took the fax out of her machine. "The first is a spell. I'll translate it and email it to you. I'm not sure what it's for or if I should speak it out loud." She moved on to the second page and read it.

"What you seek is hidden within the chamber, and protected by the twin retrievers. Five score from Lolissa into Mother's light. But first, you must meet the others at The Wheel."

"Lolissa?" Zach asked.

"It's the cabin," the girls said at the same time.

"Mom named it after us," Khloe finished. "You think the Sinew is what we seek?"

Kalissa nodded. "It has to be. It only makes sense that Mom would hide it here. It's protected behind Willow's wards."

"You did say Willow has seen more demon activity," Ayden spoke up.

"Okay. Wait for Jacen, Lydia, and us to get there before you two go looking for it," Zach said and then quickly added, "I mean it." He gave Kalissa a pointed look.

Kalissa rolled her eyes, but it was Ayden who spoke. "We'll wait. Let me know once you hear from the Raynerses." Ayden's phone beeped. He pulled it out, opened the text message, and smiled. "I'm going to send you a tag number. Let me know what you find."

"She came through." Kalissa smiled.

Zach nodded. "Will do. I have some other demonic news for you."

"What now?" Ayden and Kalissa asked at the same time.

"Sindee called. She said her source informed her of a Dark Divine round-up. Khan ordered anyone who resists to be killed," Zach said. He paused briefly before continuing. "I also ran across a name in Papa's library. Hector D. Grayson."

"Who is he?" Ayden asked

"He *was* a Khan General before Hecate killed him three hundred years ago. According to the archives, he was the one that used the Sinew to drain the Divinities of their powers. Oh, and FYI, if you are drained of your magic, you die," Zach said.

"All the more reason to get the Sinew and keep it out of the demons' hands," Kalissa said. She thought for a minute. "There's something that's been bugging me. If they seek the Sinew and want to harvest our magic, why kill our parents? Why not capture them until they got the Sinew?"

Zach scrunched up his face. "I'm not sure. Maybe there's been a change in plan?"

"Like gathering the Dark Divine together as part of Khan's army," Khloe said, reminding everyone of Sindee's message.

Zach frowned again. "I didn't think of that. I'm not sure how many there are." He pulled out a small notepad from his shirt pocket and made some notes. "Once Grams releases Papa from her evil clutches, I'll ask him. I just hope he has the strength to speak."

Kalissa and Khloe giggled.

"Okay, then," Ayden spoke with a chuckle. "We'll talk to you when you get here."

"You two be safe. I would stick close to the cabin if I were you," Zach said.

Kalissa and Ayden agreed, said their goodbyes, and shut off the video. The demons were up to something; she felt it in her bones. So she would spend the next few days with Ayden. Alone. It wouldn't do them any good to draw too much attention to themselves, or end up dead before recovering the Sinew.

With the combined strength of five Divinities, they could protect and guard the power source. But who was going to guard her heart against the one man that could possibly tear down the walls around it?

CHAPTER NINE

"I thought Khloe stopped dancing to take over your mother's computer business."

Kalissa shrugged. "She teaches when they need her."

Ayden grabbed her free hand, linking his fingers with hers. She turned her head to look into his eyes with that hint of panic still there. He couldn't hold back any longer, Noah's warning still heavy on his mind. What other choice did he have? Unwilling to spend the next day and a half to two days pretending that they were nothing more than friends and never had been, he had to do something. Insanity would take over his mind. The pull between them was too strong to push aside. Turning to face her on the sofa, he drew in a deep breath, taking in her confusion and curiosity. "You suffer from headaches. Why is that?"

"They're just headaches," she said with a smile that told him she was hiding something.

"Something tells me that it's more than that." He studied her face.

Kalissa shrugged and looked down at their linked hands. "I get them…sometimes."

"When you have visions?" he asked.

Kalissa snapped her eyes back up to his face. "How did you know?" she asked accusingly.

"A guess. I had to pull the vision of what happened to Willow out of your subconscious. Why is that, Kalissa? Why do you lock up your Divine gift?" He tried to keep his tone soft and gentle. The betrayal still lingered beneath the surface and made it hard not to be angry with her. But she was a victim in this as much as he was.

"They became too painful," she whispered after a long silence.

Ayden took a deep breath and let it out slowly. "The headaches?"

She nodded. "And the emotions." There was silence again. He wasn't sure if he understood what she was trying to say. Finally, she spoke again. Her words were more random, like she needed to get them all out in the open. "At first, after Liam died, the visions were more like memory clips. I didn't understand because I didn't remember them as mine, but I was in them. When I tried to remember or force the visions, I got sharp pains in my head. Then the visions got more frequent, and so did the headaches. A few months later, the dreams started."

Ayden's heart ached for her. Her emotions were so loud they pounded on the wall he'd put up to block them. The dreams could've been her locked down memories or something else entirely. "What were the dreams about?"

She looked at him. Her violet eyes shined with unshed tears. "Death. Everyone I care about is going to die."

His gut wrenched, and he tightened his grip on her hands slightly. "You know that visions can be changed. Nothing is set in stone."

She pulled her hands free, stood up, and walked to the bay window that overlooked the back of the property. "That's just it. I saw the deaths and nothing else. Nothing before to tell me when and where."

The memory spell. It must have had an effect on her visions. It was the only thing that made sense. "So you locked them down?" he asked.

She didn't look at him as he got up and walked over to stand next to her at the window. He spoke softly, trying to soothe her. "I think I know what's wrong with your visions."

She turned to study his face. He stepped closer to her, reached out with his fingers, and slowly traced his fingertips down her cheek to her jawline. Cupping her head, he lowered his and pressed a gentle kiss to her soft lips.

THE SECOND AYDEN'S lips touched hers in a soft, sensual kiss, an image of them as teenagers sitting in a barn kissing flashed in her mind. "Oh," she whispered, pulling back from him. "You kissed me. I mean, when we were kids."

Ayden nodded and touched her cheek with the backs of his fingers. The silver swirled in the blue of his eyes. "You were my first real kiss," he whispered, just inches from her lips.

She swallowed hard and waited for the panic to rise. Surprisingly, it never came. Instead, a strong urge to grab him, rip his shirt off his muscular chest, and nip and lick every inch of him arose. The much too brief kiss had ignited something inside her. Need boiled.

"And you were mine," she admitted. The memory of that afternoon was so clear now, as if it had happened yesterday. How did she remember something that only a few moments before, she'd had no recollection of at all?

They were both fifteen and playing hide-and-seek with the other children in the coven. Ayden was the seeker.

Kalissa hides behind the bales of hay in the loft of the coven's barn. Footsteps enter the barn, butterflies swarm inside her belly. Then she realizes there is only one way to go. She is so busted.

Ducking farther behind the hay stacks, she listens to Ayden walk around below her. She could teleport, but that would be cheating. She jumps when the ladder moves slightly, indicating that someone is climbing up it.

"I know you're up here." His soft chuckle reaches her ears, making her feel giddy.

Kalissa steps out of her hiding place and faces him. His smile reaches his baby blue eyes. She moves to the right, and then darts left to go around him. But he is too fast and grabs her waist, pulling her to him hard enough that they fall into a pile of loose hay. He kisses her before she has time to think. It's her first real, adult kiss.

"It took me a long time to get up the nerve to kiss you." Ayden's voice pulled her from the memory. She let out a soft gasp when he captured her mouth gently in a real-time kiss. His warm tongue licked her lips to encourage her to open for him. Without hesitation, she opened to the invasion and met his tongue halfway with hers. Feelings rose in her that she recognized. The electrifying desire swirled around them, intensifying their connection. It was the same as their first kiss.

The softness of a bed broke their kiss. She looked around. They had somehow teleported into the bedroom adjacent to the living room. He looked down at her from his position above her. "Did I do that, or you?" he asked with a crooked smile.

She laughed. "I think it was a combined effort." Her laughter died as Ayden kissed her again on the lips and then trailed feather-light kisses down her cheek to her jawline. She couldn't think. Being kissed by him was unlike anything she had ever known. Soft, gentle, and demanding all bound into one passionate kiss. Yet she didn't feel pressured or controlled by it. Yeah, Liam had been a good kisser, but there was always possession behind it, a need to control.

Pressing his hips into her center, Ayden kissed her neck. He slid his hand under her blouse and up her ribcage to cup one of her breasts.

"Wait, wait, wait. Stop!" The panic she'd expected a few moments ago took her over. Flashes of Liam's possessive and angry face entered her mind.

Ayden lifted up over her; worry lines formed across his forehead. "What's wrong?"

She shook her head and closed her eyes. "I'm sorry. I can't…"

Ayden kissed her on the forehead and sat up on the bed next to her. His hands clenched into fists. Kalissa sat up, folded her legs under her like a pretzel, tugged a pillow into her lap, and hugged it to her. He was mad. Embarrassment and guilt triggered her own anger. Why couldn't she let it go? She thought her fear of intimacy had gone away. Boy was she wrong.

Grow up, Kalissa! She scolded herself. *Toughen up and face your fears.* It's the only way to get past them. To heal them. The problem was, she didn't know how.

"Don't ever apologize for saying no." Ayden's voice was strained, almost a growl, but his aura shone bright blue. He wasn't mad at her. Turning to face her, he reached out and wiped a tear from her cheek that she hadn't realized had fallen. His tone softened. "What did he do to you?"

Kalissa looked away from him. There was no way she would reveal that, not yet. She shook her head and was glad that he was empathic. He would sense her pain and fear and read between the lines.

Ayden sighed and leaned into her. His lips gently pressed to hers in a quick kiss. When he pulled back, he said, "I could never hurt you."

Her subconscious grabbed on to the truth that hung on his words. She relaxed. Ayden was nothing like Liam.

The silence between them started to wear on her nerves. Thinking back on what he'd told her earlier about her visions, she asked, "Why did I not know about our first kiss?"

"We believe you may have had a memory spell placed on you."

Memory spell? She asked silently in her head, then asked aloud, "We?"

"Khloe, Papa, Zach, and I. Lo said she asked and hinted around, but you would get frustrated, and a headache would come on. She stopped asking questions for fear of hurting you. Papa said not to force the memories because the spell may cause you harm. He said that memory spells can damage the mind." Ayden got quiet, and sadness infused his expression. "I believe it's why your visions are misfiring," he added after a brief pause.

"Because of the past, present, and future thing." Kalissa's gift as a seer not only allowed her to see visions of the future but the past and present, as well. If she were under a memory spell to forget part of the past, then her visions would be affected. It all made sense to her now. She couldn't use her gift to its fullest without terrible headaches. She'd finally had to lock them down.

But who would do such a thing? And why?

CHAPTER TEN

Kalissa glided through the forest, enjoying the beautiful blue sky and warm summer breeze caressing her skin. The birds sang. Trees swayed, creating a melody of their own as the wind blew through their branches. She could hear the wildlife all around, taking advantage of the perfect, not-too-hot, not-too-cool weather.

She loved it here. The forest surrounding her family's cabin on top of the Blue Ridge Mountains was so peaceful. The air so clean and crisp. All the elements and nature were alive. Regret for not coming here the last two years filled her.

Kalissa walked down a footpath that'd been there for as long as she could remember. The trail split off in three directions about twenty-five yards from the cabin. Left led to the river that flowed through the mountains. The path to the right opened to a meadow where her family had held their rituals. But she chose to go straight, where another seventy-five yards up the path was a cave. She and Khloe had loved to play in that cave when they were little. But something called to her now. Something was in that cave, and she wanted to know what it was.

When she came to the end of the path, the cavern came into sight as she emerged from the tree line. Ayden stood next to the entrance that appeared to be blocked by something. *A spell?*

He stepped forward, closer to her, and held out his hand. "We were waiting for you."

We? She looked around. Khloe stood to their right with Zach, Lydia, Jacen, and a dark-haired woman. She recognized Jacen and Lydia from photos in the family albums. Kalissa did not know the other woman, at least not by name. She had seen her before, but couldn't remember where.

"You are the only one who can open the cave," Khloe said.

"Why me?" Kalissa asked.

Khloe gave her a sideways smile, almost a smirk. "Not sure. Plus, I already tried."

Kalissa laughed at that. It was so like Khloe to start without her. "Maybe we both need to be present."

Khloe came over to stand next to Kalissa at the mouth of the cave. Ayden kissed her on the forehead and fell back with the others. Kalissa linked hands with her sister. Just before they began their chant, a breeze blew through Kalissa's hair and a whispered voice drifted by. "They're coming."

They locked gazes. "Who's coming?" Khloe asked. Because she could control all elements, she was connected to them the same way Kalissa was connected to air so she'd also heard the voice.

Kalissa turned around in time to see several demons step out of the trees around them. Everything happened so fast as the demons rushed them. Falling into a crouch, she braced herself for impact. Adrenaline raced through her veins in anticipation. Demons weren't people, so she had no qualms about taking a few out. Her attacker barreled into her, knocking both her and him to the ground. They rolled until she managed to overtake him, then she conjured a silver dagger and plunged it into his heart.

A movement from the tree line grabbed Kalissa's attention. A larger demon had his arms raised in front of him, palms to the sky, and he was building an incredible amount of energy into a large sphere. With an evil gleam in his eyes, he directed the magical sphere at Ayden and let it go. She screamed and ran toward him, only to have hands grab her arms, holding her back. She couldn't move. She started to cry, yelling for him to move. She struggled to get free, to get to him. Another scream ripped from her throat as the energy ball sailed through the air. A look of shock and horror masked Ayden's face.

Kalissa came awake with a gasp. Ayden loomed over her with his hands on her arms. When he released her, she flung herself at him, wrapping her arms around his waist. She shook as hot tears streamed down her cheeks. The beating of his heart in her ear soothed her as she held him close so she would know that he was alive. It was just a dream. No, not a dream. It was a vision.

~

AYDEN HELD her as she cried into his shirt. Her panic hung in thick waves around her. Her screams had awakened him. Fear spiked through his whole body until he'd teleported to her side.

He brushed the hair from her face, then rubbed her back in slow, circular motions to soothe her. They sat there in each other's arms for the gods knew how long, and he would gladly stay like that forever. It felt good to hold her in his arms again. Her hair still smelled of jasmine and fresh rain. Maybe that was her natural scent. Whatever it was, he loved it.

Kalissa finally stopped shaking and fell completely still. At first, he thought she might have fallen back to sleep. Lifting her chin with his finger, he peered into her vivid violet eyes, reddened from tears, and gave her a soft smile. "Better?"

She nodded, pulled away from him, and with a frown, reached out to the wet spot on his shirt. "I'm sorry…"

Ayden cut her off by taking her hand in both of his and placing a tender kiss to her palm. "It's just a shirt." He stood up, still holding her hand. "Come on. I'll fix you some coffee, and you can tell me about your vision."

KALISSA SAT at the kitchen table with a cup of coffee and a spiral notebook in front of her. Ayden had found it and brought it to her along with a pen shortly after fixing her coffee. She asked how he'd known about her dream journal.

He smiled and said, "You told me once, plus, Noah keeps one."

All seers kept one to keep track of and decipher dreams from visions. Sometimes it was hard to tell them apart. Dreams could be very real and as vivid as visions. On the flip side, visions could be very dreamlike and unclear.

She sat at the kitchen table with the window open, taking in the pleasant morning breeze, writing down as much of the dream-vision as she could remember. Ayden left her to go shower and change. Apparently, she'd woken him up when she'd screamed out in her sleep. He'd thrown on his clothes from the day before and teleported into her room on the first floor. Although, now that she thought about it, she was a little disappointed. It would've been a bonus to press her cheek to his bare chest instead of a cotton t-shirt.

Kalissa was still dressed in her pink pajama bottoms with black witch hats and a black tank top. She hadn't bothered to brush her hair. Instead, she'd twisted the mass of blond waves up in a loose bun on the top of her head. After embarrassing herself by clinging to Ayden and crying in his shirt like a child waking from a nightmare, she was past trying to be impressive.

Ayden had still called her beautiful as he'd kissed her forehead before heading upstairs.

The change in Ayden since he'd told her about the memory spell frightened her. He seemed to fall into the comfortable role of boyfriend, like he hoped to pick up where they'd left off. Wherever that was, she didn't remember. Being with him, even for the short time of one full day, she felt things for him that she couldn't explain.

Desire flared, warming her entire body when he walked into the room. His husky voice captivated her. She was drawn to him like nobody else.

But hesitation bounced between them—her hesitation. And fear of sex. Gods, she had to get past that. He deserved more than her insecurities.

Willow came drifting in from the living room to the kitchen. Kalissa smiled at her. "How do you feel?" She smelled like the forest. The wonderful earthy and floral scent Kalissa had grown up loving. The healthy and magical glow to Willow's skin told Kalissa she'd just come back from her burrow. Her underground hideaway had a natural spring that ran deep in the earth. Through the spring, she could travel to the other side. It was where Hecate had gone to live after the Underworld was taken over by Khan. In the Afterworld, Willow could regenerate and heal faster than in the human world.

Willow did a little pose to show herself off and twirled around. "All better."

"Thank the gods nothing was broken, just bruised."

"Tell me about it. I would have been down for a couple of days." Willow wrinkled up her nose at Kalissa playfully, walked over to the refrigerator, and started pulling things out of it.

"What are you doing?" Kalissa knew what she was doing, but she still asked.

"Fixing you breakfast," Willow said without looking over at her. "You took care of me last night. I'm taking care of you this morning." She turned around and gave Kalissa a gentle smile. "Where is that man of yours?"

Kalissa grinned and turned to look out the window to hide her flushed cheeks. "He's not mine."

"Oh, but he could be," Willow said with a tiny laugh that sounded like wind chimes.

Kalissa thought differently. Especially after the vision she'd had. There was no way that she could live through another loved one dying. If she gave her heart to Ayden, that's exactly what she would have to do. She wasn't sure her heart could take it. Witches could die of a broken heart.

Before she could answer Willow's question on the whereabouts of Ayden, he walked into the kitchen. His wet hair was towel dried, leaving it in an unruly mass of golden brown waves. Kalissa bit her bottom lip to keep a giggle from escaping. It reminded her of Zach's normal just-climbed-out-of-bed look.

He shook his head. "Don't say it," he said as he walked over to the table and sat down across from her.

Kalissa tried to look like she had no idea what he was talking about. "Say what?"

Ayden smiled at her. "That I look like Zachary."

"Okay, you look like Noah…with Zach's hair." Kalissa burst out laughing. She couldn't help it. "I'm sorry. I think my sister is rubbing off on me."

He cracked a sideways smile at her. "Bethany was the first to make that observation when I moved in with them." He reached over and covered her hand with one of his. Her desire spiked like electricity racing through her body.

His free hand hovered over the notebook. She pushed the journal toward him with her mind to give him permission to read her entry. The horror of seeing Ayden die in her vision was too raw. Words tangled with each other and refused to leave her mouth.

His fingers lightly caressed her hand and wrist as he read. Worry and fear played in the lines of his face. But his touch was soothing and provocative. It was strange how his touch sparked a flame inside her that could spread and consume her like a wildfire. She looked down at his hand and then his forearm, where his rose birthmark lay perfectly etched on his sunkissed skin.

Kalissa drew her eyebrows together. He had two roses. One was a faded replica of the other, indicating that he had found his magical partner. The urge to look at her own arm, or ask Willow if she could see it nagged at her, ridiculous as it was. There was only one way Kalissa would be able to see the faded rose.

Don't go there. She couldn't give her heart to someone only to watch them die. Again. What if he turned out to be as possessive and controlling as Liam? What if she could never make love to him?

The mouthwatering smell of ham and cheese omelets brought Kalissa out of her worrisome thoughts. Willow had brought their plates to the table, set a plate in front of each of them, and went back to the island countertop to grab her own plate of food and the platter of crispy bacon. Just like Kalissa liked it.

"Hmm. This smells wonderful. Thanks, Willow," Kalissa said, breathing in the different aromas as she snagged a couple of pieces of bacon.

"You're welcome." Willow beamed with delight.

"Willow, can I ask you something?" Kalissa asked. She

hoped that Willow wouldn't take offense to what she was about to ask.

"Of course, you can," Willow answered, taking some bacon for herself.

"Did Mother…owe you anything? I mean, is there a debt to be paid?"

Willow laughed, shaking her head. "I'm sorry. I thought the question was going to be more offensive the way you looked. If there is any debt to be paid, it is I who owes it."

That confused Kalissa. She'd never heard of a nymph owing anyone a favor. As if hearing her thoughts, Willow smiled, patted her hand, and explained. "Your mother raised me as her own child. But you know that. Connie found my mom, Rose, and me in these very woods. Rose was ill and dying. She was attacked by a demon that infected her with some kind of deadly poison. I was only a couple of months old at the time. Connie took us in until my mom passed away. Connie vowed to take care of me as if I were her own child."

Willow paused for a moment. "I never knew my mother, but Connie made sure that I learned everything about her. She taught me how to use my powers and how to scry so that I could look back on my mother's life."

"I never knew. How long ago was that?" Kalissa asked.

Willow thought about it for a few seconds before answering. "I believe I was twenty-five when your mother met and married your father."

Wow. Kalissa had never known Willow's age. Her parents would have been married for fifty-two years this year, making Willow seventy-seven.

"Your mother gave me everything. Two beautiful sisters." She reached over and covered Kalissa's hand. "And half this mountain to rule as my own."

"Kalissa said you were half human?" Ayden asked.

Willow nodded and finished chewing the bite of her omelet before speaking. "My father was human, but he did not want a family, nor did he care that my mother was pregnant."

"Sorry," Ayden said softly.

Willow waved it off. "He was human. Most don't hold the same family values we do."

"Not all humans are like that," Kalissa said.

Willow smiled. "No, not all. Your father was human and the most caring and compassionate man I knew. He loved everything about our world, our beliefs, and our way of life. And he told me once that he felt more at home in our world than his own."

Kalissa looked down at her plate, pushing a piece of ham around with her fork. Gods she missed her dad. "I know. That's why he took my mother's last name."

Ayden spoke up like he sensed her shift in mood. Of course, his empathy felt the sudden sadness that washed over her, and she was grateful for the distraction. "What's on the agenda for today?"

She looked up at him, uneasiness making its presences known. "I don't know. We could explore the mountain."

Willow tsked, stood, and stacked the dishes together. "Stop worrying, Lis. All five hundred acres are surrounded with wards. What could possibly go wrong?"

CHAPTER ELEVEN

K alissa had suggested a hike followed by a picnic down by the river, but she really wanted to stay inside the cabin until the others got there. It was unlike her to hide behind closed doors. Something or someone was following her. She felt it. The tiny hairs on the back of her neck rose, and her skin crawled as if an unseen force had brushed against it. The dream-vision didn't do anything to soothe her nerves. She was a bundle of fear, desire, and distraction. She was a mess.

"Do you sense anything unusual?" she asked Willow as they cleaned up the kitchen.

"How so?"

She shrugged. "I don't know, like a presence of some kind. I have a feeling that I'm being watched."

"No. Why, hon? Are you feeling okay?" Willow reached out to place a hand on Kalissa's forehead.

Kalissa let the nymph feel her head because it was something her mother would do. Something she missed. Her eyes started to fill with tears, but she blinked them away. "I feel fine. I guess I have a lot on my mind right now."

Willow gave her a gentle, caring smile. "I didn't sense anything earlier, nor do I now. I'll be around all the same."

"Thanks."

After the kitchen was clean, Willow ran her out with a cup of tea.

Without a distraction, her thoughts turned to Ayden. It was extremely hard to stay away from him. She was drawn to him like a moon to her planet. The kiss they'd shared last night filtered through her mind, instantly warming her from the inside out. Her mouth curled into a smile as she entered her bedroom. The passion he had ignited in her was surreal. It also scared her.

When he touched her, every worry and fear melted away. Another sign of meeting a magical partner. Gods, what was she going to do? She fought the urge to run away. Running would only spotlight her weakness. No, she was stronger than that. She would overcome her phobic behavior and stomp it into the ground if it was the last thing she did.

Then there was her memory. Flashes of her past came back to her little by little, raising fear within her. She waited for the horrible pain that usually followed the flashbacks, but to her relief, it never came.

While in the shower, her second Divine Rose appeared on the inside of her left forearm and triggered the onset of visions. Memories. She staggered back against the wall for support as the images slammed into her and threw her off balance.

Kalissa rushes into the house with her heart pounding

against her ribcage. She shuts the front door behind her and presses her back against it. Khloe comes into the living room with a smirk on her face. "You're in so much trouble. I know where you were. I saw you."

Kalissa steps forward to grab Khloe's hands with hers. "Did you say anything to Mom?"

Khloe shakes her head back and forth. Before she can say anything else, their mother comes into the room. "Khloe, go tell your father dinner's ready." When Khloe doesn't move, their mother says, "Now, Khloe." It isn't a demanding tone she uses, but it is firm enough that Khloe nods and walks toward the study. Before disappearing inside, she gives Kalissa an apologetic look.

"Where have you been, Kalissa?"

Kalissa flings her arms behind her back as soon as her mother comes into the room. "At the coven," she answers.

"Why didn't you come home with Khloe?"

"I, um...lost track of time," she says softly. That isn't a lie. She was with Ayden. Every time they are together, time gets away from her.

"Give me your hands," her mother says, holding out her own.

She takes a breath to push down the fear forming in her gut. She slowly takes her arms from around back and holds them out to her mother, palms up. Her mother looks down at her hands and up to her forearms. Kalissa is surprised when her mother pulls her into a hug. "You scared me," her mother says into her hair. At seventeen, Kalissa is only a couple of inches shorter than her mother. "I couldn't bear it if anything happened to you."

"I'm sorry, Mama."

Finished with her shower, Kalissa sat on the edge of the bed, remembering being so relieved that her mother hadn't been able to see her second rose. Maybe she and Ayden were the only ones who could see them.

Oh, Gods. They were life partners.

What was she going to do? Leaving him wasn't an option. Not again. That acknowledgment saddened her. How could he forgive her? What had she done?

With a heavy sigh, she calmed herself and searched for Ayden.

Entering the kitchen, she found him sitting at the table with his laptop on. "You're not working, are you?" She didn't even try to take the annoyance out of her voice.

He closed the computer, stood up to wrap an arm around her waist, and kissed her lips softly. She winced at his fast movement but relaxed when he pulled back and met her gaze. His eyes were filled with worry. He opened his mouth and then closed it again, before taking a deep breath and answered her question. "Zach sent me the info on the tag number." Disappointment flashed across his face. "It belongs to a human. Turns out, it was a drunk driver. Charlotte PD has already taken him into custody."

"That's good, right?" She studied his facial expressions.

"I guess." He stepped back and took her hand, linking the fingers of one hand with hers and picking up the basket with the other. They headed out.

They went on their hike first before heading to the river for their picnic. A light, warm breeze drifted around them, rustling leaves and swaying tree branches.

The uneasy feeling of being watched returned. Not that

it had actually left. Being with Ayden just offered a sense of peace and security.

"Are you okay?" he asked after walking in silence for several minutes.

Kalissa nodded. "Yeah." She let out a sigh, knowing he sensed her mood. She turned over her arm and linked her fingers with his. He glanced down, squeezed her hand just a little, and then let go. A second later, he stopped and set down the picnic basket Willow had packed for them.

"What… "

Ayden turned to face her and cupped her face in his hands. "You remember?"

Kalissa relaxed. "I'm starting to." She held up her left arm with her forearm facing him. "I know this is not the first time this has shown up."

Ayden leaned in and pressed his lips to hers in a quick kiss. "Are you okay? I mean…the headaches."

She knew what he was really asking. "No, no pain. Thank the gods. I was in love with you once. But now? I'm confused. And there are things you need to know. Things I'm not sure I'm ready to share, yet." Those things would most likely send Ayden packing. So, no, she wasn't prepared to share her secrets with him.

She replayed the vision over and over in her mind, trying to figure out what it meant. True, the vision hadn't specifically shown Ayden being struck. The one question that she kept mulling over was: why were they at the cave in the first place? Unless…

"Oh my gods. The cave." Kalissa locked eyes with Ayden then she twisted out of his hands and went to the picnic basket. Reaching in, she pulled out the translated missive from her mother. She'd brought the message, hoping they could figure out what it meant. She read it aloud.

"*What you seek is hidden within the chamber, and protected by the twin retrievers. Five score from Lolissa into Mother's light. But first, you must meet the others at The Wheel.*"

"The chamber must be the cave. And five score is one hundred. The cave is exactly one hundred yards from the cabin." There was no way to avoid the vision. Her gut tightened. They had to go to the cave.

She was going to do everything she could to stop the dream-vision from coming true. Ayden had said it himself —visions were suggestions, a glimpse of what could happen. They could decide what road to take based on that peek into the future. They could prepare. Gods, she hoped he was right, and they could all walk away alive.

"And mother's light is the moon?"

Kalissa nodded. "The moon rises from that side of the mountain this time of year."

"What do you think the twin retrievers are?" Ayden asked as he picked up the basket, laced his fingers with hers, and started walking again.

"I'm not sure. But I hope they're friendly, at least to us."

"Me, too," Ayden said with a small smile.

They continued down the path to the river. Her mind was a whirlwind of information and possibilities. When they reached the riverbank, she asked, "What do you know about the Divine Rose?" He gave her a questioning look as he pulled the small blanket out of the basket and spread it out on the grass. "I mean, how is it no one else sees it?"

Ayden thought about it for a few seconds. "I'm not sure. I think it's different for every couple. Papa said his mother saw his and Grams'."

Kalissa sat down on the blanket and looked out into the water swiftly flowing along. "But no one can see ours?" She told him about the memory she'd had earlier, and that her mother couldn't see it. "I believe that's what she was looking for."

Ayden sat next to her and took her left hand in his right. For the first time, she didn't flinch away. He gave her a seductive smile before speaking. "Many believe that sex triggers it. She might've been checking to see if we had been intimate."

Kalissa pulled her hand from his and pushed at him playfully. "She was not." He raised his eyebrows at her, and she smiled. "Okay. Maybe. But we were only seventeen." As soon as she'd said it, she realized it was a lame excuse. *Magickin* developed and matured faster than humans. Plus, *magickin* didn't hold the same views about sex as humans. They viewed sex as a part of nature and a sacred part of life and love.

"I've even heard of couples whose roses were visible as they developed," Ayden added.

Kalissa looked at his handsome profile as he peered out into the water. There was so much she didn't know about him, yet she felt so close to him. She wanted to reach out and touch him, kiss him, and explore every inch of his hard, muscular body. Run her hands though his silky brown hair. But he was like a stranger to her. Would she feel differently when the memory spell was broken? Could they break the spell? They didn't even know who'd cast it or how. Or why.

Ayden took his shoes and socks off and rolled up his pants legs to his knees, then stood and walked to the edge of the bank. "Come in the water with me," he said, looking over his shoulder to her.

She shook her head side to side. "No way. It's too cold."

He turned and stepped into the rushing water, sucked in a sharp breath and laughed. "Oh, it's fine." He turned to face her.

Kalissa stood and walked closer to the edge. "It's cold," she repeated and laughed softly at his appearance. It reminded her of when they were younger and had gone to the lake. She smiled widely at the fact that she'd just had another memory without the onset of a headache. Was the spell weakening?

Ayden splashed water toward her. A half-squeal and half-laugh vacated her as she turned sideways to keep the water droplets from making contact. When she turned back to face him, her smile faded. His facial expression had changed to one of alarm. A nanosecond later, she was yanked off the ground and carried off through the forest at supernatural speed by something she couldn't see. It wasn't even completely solid.

The trees flew by in a blur of motion. Ayden yelled her name. She looked back and saw him struggle to get out of the water and run after the assailant and her, but he wasn't fast enough. Kalissa panicked and started to fight the... entity? She wasn't sure what it was, but she could tell it was male, and she knew she wasn't going to like where he was taking her.

She managed a solid kick in his stomach. He grunted, and she slipped off his shoulder slightly. Another twist and several kicks to the abdomen, and he struggled to hold on to her.

Willow swooped in behind him. "Take that, demon!" She thrust an energy bolt into his back. He dropped Kalissa, sending her rolling into the underbrush along the path they'd been traveling down.

Another shadowy creature barreled toward them, plowing into the other. The newcomer was different, felt familiar to her somehow. After a few seconds, she recognized the new one as Ayden. He was using the demon's abilities against him.

They rolled on the ground until one kicked the other off. He sailed through the air and slammed hard into the trunk of an oak tree. Sliding down to the ground, he jumped up, shook it off, and charged back at the other one.

The other crouched low—braced for impact. When the one that'd hit the tree made contact, he was thrown backwards over the other's head.

It was hard to tell them apart. Kalissa didn't know whom to root for as the two transparent, black-clouded bodies wrestled and fought one another. Her palms were sweating, and her heart raced. A crack sounded and echoed off the trees, as one got a solid punch in on the other's jaw. They were too well matched. It was a death match. She wanted to stop it but didn't know what to do.

A distraction. She could cause a diversion. But what?

Willow came and sat beside her. "Man, I wish I had some popcorn."

Kalissa frowned at the nymph. "Willow!"

"What?" Willow gave an innocent look and then released a heavy sigh. "Lis, you have the power to help him."

Doubt settled in. "No, I... How?"

"He's your life partner." Kalissa peered at Willow in question. The nymph knew. "Before you ask, no, your mating rose is not visible to me. I can see it in your aura and the way you look at each other. It was the same with your parents." Sadness passed between them. Willow took a deep breath and continued. "Close your eyes and focus. Search for the connection that draws you to him."

Kalissa hesitated, unsure how to find the connection. Another crack from a fist hitting a jaw ricocheted off the trees and pushed her into motion. If she didn't do something, Ayden and the demon would kill each other. She closed her eyes, concentrated on Ayden, and stretched out her senses.

Frustration mounting, she lost focus. Willow's voice drifted into her thoughts. *"You are stronger than you think. Open your mind to his. Accept what you deny."*

A tree branch sailed past, inches from her head, and landed with a thud in the woods. The wind from the flying object whipped her hair in her face. Her heart kicked with beats that would send her into cardiac arrest if she were mortal.

Screw trying to figure out what the hell Willow had meant with her cryptic riddles. Ayden needed help. She crouched closer to the dueling shadows. One got knocked down by a punch so hard he slid along the ground and stopped inches from her. He got up and stilled, locking gazes with Kalissa. Her heart stopped beating. That was not Ayden. She didn't try to comprehend how she knew as she scooted backwards.

A face formed out of the black cloud of a body. She cringed and fought back a gasp. Although he wasn't fully solid, his true form flashed in her mind. Marbled blue scales covered his body, and his eyes glowed crimson. One of those blue-scaled claws rose in the air and came down lightning-quick to swipe at her.

CHAPTER TWELVE

Kalissa braced for the impact of the demon's claws, eyes squeezed shut. It didn't come. She opened her lids. Bile rose in her throat, and her stomach soured. The demon lay on the ground in front of her, arm extended out, and head several feet away.

Ayden stood over the body, sword in hand; his chest rose and fell as he caught his breath. She smiled and flew into his arms. Relief and happiness raced through her.

"Are you okay?" It was the first thing out of Ayden's mouth after he'd teleported them back inside the cabin. He walked around her, touching her and checking for injuries.

"I'm fine." She took his hands in hers to halt his circling. "What about you?" Searching his face, she saw yellowish bruises forming along his right cheekbone and left eye. A deep, claw-like scratch lay over his right eye. To her relief, it had stopped bleeding.

"I'll live." He pulled her to him and held her tightly. "Are you sure he didn't hurt you?"

Kalissa had tensed for a second before she deflated, falling into him. She wrapped her arms around his waist and nodded into his chest while breathing in his scent—sandalwood and man. Comfort and warmth blanketed her as he held her. If it weren't for Willow and Ayden, she wouldn't be here. She wasn't sure where she would have ended up, nor did she want to find out. His concern for her touched something deep inside; the self-doubt and anxiety shrinking away. He could never hurt her as Liam had.

She pulled back to look into his eyes. "Who hit the tree?"

He smiled a sexy smile that made her go weak in the knees. "The shadow demon."

Kalissa narrowed her eyes at him. There was a "duh" in that statement. "How did you change like that?" She had her theories, but she asked anyway.

Instead of answering, he took her hands from around his waist and led her to the kitchen. Kalissa climbed onto one of the barstools when they'd reached the island that separated the two rooms.

Once on the other side of the counter, he explained. "I'm not sure, really. I panicked and just reacted. I mean, I got into his head and found his strongest ability and took it."

"You can do that, get inside people's heads?"

He thought about it for a second. "Not always. With other Divinities, I can just sense their Divine gifts. With demons, I have to go into the subconscious and search. Some are harder than others." He opened the refrigerator to the right of the island.

"How did that demon get past Willow's wards?"

"Shadow demons are hard to detect," he replied as he pulled some things out of the refrigerator and placed them on the counter. "Chicken stir-fry okay?"

"Yes, that's fine. Is it dinner time already?"

"Not really, but since we didn't get to enjoy our lunch, I thought I would start dinner early. Plus, I'm wound up and need something to do." He gave her a gentle smile and went back to pulling out ingredients.

Kalissa looked at the clock on the stove behind Ayden. It was 3:30. She hadn't realized they'd been out so long. They must have hiked longer than it seemed before settling in for the lunch that had been so rudely interrupted.

"Damn shadows," Willow grumped on her way into the kitchen, setting the picnic basket and blanket on the table. "They think they can just sneak up on someone. We showed him, though, didn't we?" She walked over to stand next to Ayden, giving him a little nudge with her elbow. She looked down at the chicken and vegetables laid out on the counter. "Oooh, what's for dinner?"

"Chicken stir-fry. Want to join us?" Ayden asked.

Willow thought about it for a minute and then shook her head. "No, thanks. You kids have fun. I'm going to scout around."

An hour later, Ayden found Kalissa sitting on the back porch swing, taking in the cooling evening air. Leaned against the doorframe, he watched her with a smile he couldn't get rid of. Her eyes were closed; feet folded like a pretzel under her. Dark blond curls cascaded down her back and around her shoulders. This was the most peaceful and relaxed she'd appeared since he'd picked her up from the ER. Then it dawned on him that she was meditating.

She opened her eyes and turned to him.

"I didn't mean to interrupt." He pushed off the door-frame and went to her, handing her a glass of red wine.

She smiled and took the goblet. He sat down next to her on the swing. "It's okay," she said, taking a sip of her wine.

After a long moment of sitting and enjoying the sounds of the forest, she broke the silence by asking, "What happened to us?"

He wasn't surprised by her question. He knew she had wanted to ask, he'd read it in her emotions. He took a deep breath before speaking. "We only had the summers because I lived in California. The summer before we turned eighteen was our last summer together." He stalled. He wasn't angry anymore, but it still hurt. The hurt made him cautious when he was around her, afraid she'd leave again. So many times, he'd wanted to lash out at her, tell her that what she'd done was the worst thing anyone could do. Now, he knew it wasn't her fault.

"Two weeks after school started, I called like I did every Wednesday." He stood and walked to the edge of the porch.

"What did I say?" Kalissa said softly.

Ayden closed his eyes. He heard the sympathetic apology in her voice. "You acted like you didn't under-stand why I was calling you. I thought you were playing around at first. Then you got mad at me and told me you had a boyfriend and not to call you again."

Kalissa made a soft sound. "I'm so sorry…"

Ayden turned around, only to find Kalissa standing behind him. He had blocked her from his senses so he couldn't feel her regret. He hadn't even heard her move. "Don't apologize for something you had no control over."

Kalissa took a step back. "But that was so…"

He let her trail off and nodded. "I was so angry with you. I swore if I ever saw you again, I would let you have it."

Kalissa looked down at her linked hands in front her. "Is that why you reopened the case? To piss me off? To start a fight?"

"Gods, no." He reached out and pulled her to him. Relief diminished her tension. She melted into him after a brief hesitation. Her fear abating. She wrapped her arms around his waist and pressed her cheek to his chest. It felt so right to hold her. "I had a lot of time to think. When I decided to take the position as sheriff, I asked Papa about memory spells. When I picked you up at the hospital, my suspicions were confirmed. You have no memory of us. Then Zach and Khloe agreed with what I believed happened."

"Liam."

"Excuse me?"

"It must have been Liam. He was my first…well, my second boyfriend. The first one I remember." Ayden pressed his lips together to hide a smile at her correction. He remained quiet to let her finish her thought. "He was controlling. He didn't like me talking to people he didn't know. It kind of makes sense now."

Ayden gave her a raised eyebrow expression, not sure where she was going with this. "What makes you think it was him?"

Kalissa looked out into the forest. "Let's go inside," she said and stepped out of his arms.

"You sense something?"

Kalissa shook her head. "No. Just a bird."

Ayden picked up her glass where she'd left it on the table next to the swing and turned to the door. He handed the wine to her before opening the door and following her inside to the sofa.

"Liam was an aggressive, take-charge kind of person. He was a control freak. He always questioned me after I'd spoken to Zach or Khloe without him around. He asked what they'd said. And even accused me of keeping secrets from him once." Kalissa took a sip of wine.

Ayden clenched his jaw to hold back a curse. Her words sounded as if it was nothing, but the hint of fear mixed with self-doubt hung heavily in the air. His suspicions of an abusive boyfriend were becoming confirmed by the minute.

"I didn't think anything of it until now. Liam seemed to know a little too much about the Divinities. The moment I met him, he knew I was a Divinity." Ayden frowned. Humans didn't pay enough attention to them to make that kind of observation.

"I know that's not too unusual. I mean, we don't hide what we are. Humans have known about *magickin* for centuries," she added.

"I feel a *but* coming on."

She smiled. "I found something. I went over to his house after school almost every day. One day, his father called him into the study, leaving me alone in his room. I wasn't trying to snoop. I was looking for a CD on his desk, and a piece of parchment paper slid off onto the floor. I picked it up, but couldn't read it. It was written in runes."

"You can't read runes?" Ayden asked with a smirk.

Kalissa rolled her eyes. "No. I stopped going to the witchcraft classes when I was...seventeen. And don't remember much before that."

"Well, I'm sure there are other witches that don't know how to read runes."

Kalissa smiled at him. "Yeah, all under the age of five."

"Did you ever tell anyone about the note?" Ayden asked.

She nodded. "I told Zach. We both thought it was a little odd, considering Liam was human."

"After Liam died our senior year of college, I stayed to myself," Kalissa said after a brief pause. "They said he had a heart attack," she added.

"You sound unsure about that."

"I...I'm not sure what I thought." She looked down at her wine glass and traced the rim with her finger.

"Were you bound to him?" he asked, trying to leave the jealousy out of his tone.

"I'm not sure. I mean...I don't remember. Oh, gods, I'm an idiot."

"No, you were—*are*—under a spell. There's a big difference." He took her wine glass and set it on the coffee table. For fear of what the spell would do to her, he didn't press for any more information. So far, it hadn't caused her any pain. However, there was guilt in her tone.

Wanting to chase her dark musings away, he lifted her chin with his fingers, leaned in, and captured her lips with his.

CHAPTER THIRTEEN

When Ayden's soft lips touched hers, an invigorating surge of power rolled through Kalissa, possessing every inch of her. A mixture of desire and fear washed over her. *You will not have a panic attack. You're stronger than that*, she coached herself. For once in her life, she wanted to be touched, caressed, and loved. Even if it were only for one night.

Ayden was familiar, in an old friend kind of way. A friend that made her want to explore her fantasies, instead of run from them.

When Ayden had kissed her the night before, it had been light and gentle. Now, he kissed her with intent—and with a hint of urgency and need. Her panic spiked but didn't rise to alarm until his hand slipped under her shirt and glided up to her breast.

"Stop." It came out breathlessly with a hint of terror before Kalissa could push the anxiety back. Ayden lifted his head. His baby blue eyes mirrored her fear. He knew the cause of her panic. Embarrassment and shame flooded her.

"Lis." It was a plea, and she almost cried. She wanted so deeply to be with him, to know what it was like to make love to someone without pain and humiliation. He brushed his knuckles over her cheek and kissed her lips. "I won't ask you for details. Just tell me what I can do to help."

"I…don't know," she whispered.

Ayden gathered her in his arms and sat back on the sofa. She let him draw her into his chest.

After a few minutes of silence, Kalissa took a shaky breath. She had never told anyone what she was about to reveal to him. Not even her twin. "Ayden?"

"Mmm hmm."

She lifted her head. He looked peaceful, relaxed with his eyes shut. "You're not mad?"

His lids lifted and his eyes met hers. "Why would I be mad?"

He was seriously confused by her comment. "It's just…well, Liam…I couldn't say no." The last section of the statement came out in a rushed breath. She studied Ayden as the confusion became clear and a tic appeared in his jaw. A tang of panic made her heart race, but she pushed it away with even breaths.

"Everyone deals with anger and stress in different ways. Liam used sex." She stopped, unable to continue. Mostly out of embarrassment for being so vulnerable and weak. If she'd put her foot down, taken control, and actually told him no…

Liam would have found another way to release his anger.

She'd worked to gain control of her life and the panic attacks that arose from the closeness of another person for years. Not even Zach could get near her without the air thinning the first year after Liam's death. She'd promised herself to never submit to anyone again, but she longed to know what it was like to make love to a man. To orgasm without pain.

Ayden's hand cupped her cheek. She nuzzled into his warm palm. "I could never hurt you."

The truth in his words went straight to her heart. Ayden's baby blue eyes held nothing back. "Can you show me? I mean, I can't make promises, but I want to tr—"

His lips touched hers, soft yet demanding, before she'd gotten the last word out. With a moan, she opened for him, and his tongue swept in, tangling with hers as his arms pulled her close. All her worries evaporated like water droplets hitting a hot iron. She couldn't deny her longing to be held, caressed, and loved by him any longer. Ayden ignited the flame she'd thought had died. Flame? Hell, he set off a damn inferno inside her that burned through her body with the slightest touch.

She ran her hands up his muscular arms to his broad shoulders, her fingertips barely brushing the skin. He shuddered. The sensation felt good against her aura and bounced between them until it was absorbed, merging them as one. Their magnetism mingled their Divine powers, teasing each other and intensifying the magic that ran through their veins. She coiled one arm around his neck and buried the fingers of her other hand in his silky hair, tugging slightly. He moaned softly and pulled her closer.

To her surprise and relief, the panic never came, and she wondered if he was using his empathy to calm her. If he was, she was grateful.

"Ayd?" she whispered, a breathless, almost panting question against his lips. "Are you...?"

"I'm taking your anxiety and replacing it with my pleasure." A sexy, crooked smile tugged the corner of his mouth. "Of course, it'll double your pleasure."

Mischief flirted with his words, which died when he possessed her lips again.

She wanted to feel his bare chest against her hands and test out his admission. Moving her palms down his back, she felt every tight muscle until she reached the bottom of his shirt and tugged it upwards. Their kiss broke just long enough to pull his shirt over his head. Chest bared and looking edible, he gave her a dreamy smile and reclaimed her lips. Their tongues danced as they deepened the kiss.

His lips left hers to trail light kisses across her cheek to her ear, teasing her earlobe by nipping it with his teeth before exploring downward. Her head fell back onto the sofa to give him better access as his wet, hot tongue moved over her delicate skin to the crook of her neck.

Ayden was trying to kill her with sensuality. A slow death she greeted with open arms, because without the fear, she was free to accept every caress, nip, and lick he gave her. She wanted more, and yet, he was taking his sweet-ass time, slowly torturing her. Her sex throbbed and ached to be touched, to have him inside her.

He worked at the buttons of her blouse, and the fabric shifted against her stomach until she felt the garment fall open. Through it all, he never ceased his slow, exploratory kisses across her collarbone down to the skin between her breasts. She sucked in a gasp and almost cried out when he freed her breasts from her bra, taking one of her nipples into his mouth, circling it with the tip of his tongue.

When she thought she would explode from their mingled pleasure, he released her breast and trailed light kisses down her stomach. Instead of grabbing for him like she wanted, she watched him undo her pants. A hint of panic peeked out of her subconscious. He stopped and locked gazes with her. "Are you with me?"

At her nod, Ayden slowly slid the denim over her hips, then off her legs until they dropped to the floor. He knelt down on the floor between her legs and placed tiny, feather-like kisses up the inside of her right thigh. The stubble of his two-day-old beard lightly scraped against her skin, making her flinch. His lips trailed farther up her leg to her hip until they reached her belly just above her panty line. Slowly, he removed her panties with the same sensual movements he had her jeans. Kalissa had to force herself to be patient, but it was hard. Her body screamed to bring this sluggish act to the grand finale. It was killing her. She wanted him so badly, she ached in anticipation.

Exposed and naked while he still had his jeans on, she fought the urge to cover up. She jumped slightly when his lips touched the inside of her thigh again. He smiled and asked, "You okay?" She nodded and watched him. "We can stop at any time."

As if. Never in her thirty-two years of living had she felt this much pleasure. She wouldn't be held responsible for her actions if he stopped now. She would plead temporary insanity for assaulting an officer.

He placed a hand on her other thigh and gave a gentle nudge to urge her to spread her legs apart. She complied, scooting her bottom to the edge of the sofa. When his lips touched her core, she sucked in a breath and closed her eyes briefly. His light touch against her skin made her ache for more. He moved his hand farther up her thigh to her lips to open them. She threw her head back into the sofa as he licked and sucked, sliding two fingers inside her. She gasped at the amount of pleasure that shot through her body and arched into him. Never in her life had she ever felt like this. His power went through her like a warm current in her veins. Their magic whirled around them. Just when she thought she would burst from the mounting passion, he lifted his head and moved up her body with his fingers still inside her, his thumb replacing his tongue. "I want to hold you when you come," he whispered in her ear and then kissed her neck.

Kalissa wrapped her arms around his neck and buried her hands in his hair, bringing his mouth to hers. The pleasure built as he moved his fingers in and out of her while his thumb rubbed her clit until the convulsing waves of an orgasm took her under.

AYDEN GATHERED Kalissa up in his arms, carried her to the bedroom, and laid her down on the bed. Her hand rose, cupped the back of his head, and pulled him into a deep, passionate kiss. Slowly, he drew back his empathic hold on her. He hoped she wouldn't need it any longer, now that the ice was broken.

He pulled away from her, slid backwards off the bed, and smiled at her groans of protest. Their eyes locked and stayed fixed on each other as he removed his jeans and secured a condom in place. Settling between her legs and positioning his cock at her entrance, he reclaimed her mouth again, slipping his tongue between her lips. He could still taste remnants of wine as their tongues twined and danced together. She raised her hips slightly, moving, rubbing against him as waves of passion and desire wrapped around them in a lover's embrace. Her desire ran through him as his own, intensifying his need, pushing him towards the edge of control. But the hint of fear, of the unknown, still lay under the surface, as well.

Each movement pushed them further into ecstasy until he couldn't take anymore. Her need was his need. They were connected on a level he'd never known. It was beyond his empathic abilities. Was it because they were life partners?

She made a pleading moan. He reacted and entered her slowly. Then stopped a few inches in. Kalissa became very still, her breathing coming in panicked gasps.

"Lis? Look at me." When her eyes met his, anger made its presence known again. He'd seen way too many domestic cases over the years and knew firsthand the effects they had on the victims. "Are you okay? Do you want me to stop?"

Her head shook side to side. "Don't stop. I'm okay."

He claimed her lips in a searing kiss and pushed farther inside her. A moan escaped Kalissa's lips, and he pulled out, but not all the way. He entered her again, repeating the slow in and out tempo until he'd filled her completely.

"Ayden…"

Looking down into her lust-drunk eyes, he saw her fear had turned to need. He knew what she wanted.

He increased the rhythm, each thrust becoming faster and harder until they both cried out in release. He collapsed beside her and gathered her into his arms so she lay across his chest.

"I think you broke me," Kalissa said with a laugh.

Ayden laughed at first, but then looked worried. He lifted his head to look her in the eyes. "Did I hurt you?"

She gave him a provocative smile. "No, silly. I was teasing." She crawled up his chest to place a kiss on his nose and then his lips. "Thank you."

"For what?" He wrapped his arms around her, deepening the kiss.

"For freeing me." She brought her knee up to rub gently over his still hard cock.

Ayden groaned. "You keep that up, and I'll have to take you again," he teased with his lips over hers.

"Hmmm, sounds promising." She licked his lips playfully. "But only on one condition."

"What's that?"

"Take off the kid gloves," she said. She let out a squeak when he rolled her beneath him and entered her at the same time.

CHAPTER FOURTEEN

Kalissa woke with a smile from ear to ear. She stretched and felt every muscle, sore in all the right places, and then some. Amazingly, Ayden had scared all her anxiety away. In the multiple times they'd made love throughout the night, the fear and panic no longer consumed her. She had been freed from the prison her mind had created.

Ayden belonged to her. The connection and internal need to bond with him was too great to deny.

Her smile not faltering, she reached over to the other side of the bed and frowned, patting it a couple of times. Ayden was gone. It would have been nice to wake up in his arms after the incredible night they'd had together. She climbed out of bed and searched for something to put on. The room was clean with the exception of their clothes from the night before in the chair next to the dresser. He'd brought their clothes in from the living room. That thought warmed her heart. *Neat, and he cleans up after himself.* Nice.

She walked over to the chair, picked up the first thing she touched, and put it on. It was Ayden's t-shirt. And it smelled Divine. A giggle bubbled up inside her, threatening to spill from her lips. Like the one he'd given her at the hotel, this one fit her like a nightgown, falling halfway to her knees.

A frown replaced her happy thoughts when she wondered where he was. "Damn, men. Think they can give you the best night of your life and just leave you hanging," she muttered to herself as she walked out of the bedroom and into the living room. The luring smell of bacon and eggs invaded her nose, and she froze halfway across the living room. Ayden stood on the other side of the island, preparing breakfast. She turned around to go back to the bedroom.

"Good morning."

Ayden's voice stopped her. She closed her eyes, feeling like the biggest bitch. After a few seconds, she opened her eyes, forced a smile, and turned around to face him. "Morning," she whispered.

"Why are you upset?" he asked, clearly able to feel her mood.

Kalissa walked into the kitchen and leaned her back against the counter next to him. Realization glided over her that she, too, could sense *his* mood. Right now, he was concerned about her. It was strange how connected they'd become in such a short period of time. Was it because they were magical partners? Were they starting to bond? That last question frightened her. She didn't want to bond with him only to have him taken from her.

He moved to stand in front of her. Her heart rate picked

up, and her body warmed as his aura mingled with hers, forcing all her fears to dissolve away into nothing. Ayden sent her places and showed her pleasure she'd never dreamed of—multiple times throughout the night and in multiple places. All she wanted to do was to drag him back to the bedroom and not come out. Ever.

Ayden wrapped his arms around her waist and pulled her tightly into his body. "I wanted to surprise you with breakfast in bed." He slid his hands to her ass, lifted her up, and set her on the countertop.

"Well, I could go back to bed and pretend to be asleep," she teased and then kissed his nose.

Ayden chuckled softly and kissed her lips, moving to her cheek and jawline, and stopping when he reached her earlobe. "It's too late. I've got you where I want you."

"Do you, now?" Kalissa wrapped her legs around his hips and pulled him even closer to her.

"Oh, please tell me you didn't do it on the kitchen counter." Khloe's teasing tone pulled Ayden's and Kalissa's attention from each other and toward the door. Khloe walked over, took a piece of bacon, and popped it in her mouth. She leaned her hip against the island. "So. How are the lovebirds this morning?" she asked with a wide grin as Zach came in behind her and sat at the kitchen table.

Kalissa hopped down from the counter, careful not to flash everyone in the process, suddenly very aware that she was naked under Ayden's t-shirt. Now that Zach was sitting at the kitchen table, Kalissa felt self-conscious. She excused herself and went to change.

~

As soon as Kalissa was inside the bedroom with the door shut, Khloe turned to Ayden. "Let's see it."

Ayden narrowed his eyes at her and smirked. This was a different Khloe than he remembered from his summer visits to the coven. Of course, she looked like Kalissa, they were twins, after all. But it was easy to tell them apart. Khloe's hair was slightly lighter than Kalissa's and had two pink streaks on either side of her face. She also had a nose ring, and her right eyebrow had a small hoop in it. "Did that hurt?" he teased, indicating her eyebrow piercing.

Khloe's hand involuntarily went to her eyebrow. She smiled. "Not nearly as much as I wanted it to." Ayden raised his eyebrows, but she ignored it. "Stop changing the subject and let me see it."

"See what?" Ayden asked.

"Your mark." Khloe held out her hand, palm up. Ayden hesitated, making her grow more impatient. "I can see it in your aura. Both of you. Show me your mark."

With a heavy sigh, he extended his left arm and turned it so his Divine Rose was exposed. He knew she couldn't see it, but humored her anyway. Khloe frowned. "It's not there." She looked up at Ayden.

Ayden put his arm down and went back to cooking. "That's because we're not bound together. *You* won't be able to see it." Khloe shrugged and took another piece of bacon. Ayden playfully pushed her toward the table. "Go, sit. I made enough for everyone."

"How did you know we were going to be here this morning? You have ESP or something?" Khloe teased and sat down at the table next to Zach.

"Or something," Zach snickered.

Khloe shot Ayden a suspicious look. Ayden laughed. "I have the power of adaptability. I can draw on others' powers. Sometimes, I pick up stuff without meaning to."

"Like a vision of us being here this morning?" Khloe gave him a smile that made her nose wrinkle up.

"That was the only reason I didn't take your sister back to bed."

"TMI! I so do not want to know," Khloe said dramatically and began to hum loudly with her hands over her ears. After a couple of seconds, she released her ears and laid her hands on the table.

With a shake of his head, Ayden finished up breakfast and filled them in on Kalissa's dream-vision. "I'm concerned it would be a distraction to her and me." He fixed his eyes on Khloe. "Could you talk to her?

She nodded as Kalissa came back into the kitchen, dressed in a pair of blue jeans and a white t-shirt. She immediately walked into Ayden's embrace and wrapped her arms around his waist. He pulled her in close and kissed the top of her head. Her mood had darkened again, and he wondered if she was thinking about her vision. He thought about it too and came up empty, not understanding it. Something was missing, something vital to the events that would unfold. With careful planning and everyone on alert, maybe they could all walk away alive.

∾

"I FORGOT how much I love it up here," Khloe said with her hand out the car window, letting the air pass through her fingers. They were on their way to The Wheel to meet Jacen and Lydia Rayners.

"The air is so clean. Oh! Where is Willow?" Khloe said, looking at Kalissa.

"There was a little issue on our way to the cabin." Kalissa told her about the demons following them, Willow getting hurt, and Ayden's driving skills. "But Willow's okay. She's probably just giving Ayden and me some time alone."

"I suppose. She could have at least come by to say hi. I know she knows I'm here." Khloe straightened in her seat and stuck her hand back out the window. "I missed you," Khloe said softly after a brief silence.

Kalissa smiled and took Khloe's hand. "I missed you, too. Why so early?" She frowned, thinking the Lydia and Jacen must have driven all night to be here already from New York.

"The Dark Divine round-up has Papa nervous," Khloe said with no emotion in her voice, though her uneasiness floated off her and added to Kalissa's already edgy mood.

"Are we being followed?" Khloe asked.

Kalissa shook her head. "No. You feel like we're being watched?"

"Yeah."

"Can you sense anything?" Kalissa asked. Khloe could control all elements. It was her gift. It went further than being able to work with them, though. She could actually bend them to her purpose. So, Khloe could use all the elements to search and discover if anyone was out there.

Her sister closed her eyes. Kalissa knew she was using

her senses to search for a threat. After a while, she said, "No, just a raven."

"Yeah, that's all I got, too." Kalissa frowned. It was odd that both of them could feel something but not be able to find it.

"Could be a messenger," Khloe said.

"You're probably right," Kalissa said. Ravens were messengers of the Afterworld. They were sent to deliver messages to the living from their loved ones that had already passed. The problem was, they only delivered their messages when they were good and ready.

A few minutes later, they pulled into the parking lot of The Wheel. The restaurant didn't serve breakfast, there-fore, opened at eleven in the morning. It was 9:30 a.m., so the lot only had one car parked in the middle of it. Three people stood outside the silver Audi. Two of them Kalissa recognized as Jacen and Lydia. She'd found old photos in her mother's things. The other person, a woman, looked familiar, but Kalissa didn't immediately recognize her.

"It's a good thing we left the cabin when we did," Khloe stated.

Kalissa agreed and said, "It was an estimate." She pulled up beside the Audi. "I didn't know Lydia was preg-nant." They didn't keep in touch with each other. The Raynerses lived in New York, after all. Even though they'd come to visit the Maxville Coven as children, Kalissa didn't know them well.

"Me either."

If Noah had known, he would have told them about Lydia's pregnancy, especially knowing what was at stake. Kalissa had heard that a growing fetus used up a lot of a witch's energy. She wasn't sure how much help Lydia would be against an attack. She was tempted to tell Khloe to head to Maxville with Lydia and wait for them there. It would be safer that way, and ensure that nothing would happen to Lydia's unborn child. But that was one argument she didn't want to get into with her sister at the moment.

Was it a mistake for Jacen to bring his sister here?

Lydia and Jacen, being two years apart, were as close as twins. Jacen was the oldest. Still, Kalissa could see that their auras seemed to mingle and reach out to one other. Like their magical energies were tied together.

Lydia was shorter than Kalissa's and Khloe's height of five ten. Jacen was taller than them, but only by an inch or two. The only things similar about them were their facial features and their hair. Lydia had beautiful, long, red hair. Jacen's tresses were a dark auburn.

"Why do they look like that? They're not twins."

Khloe shrugged. "Maybe Angelica bound them. It's not uncommon for mothers to bind their children together. It kinda makes sense with the demons. They would know if the other were in trouble, like we do."

She had a point. If they hadn't already been bonded through their twin connection, Kalissa was certain their mother would have done the same.

They got out of the vehicle and walked to the front of the cars where the others were waiting. "Have you been waiting long?" Kalissa asked.

"We just got here," Lydia said, extending her hand. "Lydia Rayners. This is my brother, Jacen. And this is Melaina Harris. I hope you don't mind, but Jace and I insisted on Mel coming."

"No. Not at all. But we've actually met—a long time ago."

Lydia looked at her and then at Khloe. "Oh, yeah. Duh. I'm sorry, I have baby brain." She laughed and touched her round belly.

Kalissa smiled. "No worries. It was years ago. I'm Kalissa, and this is my sister, Khloe."

She turned to Melaina and offered her hand. Melaina had American Indian somewhere in her bloodline. Her skin had reddish-brown undertones, and she had straight, midnight-black hair. But it was her eyes that stole Kalissa's breath. They were the brightest and most vivid emerald green she had ever seen. "It's nice to meet you," Kalissa said to Melaina. Melaina smiled, took Kalissa outstretched hand, and returned the greeting.

"I'm sorry for staring, but you two look just like your mother," Melaina said with a hint of sadness.

Kalissa studied Melaina for another few seconds, but it was Khloe who spoke. "You're one of the survivors. One of the six charged with protecting the Sinew."

Melaina nodded grimly. "Yes. I'm glad you found it."

"Well, we don't have it. Just a guess on where it might be. You didn't know where it was?" Kalissa asked.

"No, that was the rule. One of us hid it; the others were given directions to be able to locate it if something happened," Melaina said with a sad tone.

That explained the cryptic notes they'd been left by their parents. Kalissa got a shiver down her spine. She looked around. "Let's head to the cabin." Her radar was going off big time. There were demons in the area, and Kalissa wasn't in the mood to rumble.

Everyone turned to their right at the same time as four large demons came from the back of the building. "Are you ready to rumble now?"Jacen whispered. Kalissa shot him a look. He smiled. "Sorry, telepathic."

"Oh, great. That's nice to know," Kalissa said dryly and shook her head with a smile. She was going to have to keep her guard up. Threefold, now that Zach was at the cabin. Khloe being in her head was comfortable, but the knowledge that someone else could be in there made her a little uneasy. With two empaths and a telepath, they were going to have *so* much fun.

"Ready or not," Khloe said with an evil laugh. Kalissa decided her sister just wasn't right. Okay, so her sister had always been a little off.

The five of them stood their ground...and waited. The demons stood in place, staring at them, stalling. But why? After a few minutes of playing bet-you-blink-first, the demons charged forward. It was as if they were being commanded from the sidelines, like puppets.

Everyone but Lydia proceeded forward to meet the demons head-on. Since there were only four, it was safe enough for Lydia to hang back. Kalissa heard Jacen order his sister to put up a circle. It made sense. That way, if there were others hanging around, Lydia would be safe inside her magical bubble.

Kalissa could tell that they were Lackeys—the lower class of demons. The only way Kalissa could explain how she knew was that she could sense their power level, as if she had some kind of internal gauge that measured their strength.

These demons were holding back. It was like they

weren't sure about something, or they were just feeling out the level of their opponents' powers.

Kalissa ducked as a demon's arm came at her. She kicked and swiped out his legs from underneath him. He fell, hard. Kalissa jumped up and prepared herself for round two. She was knocked to the ground by another demon that she hadn't seen. He hit her in the side, hard enough that it knocked the wind out of her. They rolled in a tangle of body parts until he flipped her on her back to pin her to the ground with his body.

Fuck. Where the hell had he come from? That was the second time in two days she'd been taken by surprise.

A quick glance to the others said that this demon had been hiding somewhere. Khloe was overpowering the one she was fighting, almost toying with it, and Jacen and Melaina were doing a lot better than Kalissa was at the moment.

Kalissa looked up at the demon that was straddling her, holding her down. He reached into his back pocket and pulled out a magical cuff. The single silver-coated iron bracelet would mute a witch's magic and render them powerless.

"Oh, hell no," Kalissa breathed out. She would be damned if he got that cuff on her and teleported her to the gods knew where. Kicking and bucking, she tried to get the demon off of her. Anxiety filled her and invited helplessness to the party. The loss of control brought back memories of being with Liam, fueling the panic to the point of total freak out.

Out of the corner of her eye, movement caught her attention. The demon she'd knocked out moments ago recovered and stalked toward them. Her sister and the others were out of her line of vision. Somehow—maybe from the impact of the second demon knocking her to the ground—she had ended up a good distance from the others.

Just when she thought she was on her own, a voice screamed, "Take that, you bastards!" The demon pinning her to the ground went flying off with a scream that would put a schoolgirl to shame. A fireball hit him square in the chest. The impact knocked him into another demon. Both went up in flames and dissolved into a pile of ash.

Khloe came over and held out her hand. Kalissa smirked at her sister. Fire had always been Khloe's favorite element. Kalissa took her sister's outstretched palm and pulled herself to a stand. Jacen and Melaina came over to see if they were all right.

Jacen picked up the cuff the demon had left behind. "This could come in handy," he said and slipped the bracelet into the back pocket of his jeans. Kalissa was thinking the same thing. If only they could get more of those.

"Well, hell. That didn't last long," Khloe said. "I was just getting warmed up."

"Patience, little one. I'm sure you'll get another chance to pound demon ass," Kalissa said. She hoped it wouldn't be too soon. She turned to the others. "Flash your lights if you are being followed." They nodded in agreement and walked back to their cars.

Forty-five minutes later, they pulled into the cabin's driveway and parked outside the front door. Ayden stood on the porch when they got out of their cars. Kalissa climbed the stairs and couldn't keep the smile from her face. She walked into his arms, wrapped her arms around his waist, and laid her head against his chest. This was where she belonged. Her soul, body, and mind knew it. There was no way around it. He was hers as much as she was his.

The much too close call with the demons had opened her eyes. Without Khloe, Kalissa wouldn't be here to hold Ayden. She was beginning to get to know him all over again. She wasn't ready to be apart from him.

"Snap out of it, you two. We've got demons to slay and a creepy bird following us," Khloe said before she led Jacen, Lydia, and Melaina inside.

Ayden lifted his eyes to the highest branch of the ash tree to their right. He took Kalissa's hand and walked inside the cabin. Just as they crossed the threshold, Willow popped in behind them. "Hey!"

Kalissa jumped and turned to face her. "Shit, Willow, you scared me."

"Oh, I'm sorry. I was just excited. I came earlier to see Lo and you two were gone," Willow skipped ecstatically around Kalissa to hunt for Khloe.

Kalissa shivered and whirled around to look out into the forest surrounding the cabin. Something was out there. A familiar essence. Taunting, waiting.

CHAPTER FIFTEEN

Khloe led Lydia, Jacen, and Melaina through the front door of the two-story log cabin. The foyer opened to the living room. The open floor plan made the place look much bigger on the inside as compared to the outside. Khloe smiled at Lydia's amazement as she entered the mountain home.

"This is nice," Lydia said.

"Thanks," Khloe and Kalissa said at the same time and then laughed.

Willow drifted in from behind Khloe and pulled her into a tight hug instantly. Khloe hugged the nymph back and blinked away the tears that surfaced. Gods, she'd missed her adopted sister. A pang of guilt rose up in her heart. She should have visited before now. Willow was family. The last time she'd seen her was at her parents' funeral.

"Um, Khloe. You're bleeding." Lydia's voice seeped through her thoughts.

"What? Where?" Khloe pulled out of the hug with Willow and checked herself over, looking at her front and then twisting around to see her back side.

"Your head," Lydia pointed out.

Willow pulled back and looked at Khloe's forehead. "Lo, sit," she commanded.

Khloe rolled her eyes. She sat down on one of the barstools at the kitchen counter without a word. She knew better than to give any lip to Willow. Plus, it was nice to hear the motherly tone again.

Lydia sat on the stool next to her and lifted her hair to see the wound. A bowl of warm water with a washcloth drifted into sight.

"Thanks." She took the bowl and froze for a brief second.

Khloe shifted her eyes to see Zach standing there, holding the bowl, staring blankly at Lydia. He was as capti-vated as a preteen meeting his first crush. She had never seen him react to anyone like that before. It amused her. With lips pressed together to hold back a smile, she took the bowl from him. "That's Zachary," she said with a smirk.

"Hello, Zachary," Lydia said shyly as her brother move closer. Apparently, he'd noticed the attraction too and now stood behind Willow, close to Zach. Hovering like an over-protective parent. Lydia rolled her eyes at her brother. "And this is my overprotective brother, Jacen." She stressed the word 'overprotective' for Jacen's sake.

"Zach."

Lydia looked at him, confused. "What?"

"It's Zach. Everyone calls me Zach. Only Khloe and

my mother call me Zachary." He made a face when he said his full first name.

"I'm still bleeding over here," Khloe mused, feeling a little claustrophobic with everyone hovering around. She was tempted to call Kalissa, Ayden, and Melaina over to complete the gathering.

"It's nice to meet you, Zach," Lydia said, taking the cloth out of the water and wringing it out. She started cleaning Khloe's wound.

"May I ask you how far along you are?" Khloe asked to break the sudden silence.

Lydia smiled. "Six months, yesterday."

"Oh!" Willow exclaimed as if noticing Lydia's condition for the first time. She reached out and stopped when her hand was inches from Lydia's stomach. Willow looked at Lydia. "May I?" Lydia nodded. Willow smiled widely and placed her hand gently on Lydia's belly. "He's a strong one."

"You know the exact date you conceived?" Khloe asked when Willow removed her hand and stepped back. Lydia nodded and then blushed slightly. "Oh. Apologies. That was personal."

"It's okay. My Mikal died in a car crash four months ago." Lydia's expression saddened, making Khloe feel sorry she'd asked.

"Oh. I'm sorry," Grief flooded her. Lydia and Jacen had lost their parents a little over two years ago. Now Lydia had to bury her husband, too. How could she be so motivated to help collect the Sinew? Probably driven by grief and rage, Khloe decided.

"An accident?" Kalissa asked from the other side of the counter.

Lydia nodded. "Yes, but I don't believe it was related to the Divinities' accidents."

"I still think it was a mistaken identity," Jacen broke his silent lurking stance behind Zach.

Khloe smirked inwardly, remembering that Jacen was telepathic. She thought about warning Zach for a second, then decided to leave it alone. Zach would learn on his own.

"How so?" Ayden asked Jacen.

"Mikal was taking the car in for service, something that Lydia was going to do before she told him she was pregnant," Jacen took his gaze off his sister and glanced to Ayden.

"Mikal thought I should rest at home because so much can happen during the first trimester," Lydia added.

"Like I told Lydia, she was supposed to be in that car. Plus, Mikal wasn't a Divinity."

Lydia let out a sigh. "Mikal was a warlock," she volunteered. Everyone got so quiet, Khloe could hear the crickets outside. "Mikal was adopted as a baby and raised with witches inside a coven."

"He was a good man." Jacen didn't hide the sadness in his tone for the loss of his brother-in-law.

Lydia finished cleaning Khloe's wound. "It doesn't look so bad now. Do you want a bandage?"

Khloe wrinkled her nose. "Nah. I'll live."

WILLOW CLAPPED IN EXCITEMENT, making everyone jump. "The Divinities are together again." She hovered in midair and then floated over to Melaina, who was sitting at the kitchen table. "It's so good to see you again, Mel. Isn't it nice to have everyone together?" Willow was filled with glee.

"Hello, Willow. You look as beautiful as ever. Yes, it is wonderful to have the Divinities together again." Melaina looked at the group. "May I make a proposal?" Melaina asked.

"Sure," Kalissa said.

"I was sitting here, observing how comfortable everyone is with each other, and it reminded me of old times when the Divinities lived together. Jace and Dia are moving to Maxville anyway…"

"Move in with us," Kalissa blurted out, cutting Melaina off in a rush that reminded her of something Khloe would do.

"Yeah. We have plenty of room in that huge house. That way, we can be together and protect the Sinew," Khloe added.

Melaina smiled and nodded. "You sure you don't mind?"

Kalissa looked at Ayden, who gave her a smile and a short nod, and said, "Not at all."

"Well, then, it's settled," Khloe said and hopped off her barstool. "Let's go into the living room where it's more comfortable. Willow, can you fix some tea?"

"Khloe, she's not a servant."

Willow waved off Kalissa's protest to her sister's request. "I'd be happy to make tea for everyone."

"I love her tea," Khloe said. "Plus, she enjoys being helpful."

Kalissa released a sigh. "I know. I just don't think she needs to wait on us." She realized Willow might be lonely on the mountain by herself. Something she hadn't considered before.

Once everyone had taken a seat in the living room, Zach directed a question to Melaina. "Does the name Hector Grayson mean anything to you?"

A dark look passed over Melaina's face. She quickly composed her expression and asked, "What do you want to know?"

"We know he was Khan's General and in charge of harvesting the Divinities' powers with the Sinew." Zach pulled out his notepad and thumbed through the pages. "And that Hecate killed him when she took the Sinew back."

"I'm afraid that's pretty much all I know, too. He did have a son. His name was Demetrius…"

"And he has fallen into his father's footsteps, taking the position as Khan's General," Ayden finished Melaina's statement. "So he's responsible for the recent Divinity killings?"

Melaina nodded. "I'm afraid so. I've managed to escape his notice, but my coming here may have put all of us in danger." She took a deep breath and continued before anyone could comment. "Demetrius is out for revenge, retribution for his father's death. Khan wants payback for being cast out by his own people."

"What do you mean 'his own people?'" Kalissa asked. "I thought he was a warlock."

"He is. Well, at least according to the label placed on him by his mother's coven. He was born half witch, and lived inside a coven until his mother died from an illness. The Elders found out he was also half demon, so they sent him to the warlock camp. They said he was too dark to be trusted." Melaina shook her head in disgust. Kalissa could tell she didn't agree with the treatment of the young Khan.

"I've always wondered if things would have been different had Khan been raised with the spiritual love of his coven instead of being cast aside like an unwanted animal. Khan's father, the former Lord of the Underworld, was a fair ruler. As dark and sadistic as he was, he believed in the balance of the three worlds. He would never have tried to merge them like Khan plans to do."

Melaina looked at the young Divinity faces sitting around her. "Khan is a Dark Divine."

Now the Dark Divine round-up made sense to her. Kalissa told Melaina about the message Zach had gotten from Sindee. "Do you think he is gathering the Dark Divines as part of his army? Like they're his to command the same as the demons?"

"I'm not a hundred percent sure. He might not have known about them. None of us knew about them until recently." Melaina paused briefly as if thinking about it. "I can't see any reason why other than forcing them to fight in the war."

Kalissa snuggled back into Ayden's side. He wrapped his arm around her and kissed the top of her head. "Right now, we have to get the Sinew and take it home." She wondered if the others would help her chain Ayden up somewhere until after they'd gotten the Sinew. But she knew that wouldn't happen. She would have to face her vision and keep her senses open. They all had to. Or someone may not leave that cave alive.

CHAPTER SIXTEEN

Ayden took Kalissa's hand and tugged her toward the French doors. She'd noticed his mood change. He wasn't happy about something. Stopping before the doors, he turned to her with an intense stare. She suddenly felt like a wall had gone up.

"What's wrong?"

"When were you going to tell me?"

"Tell you what?"

"Don't play innocent with me. You were almost taken!"

Kalissa winched at his harsh tone. "It was no big deal. I'm here. Everything worked out." She crossed her arms. "Who told you?"

"No one." He looked out the back doors.

"You picked through my head?"

He turned back to her and shook his head. "Not you."

"That's an invasion of privacy."

"I was concerned. When Khloe purposely evaded me, I knew something had happened." He reached out to her.

She shrank back involuntarily. She couldn't stop herself. He was angry. Old unwarranted fear rose in her.

He looked at her inquisitively. "I wasn't going to hurt you."

"I know," she whispered, taking a step back.

He moved too fast for her to react and wrapped his arms around her. "I would never harm you." His tone was soft, caring.

She knew that, but the only experience she'd had with men was Liam. That she remembered anyway. When he got angry, he got forceful and demanding. Ayden was being possessive, and he was upset. So she'd reacted out of reflex; the result of a bad relationship that still haunted her to this day.

A light summer breeze flowed across her arms. Ayden guided her outside, shutting the doors behind them. His fingers slid under her chin, and he lifted her face. She peered into his blue eyes and then he pressed his lips to hers in a soft, quick kiss.

"I'm sorry. I should have told you."

"Shh. No, I'm sorry. Jacen's telepathic."

She looked into his eyes. "Yeah, I know."

Ayden pulled her tighter against him. She wrapped her arms around his waist. "I've never seen someone who can't shut out the voices before. It's intense."

"Is it that bad?" She thought back to when Jacen had read her thoughts in The Wheel's parking lot. It was rude to just pry into one's head, but if he couldn't shut out the voices... He hadn't been inside her head, she realized.

"I don't know how he deals with it. It's non-stop, like a constant chatter." Ayden gave a slight shudder.

It was a wonder that Jacen hadn't gone insane. "Did you notice that Lydia and Jacen are bond siblings? Do you think Angelica bound them to help with the voices?"

"It's possible. But I don't think it's working with Lydia's pregnancy."

Kalissa agreed. *Magickin* fetuses used a lot of energy to grow and develop. Lydia would be unable to aid her brother in shielding his telepathic ability while she was pregnant.

"Come on. Let's go inside before we're missed." He leaned in and pressed his lips to hers once more.

She moaned and pulled him tightly to her. "Let's go inside and be missed."

With a devilish smile, he gave her another quick kiss and then led her back into the cabin.

It was two in the afternoon before they'd gotten set to go to the cave. Melaina agreed with Kalissa about her theory that the Sinew was inside. She said it sounded like her mother to place it there. As for the retrievers, Mel had a hunch that it could be a set of Hecate's hounds—the Goddess's animal to call. That meant the hellhounds, as well as all others related to the canine family. It was just one more thing for Kalissa to worry about.

They'd gone over everything multiple times, including the dream-vision that Kalissa had had two nights ago. She hadn't had a vision since, but she did have memory flash-backs. Bits and pieces of her stolen past were coming back to her. It might be the spell weakening. Melaina had suggested that the spell might wear itself as she spent more time with Ayden. And the closer she got to him, the harder it became to go to that cave. Nervousness made her jumpy.

Ayden came over to where she stood on the front porch, looking out into the quiet, still forest. He placed his hand on her shoulder. She flinched but leaned back into him. "I'll be on full alert. I don't plan to leave now. We are immortal, remember."

Kalissa breathed in deeply and released the breath slowly. "Yes, I remember."

"And the vision didn't tell you who was shot." He kissed her cheek.

"I know." She took in another deep breath. This time, it was to draw strength from her element, the air around her. She silently said a prayer and asked the elemental spirits to watch over them.

The others joined Kalissa and Ayden on the porch.

"Ready?" Khloe asked. Kalissa nodded, and together, they stepped off the porch into the forest, walking down the path toward the cave.

When they came to the end of the path, nothing but a solid wall of rock stood in front of them. "It was right here. You can't move a cave," Kalissa said, pointing at the wall.

"Whoa, do you feel that?" Khloe asked, stepping up to stand next to Kalissa.

"That's the Sinew you feel," Mel replied with a soft laugh. "The cave is here, it's just hidden."

"It must be the spell. It's an illusion spell, hiding the cave from sight." Now that Kalissa focused, she could also sense it. The memory spell she was under must have placed the events of her dream-vision out of order. Or, like

Ayden had said, visions were suggestions of what could happen. They could be changed.

The snap of a twig brought Kalissa's head up. About a dozen demons stepped out of the tree line in a semi-circle in front of them. These demons were more powerful than the Lackeys they'd fought that morning, yet they weren't as strong as the Regals—highly ranked, powerful demons that served as the ruler's personal guards. The creatures that faced them now where Amiddians, the middle-class demons.

A demon charged Kalissa. She charged back, lowered her shoulder, and ran into him like a linebacker. She was quite surprised that she was able to knock the wind out of him. He fell backwards, landing on his ass. He rolled away from her and stood up. She fell into a crouch. Charging back at her, he managed to get a hit on her that knocked her backwards. Groaning from the pain in her hip as she landed hard, she pushed away the agony and shocked the demon with an energy bolt to get him to back off. As he stumbled back several steps, she conjured a sword. When he came back at her again, she was ready. With one swoop, she swung the sword at the demon. His head fell to the ground and rolled as his body sagged in a heap on the forest floor.

"Duck!"

Kalissa didn't ask why. She just hit the ground at Jacen's outburst. When she did, a fireball came whirling over her head and hit the chest of a demon who had come up behind her. The demon let out a pained screech before dissolving into a pile of ash.

Damn, she scolded herself. She had to pay better attention.

Jace appeared over her and offered her a hand up. She took it, and he pulled her to a stand. "You okay?"

She nodded. "Yeah. Thanks." She looked over at Ayden, who had just finished off the demon he fought. Fear coursed through her as another demon came out of the tree line. He fixed a stare on Ayden, raising his hands. "No!" she screamed and ran toward Ayden. Glancing back at the newcomer, she saw him raising energy for a deadly blast. In slow motion, she watched helplessly as the demon released the energy bolt at Ayden.

She screamed again, fell to her knees, and covered her eyes with her hands. Then, Lydia cried out. Kalissa raised her head to see Ayden, alive, kneeling on the ground next to Jacen's convulsing form.

Oh, no, she thought. Her eyes filled with tears, and she swallowed a lump in her throat. She got up to go to them.

On her knees next to Lydia, who sobbed uncontrollably over her brother's body, Kalissa felt completely helpless. She was relieved that Ayden was alive, grateful for Jacen's sacrifice, but saddened by Lydia's loss. She didn't know what to do, so she wrapped an arm around the sobbing witch, drawing her in for comfort. Her heart ached, and tears fell down her cheeks. Jacen's labored breaths said his chances weren't good and that he may not live through the night. The energy ball had been a deathblow, meant for Ayden. Why had Jacen stepped in front of it?

Everything around them fell silent. A flash introduced a large Regal demon. Several curses echoed among the Divinities. The new demon was easily eight feet tall. His skin had a red hue that matched those eerie-as-hell blood-red eyes. His long, straight jet-black hair fell around his shoulders. His dark aura screamed "sadist."

When he spoke, his voice sent shivers over her skin like a million tiny spiders crawling all over her body. "I see you have called in the children, Mel."

"You're stalling, Demetrius," Melaina said as she walked over to stand in front of the group, taking her place as their Elder.

Kalissa looked at the demon. That didn't look like the same being she'd seen at her parents' accident or the crime scene photos Ayden had shown her. No, that demon had looked more human. She wasn't sure why she was surprised. She knew from the demonology classes her mother had insisted she take in college that most demons were shifters. They could take multiple forms.

"I see I have underestimated you. I will not make that mistake again. Khan has a message for Hecate. He wants the Sinew, and will destroy anyone or anything to get it. You have seventy-two hours to turn over the Sinew." He gave a sadistic laugh. "Consider yourselves warned." Then he disappeared, taking the remaining demons with him.

"Or what?" Kalissa heard Ayden ask.

"I'm not sure. Let's get the Sinew and get out of here," Melaina said and bent down next to them, reaching out a hand to Lydia. When she took it, Mel nodded toward the cave. "Go. I'll stay out here with them."

"Are you all right?" Ayden asked in her ear and kissed her temple. She flinched slightly, not noticing that he'd moved closer to her.

"Yeah. Let's just get the Sinew and go home." Kalissa

began to stand up, only to have Ayden pick her up and hold her close to his body by her waist. He gave her a quick kiss on the lips before releasing her.

"Do you want me to do the chant and see if it works with only one of us?" Khloe asked with a grave look. Kalissa felt saddened by the tears in Khloe's eyes.

"Please," Kalissa said softly.

Khloe took out the piece of paper that had the counter-spell on it and recited the words. "By day, by night. Grant the Divine sight." She called the element of fire to ignite the paper into flames and then ash. Then she called air to carry the ash away, sending it out into the Universe.

A few seconds later, the magical veil over the rock wall dissolved, revealing the entrance to the cave.

Inside the cave, she explored, going off in the opposite direction as the others. Khloe had said she didn't think that was such a good idea and suggested they stay together. "When did you become the responsible one?" Kalissa had teased her sister, trying to lighten the mood.

"Since we lost one of our own," she'd replied sourly.

Lo was right. Jacen wouldn't make it through the night —if he wasn't gone already. Kalissa's heart ached for Lydia. She had lost so many loved ones in the past couple of years. It was unfair. A lump lodged in her throat. Memories of the day she'd lost her parents played heavily through her mind. Only Lydia had lost her parents, husband, and now brother. Kalissa could only imagine what she was feeling, or how she'd cope in the coming months.

A deep growl made Kalissa stop in her tracks and surface from her dark musings. A gigantic, two-headed dog came out of an opening she'd been about to check out. It stood over ten feet tall from paw to shoulder. Probably taller, Kalissa decided. The huge, box-shaped heads snarled, revealing long, sharp canines that extended from the upper and lower jaws.

Kalissa walked backward as the black and brown hellhound stalked toward her. She bumped up against Khloe.

Khloe whispered, "Stay still."

Yeah, easy for you to say, Kalissa replied in thought. The hellhounds stopped when the giant heads were inches from her face. The heads breathed in deeply, drawing in their scents. Then they sat back on their haunches and began to speak in quick sentences, one head at a time.

"Thank gods it's you," the one on the left said.

"We were getting worried," the one on the right said.

"How long has it been?"

"Too long. Where have you been?"

"Are we not good enough to visit anymore?"

Kalissa thought she was watching a tennis match with the way they spoke. "What are they talking about?" she whispered to Khloe beside her.

"I don't know."

The heads stopped talking, and the hellhound stood up and looked at Kalissa and then Khloe. Each head turned to the side as if studying them. Then they started talking again.

"You're not Connie."

"Of course, she isn't, stupid."

"I'm not stupid, stupid."

"Boys, please. We came to collect the Sinew and move

it to a safer place," Kalissa said, interrupting their argument.

They stopping talking again and glared at her. "Where is Connie?" they asked at the same time.

Khloe grabbed Kalissa's hand and gave it a light squeeze. The heads looked from Khloe to Kalissa, waiting for an answer until Kalissa finally said, "Our mother died eighteen months ago."

The hounds sat on the floor with a flop that made the whole cave quake. The heads drooped. "She was a sweet woman." Both heads snapped back up to look at Kalissa.

"Accident?" the head on the right asked.

Kalissa nodded. The head on the left made a rude sound and said, "Blah. Accident, our ass. That damn demon had something to do with it."

She stepped closer to the hellhounds. "I'm Kalissa…"

"We know who you are…now."

"Don't be rude!" the head on the right said to the head on the left and then said to Khloe and Kalissa, "You'll have to forgive my brother for his rudeness. I'm Bear. And this," he said, knocking his head into his brother's, "is Teddy."

Khloe snickered. "Oh, Lis. We have our very own giant Teddy-Bear."

Kalissa ignored her sister's teasing. "How would you like to come back with us?"

"You mean it!" Bear beamed.

"Really?" Teddy asked.

Eagerness to leave that cave flowed across their faces. They darted back into the hole they'd come out of earlier. Kalissa peeked in after them, but it was so dark she couldn't see anything. She quickly moved out of the way when Teddy-Bear started dragging a blanket with several items on top of it out of the room. There were large chew toys, balls, and a metal bowl. They dragged the blanket out and laid it down in front of them. The two heads worked together to fold over the corners to be tied together.

Kalissa bent down to help tie the blanket. When it was secure, she straightened. Bear nudged her hand like he wanted her to pet him. She hesitated at first, but then gently patted the top of his large head. He closed his eyes, let out a soft sigh, and leaned into her hand.

All of a sudden, Bear's head was pushed out of the way and replaced by Teddy's, who said, "Come on and share the love."

Kalissa laughed. "Jealous much?"

Bear nodded. "Always."

Kalissa looked around. "Where is the Sinew?"

"Around our necks," Teddy and Bear said simultaneously.

She looked at the necklace that hung around both their necks, the chain resting on their shoulders. A sphere about five inches in diameter encased in a silver medallion that looked a lot like Hecate's Wheel, hung on a thick strip of leather.

She wasn't sure what she'd expected. Maybe that it would be bigger or glow or something. When she turned around, Khloe and Ayden stood a couple of feet away, watching her and the hounds.

They walked out of the cave to where the others waited. "Everyone ready?" Ayden asked, going to where

Jacen lay perfectly still. He bent down to lift Jacen up, and Zach was there in a flash to help.

Mel took Lydia's hand to assist her in teleporting because the pregnancy made it difficult. Flashing took a great deal of energy.

Kalissa looked back at Teddy-Bear. "Are you able to follow us?"

"Like a couple of hellhounds," Teddy said with a big grin.

CHAPTER SEVENTEEN

Demetrius took form inside his office at Grayson Distributions, walked to his large mahogany desk, and sat in a high-back, leather chair. He picked up his phone and dialed the four-digit extension that would connect him to his right-hand man and business partner. "My office. Now," he demanded when the line was answered and then he hung up.

Grayson Distributions was the ultimate cover for his extracurricular activities, and to humans, it was nothing more than a large medical supply distribution company. It was also home to his bioengineering and research facility.

He'd purchased the old, abandoned warehouse several years ago. The building had been gutted, which was convenient for his renovation plans. Half the ground floor had storage rooms, and the other half was laid out as any other distribution warehouse would be, with a loading dock and packaging area.

Within seconds, Paul walked through the office door. Demetrius motioned for him to sit. "How are our guests?"

Uncharacteristically, Demetrius had offered Paul a deal: to join the Regal guards in exchange for his life. Paul had accepted on the condition that he could remain in the human realm. Demetrius agreed and presented it to Khan as a good strategy—to have a Regal living in the human realm. Khan had agreed. Besides, Demetrius liked Paul. He would never admit that to anyone other than his family, which was really only his daughter, Samoan. He had a reputation to protect.

Paul laughed. "The female still fights us. It's gotten worse since she lost her sight. The male just watches and says nothing. I don't trust him. There's something not right about him."

Demetrius raised an eyebrow at his partner. "Are you afraid of him?"

"No. I just don't trust him. It's like he's plotting something."

"Let him plot then, and leave him in solitary confinement. I have plans for that one." The isolation would drive the beast inside the shifter crazy until he snapped. At that point, Demetrius planned to introduce the shifter to the female. And he would be there to absorb their powers when they killed each other.

He opened the bottom right-hand drawer of his desk and pushed a tiny, hidden button. The bookcase against the wall beside his desk opened. He stood and walked through the opening, pressing two buttons on the keypad once Paul had followed him inside the dark stairwell. One button secured the bookcase back in place, and the other turned on the lights.

They proceeded down the stairs into a hallway that

forked off in two different directions. There were holding cells in both of the corridors. Each cell was lined with lead and iron to eliminate the possibility of teleporting in or out of the cells. The jail was perfect for holding his newly acquired guests. Of course, he kept the pair separated. The male was down the corridor to the left, and the female was down on the right.

The hallways circled around and met at an opening that housed his security surveillance equipment and his bio-lab. It was also where he kept tabs on the Divinities. He had demons throughout the city that watched their every move.

The wait had worn on his nerves. He was glad when his informant had told him the younger generation of Divinities had banded together, and that Melaina was with them. He had a message to deliver. And his boss was not the type to give second chances.

Demetrius walked down the hall to the right until he came to stand in front of one of the cells about midway down. Paul unlocked and opened the door. A corner of Demetrius's mouth lifted in a crooked grin when he saw the female pacing her cell with one hand against the wall, running her fingers along it as she walked.

Demetrius willed the lights on inside the cell. She didn't flinch, proving she was indeed blind. Her disgust mixed with a sliver of fear at his presence reached out to him, but she chose to ignore him. Demetrius was used to her rudeness. He walked over to her, and she stopped pacing and tried to keep the distance between them.

"How are you feeling today, love?" he said with a smile. At their last little meeting, she'd tried to gouge his eyes out. She was truly as fiery as the color of her hair.

However, now, she paid him no attention. That pissed him off and amused him at the same time. "Are you not speaking today?" He hoped his flunkies hadn't done anything to hinder her speech. He really liked the way her voiced sounded.

"What do you want, demon?" The question was spoken with so much venom that it almost gave Demetrius a hard-on.

"I came to give you some news." His smile widened when she looked at him, full-faced, and narrowed her eyes out of habit. "Your beautiful daughter is with child. It is a shame the father is not around to see his child brought into the world."

"You bastard! Leave my children alone." She thrust her hands out toward him. Within seconds, she was convulsing on the floor in the fetal position. The cuff she wore around her right wrist kept her from using her magic. When she tried, it sent an electric shock through her body.

Demetrius turned, walked out of the cell, and flipped off the lights before he shut the door. He put his hand flat against the door and smiled. No, he would not torture her tonight. She had done that herself. The shock from the cuff would take hours to wear off. He'd made sure of that when he adjusted the amount of electricity it released into the body.

He turned to head to the security room to find his informant. He wanted to check on what the Divinities had planned before he made his next move.

LIAM STORMED into the security center of the warehouse, slamming the door behind him. He walked to his desk next to the sofa where Samoan was stretched out, listening to her iPod. That's just what he needed. Samoan's smartass mouth. Like a physical caress, he felt her eyes following him as he sat behind his desk and fired up the computer. Her smirk said she was about to start in on him. He was so not in the mood.

The woman he loved was in the arms of another.

When he'd arrived at the cabin, he'd known Kalissa was there, but hadn't expected to see her kissing another male. Not just any male either. It was the same one he'd wiped from her memories fifteen years ago so he could claim her as his own. He'd almost lost every ounce of control and had had to stop himself from bursting through the door of the cabin to kill both of them. Demons didn't deal with jealousy well. Especially bio-fuckups like him.

She was as beautiful as he remembered, with dark blond curls that brushed her hips—just as it had when he'd first seen her. He had always suspected she'd cut it in college out of spite because he'd made a comment about how he loved her long hair. That's what he loved about her. She stood up to him, never backed down from a challenge. Most of all, she met him head-on.

He groaned when Samoan sat up on the sofa, turned off her iPod, stood, and walked toward his desk.

"Whassup?" She sat on the edge of his desk, making her very short skirt appear even shorter.

The door to the holding cells opened to Liam's father, Paul. Liam gave his father a short nod in greeting and returned to the computer screen. "What do you want, Samoan?"

"I have something for you."

"I doubt that," he assured. It's not like Samoan wasn't pretty. She was gorgeous with her long black and blue hair and cobalt blue eyes. Her elfin features from the pointed ears to the pixie-like face came from her mother's heritage, but she possessed every bit of her father's meanness. The ultimate demon seductress.

She handed him a small box that he hadn't seen her with a few moments before. He snatched the package from her and opened it. Inside, was the tiny surveillance camera he'd ordered. "When did this come?"

"It arrived this morning." She leaned over to look at the package's contents. "What's that for?"

"It's a camera. I can carry it when in my raven form," Liam answered. His raven form was the only way he could get on to Kalissa's property without setting off her wards.

"You plan on spying on the bitch?"

Liam's hand flew out, grabbed her by the throat and snatched her forward into him. She just smiled at him.

Liam could smell her arousal, and it made him sick. He released her with a shove to get her out of his face. "Don't talk about her like that," he growled.

"I don't understand this obsession. She doesn't know what you need." Samoan hopped off the desk and walked around to straddle his lap. She ran her hand down his chest to the top of his jeans. He cursed his body for responding to her touch, smell, and the glow of passion in her eyes. She leaned in to whisper in his ear. "I know what you need...and want." The door to the holding cells opened and then closed. Samoan frowned. "Saved by the parental advisory."

Samoan stood up and walked over to her father, who had a peeved look on his face. "Good evening, father." She stood on her tiptoes and kissed him on the cheek.

"I thought I told you to leave Liam alone," Demetrius said in a stern, fatherly tone.

Samoan shrugged like her father's anger didn't faze her. "I'm going out. I have my cell if you need me." She walked out the door.

Demetrius sat down on the sofa and looked at Liam. "Were you able to find anything out?"

"They have the Sinew." Liam sat back in his chair. "They're waiting for your move."

Demetrius nodded and stood up. "Then they have twenty-four hours, twenty-six if they're lucky." He turned and left.

Twenty-four hours and he'd make his move. The idiot he'd sent in to get rid of his competition had been careless. Liam had given specific instructions for Kalissa to be left unharmed. Instead, the moron had openly fired a death blast of energy, leaving his female to run to her lover's aid. Anger mixed with annoyance had coursed through him when another Divinity—the red-haired male—had teleported in front of Ayden, taking the blast.

Kalissa was alive, but so was her lover.

With two failed kidnapping attempts and one near miss on her life, Liam decided to take matters into his own hands. It was time to reclaim what was his.

CHAPTER EIGHTEEN

"You know, that really is a scary thought," Khloe said as they took form in the backyard of the Bradenton farm.

Kalissa had to agree. Knowing that demons could follow them was scary. She already knew that they could pick up on their magical signature, but not the fact that they could track them at any moment. "How many other demons can trace us?" Kalissa asked.

"There are many that can trace us, but they would need to pick up your scent first. Teddy-Bear doesn't need our scent because they're connected to us through the Sinew," Melaina said as they walked to the old barn about fifteen feet from the main house.

Khloe relaxed her shoulders. "Oh. That's good.

Zach and Ayden took Jacen inside the house, with a sobbing Lydia trailing behind. Kalissa and the others went to check out the barn.

"How is he?" Kalissa asked when Ayden returned a few minutes later.

With a grave expression, he shook his head. "He's weak. He won't make it through the night."

Her chest tightened as unwanted sorrow crept in. "Is there anything you can do? I mean, Lydia is a healer."

He shook his head. "I offered, but she refused. Said it would be a waste of energy."

Her vision blurred, her nose tingled, and she blinked away tears. There was only one reason why Lydia would refuse the burst in healing power. Jacen was far worse than Kalissa had suspected. She'd hoped that his sister could heal him, but now, that hope was gone, replaced with sadness and grief.

"Hey, Ayd, what about your Jeep?" Khloe asked, trying to change the subject. Death had fallen upon them again, and it had brought painful memories for them all.

Ayden shrugged. "I'll send Zach up to get it."

Kalissa smiled. "Does he know this?"

Smiling back, he said, "Nope."

"Oh, can I tell him?" Khloe asked. Ayden shook his head. Khloe made a face at him and said, "Fine. You're a fun sucker."

Kalissa and Khloe opened the double doors of the barn. Teddy-Bear immediately trotted inside. "It needs some work. It hasn't been used in years," Kalissa said as she did a quick walk-through and manifested a notepad and pen that floated in the air, making notes as she spoke. "We'll need fresh hay. And check the roof for leaks. Teddy-Bear, is there anything you need?"

The hounds shook their heads. "Nope. It's perfect."

"All right, then. Just let us know if you need anything,"

Kalissa said as she walked back to the door where the others still stood.

Kalissa and Mel conjured some chairs for everyone to sit in while they told Teddy-Bear about Demetrius's message. "He's not getting the Sinew, so we have to fight."

"That won't be easy," Teddy said.

Bear nodded in agreement. "There are some nasty demons out there. Many are far more powerful than you, and some make people do things...." He winced at the thought.

"So we'll take a stand," Kalissa announced. Everyone turned to look at her like *she* had grown a second head. "We can't give him the Sinew. I'm not going to sit here while Demetrius bullies his way into our lives. We're the only things standing in his way. We have to stop him."

"We defeat Demetrius, Khan will send others," Melaina said.

Kalissa crossed her arms over her chest. "And I'll be there to stop them, too." No one said anything, so Kalissa continued. "We are the Divinities. In a way, we are the protectors of all *magickin*. That is what I intend to do."

One by one, the rest of the group threw in their bids to defend *magickin* and the Sinew. Kalissa wasn't surprised that Ayden was the first to say he was in, but it did surprise her that Zach also piped up with an offer of his help as he walked across the yard toward them. He wasn't a Divinity, yet he was willing to put his life on the line to help them. Then again, he did carry the gene. That made him one of them.

"Look, I know that I'm a mortal witch, and I under-stand your concern to keep me out of harm's way, but I can be a liaison for other covens and set up a network to share information. I think they should be aware that the Divinities have reunited and are taking a stand in this war," Zach said with a look that said, *Don't shut me out of this.*

Once a cop, always a cop, Kalissa thought. "Melaina, it's your call."

Melaina nodded. "Very well, Zach, set up your network. With the Sinew here and with its own protectors —" She cut off briefly to look around the room. Teddy-Bear straightened and puffed out their chest in complete agreement with Melaina. "The demons can't touch it."

"Khloe, can you work on a security system for the house and the property?" Kalissa saw Khloe's face light up. She'd love an opportunity to show off her techie skills.

THE NEXT MORNING, Kalissa woke early, showered, and dressed in a lavender sundress that made her violet eyes stand out. She left her long, dark blond hair down to cascade over her shoulders and down her back. When she was pleased with how she looked, she headed downstairs.

In the kitchen, she started a pot of coffee and made cranberry orange muffins.

She had just pulled the muffins from the oven and set them on the stovetop when a pair of arms wrapped around her waist from behind. A smile spread across her face. She took off the oven mitts. She'd known he was there, smelled his aftershave as he came into the kitchen, and felt his presence. The bond was stronger. She wasn't sure of the hows or whys, but it was growing, making his rose on her arm darken.

Ayden placed a kiss on her cheek, brushed her hair from her neck, and kissed the tender spot just below her earlobe. "Morning, beautiful," he whispered in her ear.

Kalissa turned to face him, leaned into his body, and wrapped her arms around his neck. She looked into his baby blue eyes and the swirls of silver in them danced. "Morning."

"Hope I'm not interrupting," Melaina said in an amused voice as she went for the coffee pot.

Ayden gave Kalissa a quick kiss on the lips, reached around her, and grabbed a muffin before turning to sit at the kitchen table. Kalissa stood there for a few seconds, trying to slow her heartbeat. She wanted to drag Ayden off somewhere so they could be alone. That brought a smile to her face. It was amazing to feel so at ease with him. With no fear or panic—like they belonged together.

When she was able to breathe normally again, she placed the muffins on a serving tray, carried them to the table, and took the chair between Ayden and Melaina.

"Is something wrong?" Kalissa asked Ayden after a few seconds of silence.

He frowned and then quickly replaced it with a smile as if the question had thrown him off at first. "No. I just thought I would stop by on my way to the station."

Kalissa smiled and glanced at Mel. Mel looked briefly at Kalissa's arm before meeting her eyes. "You can see it?" Kalissa asked, talking about her new rose.

Mel nodded. "I didn't want to say anything." She paused before asking, "The memory spell is broken?"

"Not completely," Kalissa answered sadly. "But, I am starting to remember a little each day." She felt guilty about what she had done to Ayden. They'd been so in love, even at the young age of seventeen, that she wasn't sure how he was able to forgive her, let alone stand the sight of her. As if feeling her mood shift, Ayden reached over, took her hand, and brought it to his lips to place a soft kiss on the backs of her fingers.

"I have you now and forever," he said with a smile.

Khloe and Lydia came in, fully dressed and looking like they were ready to take on the world. "We're going to the coven," Khloe announced, reaching over to grab two muffins and handing one to Lydia.

A wave of grief fell over Kalissa like a heavy blanket. Jacen had passed on sometime during the night. Lydia's eyes were still swollen and red from crying. Khloe was taking her to the coven to meet Noah and Vanessa so they could make arrangements for the funeral.

After a moment of sorrow-filled silence, Melaina stood up. "Let me get my purse and I'll go, too."

About five minutes later, the three women left, yelling their goodbyes as they walked out the front of the house.

Ayden stood up. "I should be going, too."

Already? Kalissa thought and stood up to follow Ayden to the door. She watched his backside as he walked, and couldn't help but notice how his form-fitting uniform pants hugged his ass. Her eyes traveled up his back to his broad, muscular shoulders, and then she roamed her gaze down his arms to his hands. Oh gods, what those hands could do to her…

Ayden turned to face her when they reached the door

and gave a smirk that told her he knew where her mind had wandered off to. She met his gaze and smiled. He stepped into her, circled his arms around her waist, and kissed her deeply.

Kalissa returned the kiss, wrapped her arms around his neck, and melted against his body. She wanted him so badly, and decided at that moment, she would stop worrying about the past and start living for the future. Their future. He pressed into her. She sucked in a breath when she felt his arousal against her lower stomach.

Ayden pulled back to look at her. "You okay?"

"Yes…Yes, I am." She pulled his head down for another kiss.

"You keep that up, and I'll have to drag you off to your office and have my way with you," he said against her lips.

"I thought you said you had to go?" she teased.

He kissed her again and walked her backwards to the master-bedroom-turned-office. "I can afford to be a little late."

Kalissa didn't need any further enticement. She broke out of his hold and ran the rest of the way to the office. She released a squeak when she entered the room and found Ayden standing in front of her. He'd teleported. "Cheater," she said, closing the door and then locking it behind her.

When she reached Ayden, his shirt was pulled out of his waistband, and he had started to unbutton it until it hung open, giving her access to his bare chest where she placed her hands. She pressed a kiss over his heart. "How late can you be, Sheriff?"

Ayden sucked in a quick breath as Kalissa ran the tip of her tongue up his chest. "As late as I want to be."

"Good," she purred, pressing her hands against his chest while slowly running them up over his pecs to his shoulders to slide his shirt from his arms. She walked him backwards until his legs touched the sofa and gave a little push. Ayden fell into a seated position.

On her knees in front of him, she slowly unlaced and removed his shoes one at a time. She ran her hand up the inside of his thigh to his cock. His leg muscles twitched under her hands, and she loved the way he reacted to her touch. The way his eyes almost glowed with passion. Her hand cupped him through his pants. Ayden pressed into her palm with a moan. Kalissa removed her hand to unbuckle his belt and unbutton his pants.

"Wait," he said, stopping her hands. He took his gun out of its holster and laid it on the table next to the sofa. Then he removed his belt and sat it on the floor beside his shoes. When he'd finished, he rose his hips so Kalissa could slide his pants down his legs.

Paying him back for the slow torture he'd shown her at the cabin, she ran her tongue up his thigh. Ayden's soft curse brought a smile to her lips. However, making love to Ayden in an unhurried, sensual way they had at the cabin made her want more. She craved his touch now and loved the feel of him over her, under her, and inside her.

She grasped his hard length in her hand and stroked him up and down a couple of times before she licked from base to tip and then took him into her mouth.

His thigh muscles under her hands flexed and then tightened as if he were fighting to gain control. She made slow strokes with her tongue as she sucked him, and knew the moment he teetered on the edge of release. When he reached that point, she freed him from her mouth. Taking him in her hand again, she stroked him gently, teasingly. Their eyes locked. The silver in his baby blues was so defined his irises almost glowed. She had him right where she wanted, and knew she could command anything of him. The satisfaction in knowing that made her giddy.

Leaning in to take him in her mouth again, he took hold of her arms and pulled her up his chest to capture her lips with his.

"I wasn't done," Kalissa teased.

"You are," Ayden replied and pulled her dress over her head.

Heart pounding with anticipation, Kalissa laughed softly and stood up to remove her panties. She moved closer and straddled his lap, but didn't sit. She wasn't done teasing him yet.

She let out a surprised gasp when Ayden's mouth covered her left breast. His fingertips raked down her back and over her ass and pulled her closer to him. Fingers sliding around the curve of her rear to her center, he slid his middle and ring fingers inside her. A gasped moan left her as he moved them in and out while rubbing her clit with his index finger. She had lost all her control over him, but she didn't care. He picked up his pace until an orgasm cascaded over her.

Ayden captured her mouth, thrusting his tongue inside. Kalissa rubbed her sex on Ayden's throbbing shaft between them. Aching to have him inside her, she rose up so her entrance was over his head and lowered herself down to take all of him inside.

She moved her hips in a slow rhythm, riding him to

release. And loved the way he made her feel, his energy and power when it merged with hers. They were one, connected like two perfectly fitted puzzle pieces. The air filled with their magic, and it only got more intense as they moved closer to their climaxes.

Kalissa rode him, slowly at first. She wanted it to last as long as it possibly could. It felt too good to be loved the way Ayden loved her. He didn't have to say the words for her to know it. Their growing connection broadcasted their feelings to each other. They were bonding. Each time they touched, kissed, and made love, their link strengthened.

She figured Ayden had had enough of her slow movements because he took hold of her hips and picked up the pace. Kalissa matched his thrusts until they both cried out in release.

Kalissa collapsed against Ayden's chest. He encased her in his arms and kissed the top of her head. "I love you."

She lifted her head to look at him with a wide smile. Her heart swelled. "I know," she teased and kissed his lips. "I love you, too," she said against his lips.

"I should be going," he said, sounding like he didn't want to go.

"So should I," she said back with a grin. She gave him one last quick kiss on the lips and climbed off his lap. Giving him a devilish grin, she asked, "Shower first?"

"You keep that up, and I'll have to move in just so I can get enough of you," Ayden said, and then frowned at her hesitation.

Kalissa looked him full in the face and thought, *Why not?* Ayden reached out and took her hand. He was about to apologize for saying it, she just knew it, so she cut him off before he had the chance. With a quick kiss, she said, "Okay."

"Okay?"

Kalissa nodded and held up her left arm with her newly paired roses facing him. "All right. Move in. These tell me we're stuck with one another."

"You do have a choice," he said.

"And I choose you. I want to spend every day for the rest of my life with you." *Naked and in your bed—no,* our *bed*, she left unspoken. She was sure he'd picked up on that. They were still connected from the sex.

"Okay," he said, smiling like he had just won the lottery. He gave her another quick kiss and asked, "How about that shower?"

CHAPTER NINETEEN

After the shower with Ayden, Kalissa went to her office and sat behind her desk. Earlier scenes of them together on the sofa made her smile. It also made her want to chase down his police cruiser for a replay. Then there was the shower. Ayden had taken her two more times. Damn, that man sent her sex drive through the roof.

And he was moving in, tonight. What was she thinking? Right, she wasn't. Looking down at her left forearm, Ayden's rose was as vivid as the one she'd been born with, proving they were magical partners. In the eyes of *magickin* they were married, just short of a hand fastening.

She loved him. Truly, with all her heart, she knew they belonged together. With a sigh, she pushed her thoughts to the side and got to work.

The smell of espresso and pastries welcomed her as she walked through the door of Coffee Café. The lingering aromas reminded her of her father, and the warmth, strength, and love he'd given to their family. Loss and grief tried to reawaken her sorrow, but she swallowed the lump in her throat and focused on the positive. And revenge on the demon that had taken her parents from her.

Kalissa placed the payroll checks inside the safe, grabbed an apron, and put it on. Walking out from her small office, she made her way to the bar where Zach's sisters, Bethany and Annemarie, sat enjoying iced lattes. Bethany perked up with a bright smile and a knowing gleam in her eyes. It would surprise Kalissa if Ayden's name didn't show up in their conversation.

"Good morning, Lis." Bethany Manus sounded way too chipper. "How are you?"

"Good, and you?"

"Oh, I can't complain." The smile faded, replaced by sadness. "I met Lydia as we were leaving. It's so horrible what happen to her brother."

A wave of guilt washed over Kalissa. "Yes." It was all she could say. A mixture of emotions whirled around inside her. She was saddened by Lydia's loss, yet happily falling in love with Ayden. Deeply. She felt she didn't have the right to be so happy when Lydia was in so much pain.

Bethany covered her hand with one of her own, bringing Kalissa's gaze to hers. "She's in good hands. Papa and Grams will put together the most beautiful ritual for his passing to the Afterworld."

Kalissa smiled. *Beth was right.* "She is. And Khloe seems to have developed a quick friendship with her."

"A partner in crime?" Bethany made it a question.

"Not so much. Lydia doesn't seem as impulsive."

"That's good. Maybe she'll find a way to ground our Khloe." Bethany took a sip of her latte before continuing. "Tell Lydia if she needs a midwife, I would be honored.

Better yet, come to dinner tomorrow night. That way, we can all catch up."

"That sounds great," Kalissa said.

"Great!" Bethany said. She looked at her watch. "Oh, dear. We should be going. I'm sure Cassia is giving her grandmother a run for her money about now."

Kalissa laughed. Cassia was the most active toddler she'd ever seen. She was cute as a button, and smart beyond belief, and already thought she knew it all. "Are you sure she's not a Divinity in disguise?"

Bethany smiled. "Yeah, I'm sure. Papa says she has a great chance of having Divinity children. Something about the gene being stronger in her. I don't understand the genetics of the whole thing, but Papa knows, and I trust his judgment."

"That makes two of us."

"You know what?" Annemarie broke her silence. "Kalissa's smiling."

Bethany looked at Kalissa, studying her with a wide grin. "I think you're right, Anne. You know, Ayden was up and about awfully early this morning. I do believe it was before the sun rose. He also looked a little more chipper than usual."

Kalissa's heart fluttered at the mention of Ayden's name. She managed an eye roll at them. "I thought you two were leaving," she teased.

"Okay, we're going." Bethany laughed as she stood and collected her purse. "Talk to ya later."

"Bye." Kalissa shook her head at Zach's sisters as they walked out of the Café.

Had it really been that long since she'd been happy?

She frowned to herself and wondered if she really was as gloomy as Scrooge during tax season. Although she didn't really socialize with many people, she admitted she was too serious at times, but she'd never thought of herself as depressed or unhappy in any way.

Another habit she'd developed while dating Liam.

She shook out of the depressing thoughts and looked at the clock on the wall. It was 11:15 a.m., and almost time for the lunch rush. The Café was located on Highway 301 and got a lot of lunch traffic. The time would vary from day to day when 'lunch' actually started, but since it was Thursday, Kalissa suspected the rush would start piling in just before noon as usual.

As always, Kalissa was right with her prediction. The first lunch crowd arrived ten minutes before noon. She always enjoyed working at the Café. Today, she enjoyed the distraction from the recent demonic activity. The strong feeling of being watched still hung over her. Her senses had been on full alert since she'd left home.

It was after 1:00 p.m. when Ayden came in for lunch. The sight of him walking through the doors made her pulse pick up, and she could feel her cheeks heat and turn pink.

He strode to the bar with the power of the enforcer he was. Strong, confident...impressive. She knew all too well what kind of strength that large muscular frame possessed. He took a seat on a high-backed barstool and waited.

She finished with the customers she was with and then went over to pour him a cup of coffee. "Hello, Sheriff," she said with a smile.

"Hi." He returned the smile with a little more heat.

"Zach says Bethany is planning some dinner party tomorrow night." Kalissa nodded. "Are you going?"

"Yes."

"Great." He leaned over the bar countertop and gave her a quick kiss.

Kalissa glanced out into the dining area of the Café. Feeling that eerie chill up her spine again, she scanned the people enjoying their lunch. In the far right corner at the front of the Café was the 'gossip group' of Maxville. They were watching her and Ayden, most likely getting ready to make them their next rumor mill victims. Kalissa smiled and waved at the group of four women. A mixed-age group, two of the ladies were in their late thirties—best friends from grade school—and the other two were their college-bound daughters. They returned Kalissa's wave with wide smiles and a few giggles. Kalissa shook her head and moved on to scope out the rest of the diminishing lunch crowd.

There. Sitting at a two-seater table in a dark corner, reading a paper and drinking coffee was the source of her uneasiness. She moved around the bar into the dining area and stalked toward the guy. He noticed her coming toward him and bolted out the side door next to the table where he had been sitting. Kalissa ran for the door with her heart beating so hard she thought it would jump right out of her chest. Exiting the Café onto the walkway, she looked around, but he was gone. It was like he hadn't been there at all.

It wasn't until Ayden came up next to her that she realized she was having a difficult time catching her breath. A panic attack. Damn, what was wrong with her? She'd sworn that man sitting at the table looked like Liam, but...different.

"You okay?" Ayden asked. He extended his hand to her but didn't touch her.

Kalissa took his hand and stepped into the warmth of his body, needing to feel the safety Ayden provided. It was something she hadn't felt in a very long time. Maybe it was the fact that he was a Divinity, or maybe it had something to do with their bond. He wrapped her in his arms, warmth and security enclosed her.

"Please tell me you saw that man," she whispered into his chest.

"Yeah, I saw him."

Kalissa relaxed a little. "Good. I'm not completely losing my mind."

"Have you seen him before?"

She looked up into Ayden's baby blue eyes, her pulse still racing. "He looked like someone I once knew." She stepped out of the security of his arms and looked inside the Café. Everyone turned their heads away quickly, trying not to look as if they'd been watching them. Everyone except the rumor patrol. By this time tomorrow, the good people of Maxville would be planning her and Ayden's wedding. "You know we're the next scandal of Maxville."

Ayden looked around and then laughed. "Yeah, it appears that way." He turned back to Kalissa. "Are you all right?"

Kalissa nodded. "Yes. I'm only going to be here a few more minutes, and then I'll head home."

He kissed her on the forehead and said, "I'll see you tonight."

"Don't be late," she teased.

"I won't," Ayden said before walking to his patrol car a few feet away.

Kalissa shivered without the heat of his body, gave one last glance around, and pivoted to go back inside the Café.

∾

"You are such an idiot."

"Are you following me, Samoan?" Liam let out a growl as he transformed from raven to human but didn't turn to look at her.

"Only for the last thirty minutes." She pushed away from the wall. She'd found him and the two Divinities inside the Café, so she'd decided to make herself comfortable and enjoy the show. When the female had noticed Liam and started walking toward him, Samoan had filled with excitement. Liam alone would be no match for two bonded Divinities, despite him being a Dark Divine. That meant she would have to rescue his ass. She itched for a good fight.

"I don't need a babysitter," Liam spat out.

She ignored him. "Was that her?"

Liam didn't answer and continued his long strides down the street to his Jag. She took that for a yes and followed him. "Your job is to spy, not stalk."

He whirled around to face her. Midnight blue eyes bored into her and flashed to red. "I know what my job is. If you must know, I was able to get some valuable information."

"Oh, yeah? Like what?" Samoan asked.

"That is between me and your father." Liam reached his Jag and pulled open the door.

Samoan smiled at him as he climbed into his car, slammed the door shut, and drove off. "No, Liam. It is now my business. Dear old Daddy has given me a babysitting job." She laughed. Demetrius was right. Liam was digging his own grave.

CHAPTER TWENTY

"I know what I saw," Kalissa blurted out for the third time since telling Khloe about the man at the Café.

"It can't be him. He's dead! You were there when his heart stopped beating." Khloe had real panic in her voice. She wanted to believe what she said, but Kalissa felt her sister's doubt as well as heard it in her words.

"I know," Kalissa said quietly.

"He could be a relative. A cousin or some family member of his father's," Khloe said.

"Maybe," Kalissa replied. She wanted to change the subject but didn't know what to say.

"Did you tell Ayden?"

"About who I thought I saw?" Kalissa shook her head. "No. I'm still not sure if it was him."

There was a loud thump followed by rattling windows, and it caused them to stop talking. Khloe looked to Kalissa. "I didn't do that," she said defensively.

Kalissa laughed. "It sounded like something fell outside. A very large something."

"Guys, you've got to come see this," Lydia called from the back door.

Kalissa and Khloe looked at each other and shrugged. They hurried downstairs and to the back door. Lydia and Melaina stood on the back porch, looking into the yard. Kalissa followed their line of sight to see something truly unexpected. Teddy-Bear lay flat on their back with all four legs in the air. Rolling back and forth, they laughed while they scratched their back on the ground. Their paws were waving wildly in the air as they played. By the looks of it, they seemed very happy with their new living arrangements.

Their body froze when they noticed they had an audience. "Hey, Ted, the peeps are watching us," Bear whispered loudly.

"I noticed," Teddy said. They flipped over and stood. "Is something wrong?"

Kalissa shook her head, a wide smile on her face, her past worries temporarily pushed to the back of her mind. "No. We were just noticing how happy the two of you look."

"Who wouldn't be happy?" Bear rolled his eyes.

"We have more freedom here," Teddy answered, and then they were back to one of them starting a sentence and the other finishing it.

"No outside peeps to notice…"

"…a two-headed, truck-sized hound romping around in the backyard."

"Well, romp all you want." Kalissa swept her arm toward the property. "There's plenty of room to do it. Just be careful about jumping too close to the house. It shakes the whole thing."

"We will, little mum," they said in unison and trotted off to play in the wooded area of the grounds, their huge tail wagging happily behind them.

Kalissa laughed at the two of them and could totally see why her mother loved them so. This was a diversion she needed. Togetherness and the feeling of family were seeping its way back into their lives, and it felt wonderful. She turned around to head back inside. There was a knock at the door that made her heart flip in the confines of her ribcage. Kalissa looked at the clock and smiled as butterflies fluttered in her belly. It was four in the evening, and time for Ayden to show up. Going to the front door, she felt like she was fifteen again as she reached out to the doorknob and opened it.

She frowned at Zach, standing in the doorway, holding a couple of suitcases. Zach smiled at her. "Ayden said he changed his mind. I'm moving in, instead."

"Oh, hell no!" Khloe came up behind Kalissa.

Kalissa sighed and turned to the others, now standing behind her. "I'm sorry. I forgot to mention it. Ayden is moving in."

Khloe waved her sister off. "We already knew that. I said 'hell no' to Zach moving in. Good gods, I see enough of him as it is." Khloe laughed and dodged Zach's foot when he swung it out at her.

Kalissa laughed and stepped aside for Zach to come in. She looked out to the driveway and saw Ayden pulling two more suitcases out of his Jeep. "When did you get the Jeep?" she asked Zach.

"I teleported to the cabin last night and drove it down. Good thing I have a great boss to give me the day off to pick up *his* Jeep," Zach said loud enough for Ayden to hear him.

Laughing again, she waited anxiously for Ayden to climb the stairs to the porch. When he did, Kalissa was overcome by his power. Melaina was right. Ayden's gift was very powerful. Kalissa didn't know how he dealt with all that power.

"I learned to lock it down," Ayden said when he wrapped his arms around her waist and pulled her into his body. Kalissa frowned at him for reading her mind. "I'm sorry. I think it's our bond."

"Oh," she whispered and then nipped at his ear playfully. Another thing to get used to. Her bond with her twin was something she'd been born with, but the connection with Ayden was new.

"Anyone hungry?" Lydia asked sheepishly.

Kalissa laughed. "Yes, I am."

Lydia smiled. "Oh, good. I thought I was the only one."

"Don't worry, I eat like a pregnant woman, too," Zach replied.

Khloe laughed and said, "That is so true." She linked arms with Lydia and tugged her toward the kitchen. "Let's go make a snack."

They disappeared into the kitchen with Zach right behind them.

LIAM'S MOOD had turned from bad to lethal by the time he pulled into the driveway of his Jacksonville home. He'd watched as Kalissa had gotten cozy with the sheriff of Maxville at the Café. It took every fiber of self-control he possessed to keep from revealing who he really was. If he did that, he would never be able to take her as his mate. Besides, he was not ready to reveal too much to her yet. She'd recognized him at the Café. The icy stare she'd cast him spoke volumes.

On top of that, Samoan had shown up with a stick up her ass.

Demetrius had something cooking, and the Divinities were in for a big surprise. Liam planned to be there when things went down, waiting for the right time to strike.

He walked through the front door of his two-story, Victorian-style home into the foyer. Liam had moved into the eleven-thousand-square-foot house about five years ago. There were no neighbors for miles.

His father had moved into one of the apartments above the warehouse about two years ago to be closer to Grayson Distributions and farther away from the memories of his wife. The regret had become too painful for Paul to stay in the home that he'd designed for his wife in hopes of keeping her happy.

Now, Liam would give the mansion to his Kalissa as their wedding gift.

His biker boots fell heavily on the white marble floor as he made his way to his office. It was one of two rooms he truly called his. The other room was his bedroom suite, directly above the office. The rest of the house held painful memories of his mother and her rejection when she'd found out that her husband and child were demons. The most undesirable room was the kitchen.

Arriving home about fifteen minutes before his father, he entered through the front door to a well-lit house. It was just past midnight. His mother should have been in bed asleep. The eerie silence set him on edge, making his pulse race.

"Mom?" he called out. Something was wrong. He felt it. His mother was supposed to be safe, protected by Khan's Regals. Any demon who touched her signed his death warrant.

Stalking farther into the house, he stopped even with the kitchen entrance. Death drifted in the air, making his blood boil. He would rip through the Underworld to get his hands on any creature that had touched her in any way.

Taking a sharp turn, he rushed into the kitchen, only to stop cold. Emotions mounted in him, overflowing to become tears streaming down his face. He shook uncontrollably and let out a cry of agonizing pain.

In the center of the large kitchen, dangling by a decorative support beam with a thick rope around her neck, was Barbra Loomis—or rather her lifeless body. An overturned chair lay beneath her feet.

Liam had had to leave the house before his father got home, because he knew he would have killed him. After that night, their father-son relationship changed.

Sitting down in front of the computer, he fired it up, took out the digital camera from his shirt pocket, and plugged the USB into the computer. As he waited for the pictures to download, his phone rang. He pulled the phone out of his pants pocket and answered it.

"Yeah?"

"Any news?" Demetrius asked in his usual neutral tone. The demon never showed any emotion unless it concerned his daughter.

"The Sinew has a keeper. Besides that, they are still waiting for your next move." Liam sat back in his high-backed, black leather chair, his jaw clenched. The demon General never gave information, he just demanded it. But Liam knew the Echens would be released soon, and he was going to be there.

"Yes. I know of Hecate's hounds," Demetrius replied in a flat tone. After a few moments of silence, he added, "Do you want to speak to your father?"

Liam released a heavy sigh. "Nope."

"Very well. Keep me updated on the Divinity activity."

Liam didn't have time to reply before the line went dead. That was Demetrius, though. He was never one for small talk. The only reason he'd asked if Liam wanted to talk to his father was that it was getting close to the anniversary of his mother's death. Liam didn't want to talk about it. He blamed his father for her death. If only he had manned up and made the woman his bonded mate, Liam would have his mother with him now.

Instead, Paul had wanted to live a normal *human* life with his human wife and half-human son. Paul had kept Liam in his human state by feeding him a potion made specifically for slowing the demon DNA in human-demon halfbreeds. Only Paul ignored the warnings of the damaging effects the potion had on the mind. The one thing they'd never anticipated was the change in Liam's

DNA. Somehow, he was stronger and possessed powers normal demons did not.

Liam also blamed his father for him losing Kalissa. She would be by his side now instead of the male he'd stolen her from fifteen years ago.

I'll just have to steal her all over again.

A beep from the photography software indicated that the photos on the camera were downloaded. He unplugged the USB cable and began to choose his photos carefully. After a couple of changes through editing and cropping, he printed two photos to add to the collection in his bedroom.

Walking out of the office, he headed upstairs to his room and stuck the photos onto the large mirror over his dresser. They fit in perfectly with his growing collection. He reached out to his favorite photo. It was of Kalissa and her sister on a shopping trip. Kalissa had been happy that day. She had the most beautiful smile. Stroking her laughing face with his thumb, he vowed, "We will be together again, my love."

CHAPTER TWENTY-ONE

Lydia stood at her bedroom window watching the pinkish orange sky fade into darkness. Twilight was the death of day and the birth of night. All passing ceremonies were held around this time. The symbolism of death and rebirth, the cycle of life.

Noah, Vanessa, and a few other coven members arrived an hour before sunset to help with preparations for Jacen's passing ceremony. Lydia wanted it simple, but after meeting the Danielses, she knew their taste for simple was a little more elegant than hers. Khloe advised her to let the Elders handle it and take it easy.

Relaxation had been missing from her life since the day she'd lost her parents. It hadn't been good enough for the demons to take them away. No, they had to come back and take her husband and now her brother. Although Jacen's death had been more self-inflicted, leaving a hole in her heart and an emptiness in her soul. She was a little angry with him but understood why he thought he had to do it.

They'd been bonded siblings since they were teens. Their mother had hoped it would quiet the voices of his telepathic ability. It had helped some, and with Lydia's help, he was able to mute the chatter to a hum. But as they'd gotten older and started their own lives, the bond had weakened, and his control over the noise slipped. If only she could have done more for him.

"We could have found another way, brother." She sighed, moved to her bed, and removed a family photo along with a single picture of Jacen from one of her albums. She wrapped a black cotton handkerchief around the photos in a protective shroud so they could be placed with his body.

A soft knock on her bedroom door put a rush in her step. She'd taken much too long preparing herself. "Come in."

The door opened, and Khloe walked inside. Her new friend had released her glamour spell, revealing her natural, dark blond hair that matched Kalissa's perfectly. The only way to tell them apart now was the fact that Khloe's hair was shorter, falling about two inches below her shoulders and her eyes were teal, opposed to Kalissa's violet.

"The only magic inside the circle is that of the Priest and Priestess," Khloe said with a smile and an eye roll.

Lydia laughed softly. She knew the ritual rules, but Khloe was complaining, politely. One last look in the mirror to check her long, fiery red hair and to smooth her black, floor-length gown over her baby bump, she was as ready as she'd ever be to say goodbye to another loved one.

They were burying Jacen in a tiny cemetery about two hundred yards from the Bradenton home where Kalissa and Khloe's parents had been laid to rest. Because Connie Bradenton had listed the land and farmhouse as part of the coven with the town's property appraiser's office, they could have a legal, private burial ground on the grounds.

In the backyard, four elfin males waited beside Jacen's casket. They were beautiful in a masculine kind of way, with hair that brushed the tops of their broad shoulders and pointed ears that stuck out slightly through the dark strands. Their skin glowed with otherworldly magic.

Taking her eyes from the elves to look around, Lydia was surprised at the amount of people who had come to pay their respects. Most of the faces were familiar from her visit to the coven that morning. A sense of belonging filled her heart and tears threatened to overspill her lids. She'd always felt like an outsider among Mikal's people.

Her eyes found Zach talking quietly to Ayden off to the side. As if feeling her stare, his gaze shifted to meet hers. A moment later, he headed her way. His ruffled light brown hair begged for fingers to run through it. The gold in his brown eyes intensified as he stalked toward her. Warmth flushed over her skin, and she knew her cheeks blushed. She looked away. This was wrong on so many levels. Why did she have the urge to drag the deputy off to a private room?

"Hi." His husky voice brought her eyes back to his. He reached out to take her hand but let his drop before it made contact. Uncertainty marred his features.

Nervously, Lydia took his hand and gave a slight squeeze. "Hello, Zach."

His smile sent a flare of desire through her. The baby stretched, and she gasped at the sudden discomfort and rubbed circular motions over the protruding section of her swollen belly.

Zach was about to say something, but Noah appeared beside them. "Lydia, we are ready to begin when you are."

She nodded and stepped away from Zach. "I'm ready."

In single file—with Noah and Vanessa leading—they followed the casket through the woods to Jacen's new resting place.

They came to a stop at an open grave inside a gated cemetery. Only two headstones sat in the middle of the area. Jacen's grave lay to the left of Connie and Troy Bradenton's.

The elfin men lowered the casket into the hole and stepped back, beyond where the circle would be cast.

Vanessa conjured a small altar table and began placing ritual items on it while Khloe passed out small white candles. The Divinities lit their wicks with the will of minds and then turned to the guests and illuminated their tapers.

"Brothers and sisters, we gather on this night to bid farewell to Jacen Rayners—Divinity, brother, son, and friend." Noah's deep, confident voice boomed through the silence of the night. He held his hand out to Lydia. "Would you like to light his candle?"

She nodded, not trusting her voice, and stepped closer. Instead of using magic, she reached out a shaky hand and dipped her candle to the one in the middle of the altar, meshing flame to wick. With a shuddered breath, she stepped back.

Once the candle flared to life, Noah spoke. "Just like the flare, Jacen's memories will burn in the hearts of those who knew him and loved him."

Everyone raised their arms with lit candles still in hand and chanted, "May the Divine embrace Jacen, surround him with their love, and give him ease so that he may be free to journey on to a new adventure."

Arms lowered, and Noah completed the ritual. "Death is not the end, but the transition from this life to the next. We bid Jacen safe passage into the Afterworld and to his next life."

When the circle was broken, the guests smiled sweetly and offered their condolences as they made their way toward the house for snacks and refreshments. Lydia's heart swelled at the amount of love and friendship the Maxville Coven offered her.

Spotting Ayden and Kalissa, she pulled them to the side. "I want you to know that you shouldn't feel guilty about Jacen. He, um…the voices were too much for him. I believe he was looking for a way out." Sadness wrapped around her as she spoke the words out loud.

A sobbed gasp escaped Kalissa, and she pulled Lydia into a hug, causing the dam holding back the flood of tears to break. "I'm so sorry. We are all here for you. Anything you need."

Nodding, Lydia allowed the other woman to hug her.

After several moments, she pulled back and wiped the tears from her cheek. "I am grateful for all of you. He just couldn't…"

Ayden rubbed her arm. "I know. I heard his thoughts,

too. I didn't understand them at first, but now they make sense. He felt you would be safe and happy with us."

Lydia sniffed and bobbed her head. "I know. Thanks."

As they made their way back to the house, a calm fell over her. Jacen was free from his torment but hadn't left her alone. She had a new family and new friends. Her son would be raised in a positive and strong household. And if it were the last thing she did, her mother would be found. And the demons would pay for their crimes.

CHAPTER TWENTY-TWO

K alissa flung her eyes open, unsure what had startled her awake. The bed dipped beside her, and she smiled. She wasn't used to waking up next to a man. And certainly not used to Ayden being that man.

"Sorry. I didn't mean to wake you," he said and leaned over to place a light kiss on her forehead.

She wanted to pull him down and possess his lips and other parts of his anatomy. He was dressed in his police uniform and smelled delicious. *Why can't life just stand still for a couple of decades?*

"You want me to fix you coffee?"

He shook his head. "I'll get some at the station."

"You're a very brave man," she teased.

He laughed, and it made her want him even more. The flash in his eyes told her he'd felt her desire. "I'll see you tonight."

Once he was gone, she felt empty and alone. She missed his presence, his smile. The bond between them was strengthening and was much stronger than the one she shared with her twin.

After tossing and turning for about thirty minutes, trying to go back to sleep, she gave up. She rose, stretched, and smiled widely when she caught the scent of Ayden's lingering aftershave.

Inside the bathroom, she brushed her hair and put on her robe before she headed downstairs.

When she reached the bottom of the stairs, she was assailed by the wonderfully rich smell of coffee. She gravitated to the coffee pot like it was a beacon calling out to her. Khloe stood with her back against the counter, sipping on a cup of coffee, dressed in her usual black, baby doll nightgown. Her hair was a ruffled mess on top of her head. Kalissa held in a laugh as she walked by her. At least Khloe had put on a robe, even though it was sheer black and wasn't tied closed.

"I remember the first time Zach saw you like that." Kalissa laughed as she poured her coffee.

"He got used to it," Khloe said with a smirk. Zach hadn't known whether to laugh at her or run. He'd decided to say nothing and kept his distance. He'd grown up with them, the brother they'd never had. Khloe hadn't thought about his reaction.

"It was his fault, showing up here and waking me up at four in the morning. He was lucky I didn't zap him with a lightning bolt."

"What time is he supposed to be here?" Kalissa asked, taking her seat at the kitchen table. Zach had the day off and was coming over to help with the security system Khloe had designed.

Khloe tilted her head to look at the clock on the stove. "Any minute now."

A few seconds later, Zach walked through the back door. He looked at Khloe and laughed as he sat down at the table across from Kalissa.

"Hey! You could hang a sign out front that reads, 'Medusa lives here,'" Zach said with a burst of laughter.

Before Kalissa could stop her sister, Khloe threw a tennis-ball-sized energy bolt at him. Zach reacted with inhuman speed, something Kalissa had never seen him use before, and lifted his hands to throw up some kind of shield. It was like a magical circle, but stronger. The energy ball hit the shield and disappeared.

Khloe smiled. "You've been practicing."

Zach dropped his shield…circle…whatever it was and shrugged. "A little."

"Someone mind telling me what just happened?" Kalissa asked.

Zach looked at her and then out the window. "I'm a fucked up Divinity." Kalissa raised her eyebrows at him. "The Divinity gene is strong enough in my DNA to give me powers like you, but not strong enough to make me immortal. Papa believes Cassia is the same way."

"Apparently, Zach's Divine gift is a shield. He can throw up a circle in half a microsecond that is stronger than any normal magical circle. He can also absorb the energy directed into himself and return it to its owner," Khloe said

"How long have you known about this?" Kalissa asked her sister.

She gave a half shrug. "Most of my life." Kalissa gave

her a look. Khloe sighed and continued. "I told you once. But you don't remember." There was sadness in her voice.

Kalissa turned to look out the window, bitterness not far from showing itself. The memory spell. It had affected a lot more of her than just her love for Ayden. "What else have you told me that I don't remember?"

"I'm not sure. We'll take it slow. Give it time. Everything will come back to you," Khloe said, turning to refill her coffee cup. "Anyway, little Cassia is the same as Zach. She has all that power inside that little frame. Lynzee is teaching her to use it and suppress it. Also, like Zach, she's mortal and doesn't carry the Divinity rose on her arm."

That made sense and brought to mind something she'd never considered. "Is that why you can teleport?" she asked Zach.

"Yeah," he answered.

"You're not fucked up. You're a rare commodity." Zach made a face at the choice of words. Kalissa laughed and explained. "You are our secret weapon."

"Who would ever suspect a mortal witch to have the same powers as a Divinity?" Khloe added.

"I guess." He looked around. "What's for breakfast?"

"I was waiting for Lydia and Melaina to get up," Khloe replied, setting her cup down to go to the pantry.

"How is she doing?"

"Hanging in there. How are you this morning, Zach?" Lydia spoke as she drifted around the island to the kitchen table.

He stood and offered her a seat. Kalissa smiled at the way his eyes lit up when he saw Lydia.

"I'm good. What would you like to drink?" he asked,

going to the refrigerator.

Kalissa leaned into the table across from her and whispered, "I think you have a personal servant."

Lydia smiled weakly, but Kalissa could see the slight blush that rose in her cheeks.

"Here, Zachary. Make us pancakes," Khloe said, moving to sit at the table. "Might as well take advantage of it, right?"

She has a point, Kalissa thought. At this rate, they could have a personal chef, too.

It was one in the afternoon. Lydia, Melaina, and Kalissa had settled down to watch a movie when Teddy-Bear walked into the living room and curled up on the floor in front of the TV.

Kalissa looked at Lydia and then Mel; both had the same confused look on their faces. Kalissa finally asked, "TB, when were you going to tell us you could change sizes?"

Their heads lifted and tilted to the side in unison. "You didn't know?" they asked together.

"No, I didn't know," Kalissa said. Mel and Lydia agreed that they hadn't known either.

The hounds lowered their heads back onto their paws and said, "Now you know."

Kalissa laughed out loud. They were quite a pair. They said what was on their minds and didn't care how it sounded.

"What else can you do?" Kalissa asked.

"We can separate into two hounds. But we don't do that too often. It's our only weakness. If you know what we mean," Teddy said.

Kalissa nodded. They had been born Siamese twins. Their existence depended on each other. If they were separated for an extended amount of time, they could die. All the demons had to do was catch them apart, capture them, and keep them separated until they died.

The rest of the day was lazy. Kalissa seriously thought about going to the Café to work, but changed her mind when Khloe came in with a bottle of wine for Mel and Kalissa and tea for herself and Lydia. The rest of the afternoon was spent watching old movies.

Tension lay heavily in the air. Everyone was on high alert, waiting for the other shoe to drop.

"Why are the demons being so quiet?" Kalissa said when the stillness finally got to her.

"Demetrius is a plotter, and very seldom strays from his plan. He wouldn't leave us wondering for long," Mel assured everyone.

It was nice to just act normal for one day, but the closer to nightfall it grew, the more uneasy Kalissa became. She didn't trust the demon. He was cooking something up.

Despite everyone's worry, they went on with their plans to go to the coven for dinner. Kalissa was sure they were still being watched. She didn't know how someone could get onto the property without her wards going off, but an unknown aura would brush against hers every so often. The unshakable dark presence made her skin crawl.

Someone or *something* was getting around her safeguards.

CHAPTER TWENTY-THREE

The coven was only a ten-minute drive from the Bradenton house, which was now known as the Divinity house. It was becoming hard for Lydia to teleport, so Zach had offered to be their chauffeur and had brought one of the coven vans they used for youth outings. Bethany had said it was better that Lydia didn't teleport anymore until after the baby was born.

The Maxville Coven was more like a small village and operated like a community. There were about two dozen smaller cottages randomly placed throughout the hundred-acre property. Each cottage was as individual as the family that lived in them. The main house was where the Daniels-Manus family lived.

The coven was the *magickins'* safe haven. It was where they could live comfortably without human prejudice. The property was heavily guarded by wards and large, old oak trees. The only difference between the coven's wards and Kalissa's was that the Sinew had created these before her mother hid it.

The large main house reminded Kalissa of a ski lodge in the mountains. After the coven attacks a little over three hundred years ago, it had been used as the Divinity home for centuries until they'd decided to split up and have families of their own.

Zach parked the van in the circular drive. They piled out and walked up the porch stairs to the front door and entered into a larger foyer. The natural log cabin feel continued inside the house. Everything from the furniture to the staircase railing and even the hardwood floors was made from the trees that had been cut down to build the house. Each piece was handcrafted with love and magic, which gave the house a spirit. Kalissa felt it when she crossed the threshold. It felt like the walls were alive, but it wasn't an eerie feeling. It was comforting and welcoming.

The large, hand-carved wooden staircase stood in front of them, leading to the second floor. It split off into the separate wings of the upstairs and circled around to another staircase above the door that led to the third floor.

A high-pitched squeal followed by a tiny giggle brought their attention to the three-year-old toddler, who came running out of the living room. She was dressed in pink, footed pajamas and carried a baby doll in the crook of her right arm. Ayden stepped into her path and scooped her up in his arms as she ran by. Another excited squeal escaped as she looked at Ayden and threw her little arms around his neck. "Ayd! Save me. The dragon is coming!"

"Oh, no. Where should we hide?" Ayden asked, playing along.

"Come on, princess. It's time to wash up," Bethany said,

walking into the foyer. Her face brightened into a smile when she saw Lydia. She held out her hand. "I'm so sorry I had to run yesterday. And again at your brother's passing…"

"That's okay," Lydia said softly and accepted Bethany's hand.

"Dinner is almost done. I'll be right there. I'm going to get Cassia washed up." She took Cassia out of Ayden's arms and turned back toward the living room.

Everyone followed Bethany and was greeted by Noah and Vanessa.

"Melaina, it is so good to see you," Vanessa said, pulling Melaina into a tight embrace.

For the average human, Vanessa looked thirty-something instead of three hundred nineteen. Her chestnut brown hair was curled into large ringlets at the bottom. She had the same golden brown eyes as Zach.

When Vanessa pulled out of the hug, she had tears in her eyes. The two women were sharing their sorrow for the friends and loved ones they'd lost. The scene pulled at Kalissa's own heartstrings.

Noah stepped up beside his lovely wife, drew her to his chest, and kissed her on top of the head. Looking at Noah, Kalissa could see where Ayden and Zach got their looks. Noah wore his light brown hair long. Most the time, it was tied back in a loose ponytail. Noah's eyes were the same baby blue with swirls of silver as Ayden's.

Noah held his free arm out to Melaina. She walked to him and let him hug her. For the first time, Kalissa realized how close the surviving six Divinities were. They were family, friends, they loved and cared for each other. The bond between the three Elders in front of her was still very strong.

Vanessa pulled away from Noah first, looped her arm with Mel's, and led her into the living room.

Noah motioned everyone to take a seat while they waited for dinner to finish. "We've had too many lives lost," Noah said absently and to no one in particular.

"Why did our mother hide the Sinew," Khloe asked after they'd taken their seats.

Noah sighed. "We didn't really know what to do with it. After we rebuilt the coven, Hecate paid us a visit, apologizing for leaving us so abruptly the night of the attacks. She didn't give an explanation, but I figured it was because she was wounded." Noah turned to the group. "She told us the demons had used the Sinew to harvest the Divinities' powers, which killed them. Our magic is our life force."

It was the same thing Zach had said when Ayden and Kalissa had arrived at the cabin. Kalissa was glad the Sinew was safe and protected. The Divinities had reunited and, for the first time in centuries, they had taken a stand in the war against the demons.

"Will you tell us what happened the night of the attack?" Khloe asked softly. Kalissa had always wondered herself but was too afraid to ask. She wasn't afraid of Noah, but she was nervous about how he would feel if she asked.

He looked at her, and after a brief pause, nodded and began telling the story as he'd seen it three hundred years ago.

There was a loud, thunderous boom so close that it shook the house. Noah ran out of his bedroom toward the front door. He got to the entryway and stopped. The crystal vase that held twelve long-stemmed red roses lay on the floor in front of him. The vase had shattered into a million pieces, scattering its contents over the hardwood floor.

Another rumble from the windows, and visions flooded his mind like a dam breaking. The images came at him like a slideshow on fast forward. Some of the scenes he recognized from dreams he'd had over the past several months; others were new. They all had something in common. Fire. He focused on the newest one and controlled the speed, slowing the images down so it was easier to focus on just one. It cleared, confirming his greatest fear. A fireball the size of a Volkswagen Beetle flew through the air, landing on top of the community center. With even, steady breaths, he calmed his panic. He knew it was coming. He had seen it many, many times since his visions had started coming to him at the age of ten. He just never thought it would come so soon.

He focused harder on the images in his mind to get a clear visual of the present moment. If he concentrated hard enough, his visions were so real it was like he was there. Choking on the amount of smoke from the scene as he stood in the middle of the large gymnasium, he took in his surroundings. The building was completely engulfed in flames. He felt the scorching heat of the flames crawling up the walls and out the gaping hole in the ceiling. The smoke was so thick he couldn't see past a couple of feet in front of him.

He broke off from the vision and ran out the front door. Once outside, he saw large flames shooting up into the sky where the community center was located. Noah was overcome with fear and sadness. He took off toward the center but was cut short when a large cat knocked him down.

"Get off me, Kris. Now!" Noah demanded.

In tiger form, Kristof Rayners outweighed him by a hundred pounds.

The huge, white tiger's head shook side to side in a no. After a few seconds, Kris changed to his human form, willing clothes to cover his body at the same time. "It's too late. They're gone," he choked out, looking Noah in the eyes. Kris's emotions pooled over onto Noah. Somehow, Divinities were connected. Kris was wracked with sorrow and fear. He wanted blood from whoever had done this.

Every coven member had been at the community center for their monthly meeting. As an Elder, Noah's mother had to be there.

"No." Noah struggled to get up. "We have to try."

"I already did." Kris stood up and held out his hand to Noah. "We have to get the children to safety."

After a few seconds, Noah stood up, took one last look at the burning community center, and followed Kris to collect the children.

The coven children were to meet at a centralized location. Every other week, they had drills in case of an attack. Noah hated the drills, and knew the other children did, too, but they were necessary.

Noah and Kris reached the playground a couple of feet from Noah's house. The children were huddled together, secure behind a magical circle. The sobs from the toddlers pulled at his heart. He wished he could turn back time and take their pain away.

"Is everyone okay?" Noah asked when he reached them.

"As well as one would expect," seventeen-year-old Melaina said with an eye roll as she tugged eight-year-old Angelica Preston behind her to open the circle. "We just lost our parents and friends and have to spend gods know how long in a room eating canned food."

"We both saw this coming," Noah said softly. He understood her anger. He was angry, too. Melaina was also a seer, and she had seen this outcome just as Noah had. The Elders took precautions by strengthening the wards and performing bi-monthly rituals to bring extra protection to the coven. Noah feared that the additional security had only held off the demons until they found a way around it, or possessed enough power to break through the wards.

Noah reached out to Melaina. She shook her head. "I don't want to cry right now. The others need us to be strong."

Heavy sobbing from behind Melaina made Noah swallow a lump in his throat. He would break down later, but Mel was right; the younger children needed him, Kristof, and Melaina to bring them to safety. He stepped around Melaina to find thirteen-year-old Connie hiccupping with sobs while being hugged by her best friend, nineteen-year-old, Vanessa. Noah was flooded with relief to see Vanessa alive. He fought everything inside to keep from pulling her into his arms.

Noah was just about to ask where the sixth Divinity was when he heard footsteps running up the dirt path behind him. Ten-year-old Caleb Rayners, Kristof's baby *brother, was carrying a wooden box in his hands. Kris cursed and walked over to his brother. "Where have you been? I told you to come straight here."*

"I'm sorry, Kris. I th...thought we m...might need this," Caleb stuttered out, trying to hold back the tears. He held up the box to Kris.

Kris took the box and squatted down, eye level with Caleb. "We could have managed without this. I cannot bear to lose you, too."

"I'm sorry," Caleb whispered. "I saw them. They're here."

Kris pulled back and turned to look into Noah's eyes. He turned back to Caleb. "You saw them how?"

Caleb glanced at Noah and then back to Kris. "In my mind's eye. You know, like when you dream or meditate."

Kris looked up at Noah. A mutual acknowledgement of Caleb's newfound gift passed between them. "We'd better get inside," Kris said and stood.

Noah nodded. He figured it could be a good thing to have three seers. He also recognized the box that Caleb had gone back to get. It was their mother's runes and crystals. Noah didn't understand why the kid wanted them. Noah and Mel didn't need those things to see the future.

They got everyone inside and down to the panic room in the basement.

"Connie?" Noah spoke softly. When she looked up at him with her tear-filled eyes, Noah took a deep breath. "Can you help Vanessa with the little ones?" Connie nodded.

Vanessa grabbed his hand. "You're not going back out

there." It was half question, half demand. She looked him in the eyes and shook her head. "I can't live without you."

He cupped her head in his hand and kissed her on the lips. Pulling back to look into her tearful eyes, he said, "You won't have to."

"Noah?" Kris called from the door.

Noah gave Vanessa another quick kiss before turning toward the door. "I love you," he said before sealing her and the other children inside.

They exited Noah's house and stood on the front lawn, looking out at the destruction. It looked like a bomb had gone off. The houses were on fire and half tore down. The community center was a pile of smoking rubble.

Noah's sadness turned to fury. The demons were going to pay.

Hecate appeared in front of them. "Are you ready, my children?"

They were surprised to see her there, and wondered why she had come. They went down to their knees and bowed their heads without questioning her. "Yes, Goddess."

"Then stand and let's kick some ass," she prompted.

They didn't have to look very far. A group of demons stalked toward them like a wave. Noah felt a surge of power rise up in his body. It ran through his veins, building and strengthening. On instinct, he thrust his hands straight out in front of him toward the demons. White light left his palms and hit the first couple of demons, sending them flying backwards into the demons behind them.

He looked down at his hands, stunned for a few

seconds before looking at Hecate. She was engaging four demons. They charged her two at a time and then all four at once. She was too fast for them, or so he thought before she took a hit in the side that made her cry out. Noah made a move to go to her, but her voice filled his head, stopping him. "Don't worry about me. Use your magic. Think about what you want and will it so."

He looked over at Kris and Mel. They'd also heard Hecate's command. They nodded to Noah, and together, they fought the demons with powers they never knew they possessed.

One of the demons cut Kris across the back with a sword. Kris whirled around to face the demon. His eyes glowed amber like dancing flames. Noah had only seen Kris's eyes like that when he was in animal form or when he was calling out to his element, fire.

"Back off!" Kris demanded. Noah and Mel backed off slightly. When they did, Kris threw his hands out in front of him and then spread them wide, sending flames out like a blowtorch to encircle the group of demons.

It was the coolest thing Noah had ever seen. Kris was a human flamethrower. He wished his element was fire instead of earth. Then he had an idea. He called out to the earth and the forest that surrounded the coven. He willed the vines covering the trees to him. The vines snaked and twined along the ground, unseen by the demons until they took hold, wrapping and twisting around the demons legs up to their torsos.

Mel took that opportunity to call her element. She called a light breeze to blow Kris's fire toward the demons. The oxygen from the air fed the fire.

All together, they sent everything they had into what they'd created. The vines twined around while the air intensified the flames and pushed them over the demons, burning them all in a matter of minutes.

Everything fell quiet. The three of them looked up to see Hecate walking toward them. She was still as beautiful as she had been before the fight began. Then again, she was a goddess. She stopped in front of them and held out an amulet of some kind. Being about five inches in diameter, it was too big to be worn as a piece of jewelry, and Noah wondered what it was. The center was a crystal sphere that seemed to glow with multi-colored energy waves. Surrounding the sphere was a labyrinth-like symbol: Hecate's Wheel—the symbol of knowledge and life.

"This is the Sinew. It is the source of all magic and knowledge. Guard it with your lives. The demons must never have it again." Hecate gave them the Sinew and vanished.

The stove timer went off, causing everyone in the room to jump. Vanessa stood up. "Dinner's ready."

Everyone took that cue to move to the dining room.

CHAPTER TWENTY-FOUR

After dinner, Ayden was finally able to get Kalissa alone. He asked her to go for a walk, and she said yes without hesitation. He smiled, knowing she was as glad to be alone as he was.

It was nice to have everyone together. It was like old times. When he'd come to visit as a child, they would have dinner parties all the time. Kalissa's parents, his parents, and sometimes, Melaina would come down from Maine to visit. Back then, he and Kalissa would sneak off after dinner.

"I remember doing this," Kalissa said.

"You mean sneaking off after dinner?" Ayden asked with a chuckle. "I was just thinking the same thing." He stopped, drew her into his arms, and gave her a soft kiss on the lips. "So, you know where I am taking you?" He watched her flush and look away. "I'll take that as a yes." He pulled her toward the barn.

"I also remember that Zach used to come looking for us." Kalissa giggled.

Ayden's heart swelled at the sound. He didn't expect to ever hear her laugh again. The sound of her laughter drifted out to him like a soothing caress, and the light in her eyes when she was happy guided him home. From this day forward, he would make sure that light burned for the rest of their existence.

"Wow," Kalissa said, walking through the barn's eight-foot-tall double doors. "Noah's barn is three times the size of mine, and in better shape. I really needed to fix it up. Don't ever show this barn to Teddy-Bear. They'll leave and come here to live."

Ayden chuckled and quickly followed her as she walked over to the ladder in the middle of the barn that led up to the loft. When he reached the top, Kalissa was peering out the opening that overlooked to the back of the property. He walked up behind her and wrapped his arms around her waist. She sank back into his chest with a sigh. His lips brushed her cheek and moved down to her neck.

A small moan rose in her throat, and she pressed into him more. She reached behind her and ran her hand up his thigh to the growing bulge in his jeans and cupped him.

Ayden turned her to face him so he could capture her lips with his. Kalissa wrapped her arms around his neck and buried her fingers in his hair. She immediately opened for him and returned the kiss with her own eagerness.

He lowered his hands to her hips and cupped her ass to lift her off the ground. Kalissa's legs clamped around his waist, pulling their bodies closer. Holding on to her back for support, he lowered them to the floor of the loft. He broke the kiss to look into her eyes. They were so full of passion and need that they almost glowed. Never had he thought to see that dreamy-eyed desire in her eyes again. The more he had her, the more he wanted. He loved her, and he was going to show her how much for the rest of their existence.

"What is it?" she asked in a whisper.

He smiled widely at her, stroking her cheek with his hand. "Just admiring how beautiful you are."

He lifted her torso off the floor and removed her shirt, then lean down and kissed her lips. Her skin smelled of vanilla and jasmine as he trailed kisses over her cheek, down her neck, and farther to her breast. The scent intensified the more she was aroused, making him grow harder as it crawled inside and wrapped him in its grip.

The clasp on the front of her bra opened by his will to free her breasts. He captured a pink nipple with his mouth and gently sucked. She arched her back and moaned. Her soft curves under him felt too right. The way she moved. The sounds of pleasure she made when he caressed her.

He slid his hand down her side to her hip, gathered her skirt, and pulled it up to slide his hand up her inner thigh. The strip of her panties was the only barrier, but not for long as he pushed them to the side to rub his fingers over her clit. She was wet and ready for him. Her hips lifted and pushed into his hand, meeting his strokes. He wanted to taste her again but knew they didn't have much time before someone came looking for them.

After the last shudder had left her body, he pulled his hand away to undo his jeans and release his hard cock from its confinement. He leaned down over her, pressed his lips to hers, and slid inside with a quick thrust.

Damn. He was lost. Kalissa sent him places he'd never

dreamed of, the way she captured his heart and commanded him when he was in her. She wrapped her legs around him to take all of him and met every thrust he gave her until they both climaxed and were left a trembling pile of bodies.

~

LYING DOWN BESIDE KALISSA, he pulled her to his chest. "Love you," he whispered in her ear.

She snuggled further into him. "Love you, too." She brought his hand to her lips to place a kiss to his palm.

A few seconds later, his phone rang. He smirked. At least, his cousin had sense enough to call. He answered the phone. "Yeah."

"I...get up to the house ASAP," Zach said in a rush that told Ayden something had happened.

Ayden closed his phone. Kalissa had heard what Zach had said, so Ayden didn't need to explain. They dressed and made sure the hay was out of their hair before heading back to the house.

Ayden and Kalissa entered the foyer of the house. Zach was waiting for them. He looked from Kalissa to Ayden and frowned. "The Riverside Coven has reported some kind of disturbance near Friendship Fountain."

Ayden cursed softly and followed Zach to the living room with Kalissa on his heels. "Zach and I will go check it out," Ayden said.

"Not alone, you're not," Kalissa said with her hands on her hips.

Ayden was about to argue with Kalissa when Mel

spoke up. "I'm coming, too. It is better that we're together. If it's a portal of some kind, then it will need to be closed. Lydia and Khloe can stay here." The last statement was said with a pointed tone that said, "*don't ask*."

Khloe looked like she wanted to argue but looked at Lydia and decided not to. "Lydia and I will stay here for a little longer," she said and then spoke to Lydia. "Let me know when you get tired and we'll go home." Lydia nodded.

Kalissa leaned over the back of the couch and kissed Khloe on the cheek. "We'll be back soon."

Khloe grabbed Kalissa around the neck with her arms. "Please. Be careful."

"We will. Love you." Kalissa pulled out of the embrace and teleported to downtown Jacksonville with the others.

One by one, they materialized several feet from Friendship Fountain, away from human eyes. Although humans knew about witches, they did not know about the Divinities' powers. Many humans associated Divine powers with demons. Other humans liked to pretend that the preternatural didn't exist. That was the main reason Khloe hadn't been allowed back in the public school system to teach dance after her little display years and years ago. Humans thought magical teachers were a bad influence on their children.

"So, what did Khloe do?" Ayden asked, obviously reading her thoughts.

Kalissa looked at him. "What do you mean?"

Ayden smiled. "Sorry. I picked up on your thoughts again."

Zach laughed. "You remember when I told you about the boy who got trapped inside a ring of lightning?"

"That was Khloe? How old was she?"

"Six." Kalissa had to laugh. "Bruce had been picking on both of us for weeks. Then, finally, one day on the playground, he pushed Khloe's last button."

"And she called a storm," Ayden said, shaking his head.

"Accidently. Her emotions can unintentionally set off her gift. If she's sad, it rains on the house. If she's angry, lightning," Kalissa mused.

"She was lucky that Aunt Joelle was the school nurse, or they would have cuffed her until Connie got there," Zach said.

Ayden knew the cuffs Zach was talking about were the same ones Jacen had taken from the demons in Georgia. High school witches that went to public schools had to wear them during school hours. That's why most of them were homeschooled.

"The school told our mother that before she was allowed back in school, Khloe's powers had to be bound. Mama said she'd be damned before she limited her daughter's powers for the human's silly fears." Kalissa smiled. That was her mother—the voice of reason and despair. She was always the first parent at the school to protest against the 'magical guidelines that were beneficial for everyone' types of things. The truth was, it was always more beneficial for the humans. Mom refused to back down and take their prejudiced notions.

If the humans knew the Divinities possessed the powers of the gods, a whole new paranoia would arise.

Witches everywhere would be collected and tested—possibly locked away.

"There it is," Melaina said when they rounded the corner.

Kalissa looked to where she pointed. Next to the fountain, about two feet from the river's edge, was an oval-shaped energy field. Kalissa didn't know how to describe it. It had no color. To the human eye, it wasn't even there, but Kalissa could tell that something was there. She could see the outline of a gateway and waves of magical energy that ran from the outer walls to the center, like ripples in a pool of water.

She reached out with her senses to see who had opened the portal and who, or *what*, had come out of it. The vision slammed into her, and she fought a gasp as images raced through her mind. After the images had slowed down, she was able to focus on the scene. The portal had been opened from the inside, or maybe from a distance. Kalissa couldn't tell. A few moments after the portal had opened, two demons came out. They were human-like, with short, dark hair and dark eyes. But they weren't human. Maybe whatever made her a Divinity also allowed her to tell demons from humans and vice versa.

It'd been a long time since she'd had a vision so clear, and never had one hit her so hard. Was it the energy from the portal that caused the spike in her powers, or the bond with Ayden? Another possibility was that the memory spell no longer dampened her visions.

The first person she saw when her sight pulled back was Ayden. She smiled at him and had to fight the urge to go to him, kiss him, and wrap herself around him. It was a hard battle, but she managed. Life without him would be so…empty, lonely. She loved him, and wanted to spend the rest of her very long existence with him.

Shelving her need for him for later, she cleared her head before speaking. "The portal hasn't been open for long. The disturbance the witches felt was probably the portal opening. There were two demons that came out about an hour ago." She described the demons to the group.

Melaina cursed. "Sounds like Etchens."

"What are they?" the others said at the same time.

"They're Amiddian demons. They aren't high enough in power to be Khan's personal army, but not low enough to be servants, either. However, Khan's guards, like Demetrius, won't think twice about using them for their own benefit." Melaina paused for a brief moment before she continued like she was trying to remember something. "Etchen appear human. The only way to tell them from humans is by their aura. Their auras, like most demons', are darker than humans' auras. But some have been known to adapt another's aura by taking the human's essence as their own. They are dangerous because they can enter a human's mind and implant a thought that will grow like a virus."

Kalissa bet the thoughts weren't of flowers and puppies. It would be more like death and destruction. "They can take human essences, like vampires?"

"Not exactly. They don't have to bite mortals, but they will if necessary. They prefer sex, or in some cases, a kiss," Melaina answered.

Khloe shivered at the thought and asked, "So, Khan

released a couple of Etchen to plant thoughts in the humans to destroy each other?"

Melaina nodded. "The virus will grow rapidly and spread from person to person. Humans will turn against each other and destroy a city within days. They could move on to other cities and start a chain reaction around the world."

That's just awful, Kalissa thought.

"Kalissa and I will close the portal while you go hunt down those demons," Mel said to the men, who nodded and set out in search of the Etchens.

Kalissa turned back to look at the portal just as two Lackeys came out. They spotted her and started to run. "Oh, no you don't!"

She threw her hands out to blast them with an energy bolt. Instead of knocking them to the ground as she'd planned, the energy blast made them explode into black dust. "What the…."

Mel laughed out loud. "Ayden has amped you up. You'll have to learn to control the extra strength. Let's close the portal and go find the guys."

CHAPTER TWENTY-FIVE

A cross the river from Friendship Fountain was the downtown nightlife. The Landing had a courtyard with an open stage for live bands, and restaurants with outdoor seating on both the ground floor and the second level. Loud music blasted out of the speakers from the stage. Several groups of people were in the middle of the courtyard, dancing, laughing, and having a few too many alcoholic drinks—completely unaware of the danger that walked the streets.

If the demons wanted to infect a large group of humans, The Landing was the place to do it.

"You see anything?" Ayden asked as they walked along the Riverwalk.

Zach shook his head. "But there is definitely demonic activity around."

Yeah, Ayden had picked up on that, too. "Wanna split up?"

"Okay, but don't go too far," Zach said, leaving to walk around the courtyard.

Ayden felt a pleasantly familiar presence behind him. He turned to find Kalissa standing there. He encircled her waist, pulled her to him, and claimed her mouth as if it'd been days since he'd seen her last. She melted into his kiss and wrapped her arms around his neck.

"Incoming." Zach's voice invaded Ayden's mind. That was another ability Zach seemed to have, communicating telepathically with his siblings and the Divinities. Although he claimed not to be able to read thoughts, Ayden had his suspicions. He looked up to find Zach across the courtyard, motioning with his thumb to the right. Ayden moved his lips to Kalissa's ear and whispered, "There are two demons to our right."

Kalissa looked to the right. "That's them. We need to lure them away from the humans." They were the same ones from her vision. She gave Ayden a quick kiss on the lips before pulling free from his arms and signaling Melaina to follow her.

Kalissa and Melaina masked their magic and walked past the Etchens, giggling and stumbling like a couple of drunken humans. They were trying to catch their attention. It worked because the Etchens started following them. Ayden was instantly flooded with fear for the woman he loved. The stubborn female wouldn't take no for an answer.

He and Zach tailed the Etchens as they followed the women to a dark and empty area of the Riverwalk. Kalissa and Mel continued their false drunken steps towards an alley across the street.

The demons looked a little confused until Ayden and Zach entered the alley, blocking their exit. The expressions on their faces were priceless as the light bulbs came on inside their heads, realizing they've been trapped.

The Etchens looked at one another and then at Kalissa and Melaina. Melaina moved closer to Kalissa and whispered, "Don't look in their eyes. That's how they get in and control your thoughts."

Kalissa nodded and shifted her gaze to Ayden, standing behind the demons. Ayden gave her a tender smile that reached his eyes before he snapped his attention to the Etchens. He had obviously caught something she hadn't.

She gasped as one of the Etchens took hold of her mind. Apparently, Mel had been wrong about looking into their eyes. Voices and images flooded her mind. Images of her parents' dead bodies flashed. *They did nothing to help*, the voice snarled in her mind. Shaking her head, she refused to listen.

Kill them before they kill you. It was a different voice. A fragment of another image flashed in her mind. She was taken back to the cave where Ayden thrust a death bolt at Jacen.

"No!" she screamed, knowing it was the Etchens who were sending the false images to her. Trying to get her to turn on the man she loved. Pain hit her temples, causing her to double over. Then the scene played over. Ayden killing Jacen and stalking toward her with his hands raised.

Tears ran down her face. She reached out to Ayden through the bond, trying to find a way out of this hell.

The more she fought the visions, the more intense the

pain got. She fell to her knees with her hands over her temples. Her head felt like it was going to split open. Then, everything fell quiet. The pain and the voices stopped as quickly as they had started.

She took her head out of her hands and looked up from where she knelt on her knees. Ayden had distracted them, and was now under the same attack Kalissa had suffered a few seconds ago. "No!"

Mel grabbed her hand. Kalissa shook her head.

"He'll go insane." Kalissa started to go to Ayden. "The voices...they're horrible."

"Calm yourself or you'll only make thing worse."

She looked into Mel's face. Taking a deep breath, "What can I do?" she pleaded.

"Concentrate. Find the connection to Ayden and then his gift."

Kalissa looked at the Elder with confusion. "I don't know how."

"You are his magical partner. You'll find it."

Kalissa looked back at Ayden, struggling to gain control. She really didn't want those voices in her head again, but she had to help him. Opening up her mind, she searched for Ayden, for the line that bound them together. In the depths of his subconscious, she found it and gripped it tightly. His pain and struggle slammed into her as if it were her own. She vaguely heard Mel tell her to hold on.

"Get...out...of...my head," Ayden said through clenched teeth.

Kalissa used their connection to amplify his ability. He responded by tugging on her magic, drawing it inside himself. The tug made her gasp, and she almost let go.

Together, they pushed back on the Etchens' hold on his mind.

"Now," Ayden gritted out. She pushed with him to force the attack back to the Etchens. Their magic merged and grew. With one last shove, they sent the energy into the demons.

Both demons dropped to their knees and howled in pain. Kalissa glanced to Melaina and shared a knowing look. They raised their hands, and at the same time, shot both demons with an energy bolt. The creatures disappeared into thin air.

Ayden sagged into himself. Zach rushed over and pulled him to his feet, letting him lean on his shoulder.

"See you at the house," Ayden said hoarsely.

"Love you," Kalissa said as Zach and Ayden faded out.

Kalissa paused. There was something in the air.

Melaina noticed Kalissa's hesitation. "What is it?"

"Do you feel that?"

Melaina shook her head. "No. Did you have a vision?"

Kalissa sighed. "No, maybe I'm just being paranoid. I'm wound up, I guess."

"Come on. I know just the herb to calm your nerves."

Kalissa smiled at the thought of Melaina's herbal teas. Curling up next to Ayden with a cup sounded good right now.

She let out a gasp when a figure stepped out of the shadows. It couldn't be... She'd been there when his heart had stopped beating. "Liam?"

Melaina shifted beside her nervously.

Liam smiled brilliantly and walked closer to her. "Hello, Isa. Miss me?"

Shaking her head vigorously, she took a step back. "How...?"

A dark shadow fell over his features. "What neither of us knew was that my father is a demon. My demonic powers were unlocked the day I died."

"Stay away from us," Melaina warned. Liam ignored her and proceeded forward. Melaina tried to blast him, only to have it backfire, knocking her into the wall behind them.

Kalissa wanted to go to her but didn't want to turn her back on Liam. "What do you want?" She glanced back at Melaina and was relieved to see her breathing.

Liam stood a few inches from her. He reached out and stroked her cheek. Kalissa flinched away from his touch. "I have come for what is mine." He grabbed her by the waist and vanished.

AYDEN AND ZACH flashed into the living room. Lydia jumped up off the sofa and came around to stand in front of them. "Are you okay?"

"I'm fine," Ayden said waving off Lydia's concern. Zach helped him sit down on the sofa.

Zach gave them a short version of what happened downtown. "We were able to defeat them." He looked at his cousin and asked, "Do you need anything? Water?"

Ayden shook his head.

Khloe perched herself on the edge of the coffee table in front of them. "Where is Kalissa?"

Ayden frowned. "She and Mel were right behind us." Panic flooded him like a dam breaking. *Kalissa.*

Khloe had sensed his emotions and her bottom lip trembled. She started to shake. Lightning flashed outside. "Oh, gods, something happened."

Ayden leaned forward and cupped her head in his hands. "Try to calm yourself. I'll find her."

A shift in the air had him whirling around. Melaina materialized and staggered back against the sofa, holding her stomach. "Liam…he took her."

CHAPTER TWENTY-SIX

K alissa paced the large master bedroom suite in the house Liam had taken her to. He'd teleported them to the bedroom and left her there. He told her the doors and windows of the house were protected by a spell. She could leave the bedroom, but couldn't leave the house. The bastard had covered his bases.

The first thing she noticed when she arrived, was that she was in his bedroom. *As if...* Then she saw the pictures of her on his dresser mirror. They were recent photos. Shots of her at work, walking to her car after work, going to the police station after her parents' deaths. The most disturbing one of all was the one of her and Ayden at the cabin in Blue Ridge. He'd been stalking her.

Fucking psycho...

The bedroom door opened, and Liam came in with a tray of food. "I thought you might be hungry," he said as he carried the tray to the small table next to the window. He hadn't changed much since she'd last seen him. Though his blond hair was longer, brushing the tops of his shoulders, his blue eyes were darker, making them almost navy blue. Everything else was the same, including his ego. *No surprise there.* What did she ever see in him besides a handsome face?

Oh, yeah, she had been under a spell.

She watched him walk over and set down the tray. He turned toward her. She tensed. It was a reflex. She didn't want him touching her. He'd lied to her. Put her under a memory spell. Now, he'd kidnapped her and taken her from her family and her true love.

He reached out to touch her face. She blocked his hand with hers and pushed it away. He laughed and reached for her again. She wasn't fast enough to block him the second time, and he grabbed a handful of her hair, jerking her against his body.

"You will not deny me." His breath was warm against her skin. She tried to pull away, but he had a tight grip on her hair at the roots so she couldn't move. This wasn't the same Liam. He was more aggressive and very angry.

He released his grip on her and gently ran his fingers through her hair. "Why do you make me angry? Do you think I want to hurt you? I love you, Isa, and it kills me to use force, but I will if I have to."

That was another thing she'd grown out of—the nick-name, Isa. The sound of it made her skin crawl. "Then why didn't you stay dead?" Kalissa spat the words at him.

He backhanded her hard enough that she fell back on the bed. Picking up the tray of food, he flung it across the bedroom, sending it crashing into the wall and sliding to the floor. Stalking over to her, he yanked her up by her forearm. He opened his mouth and then closed it. A look passed across his face but was gone instantly. She was sure it was regret.

He pushed her away, letting her drop back on the bed, and stormed out of the room.

Raising a hand to the right side of her face, she felt the warm, rising lump forming. She was utterly shocked. He'd never hit her before.

Oh, gods, I wanna go home.

AYDEN PACED his grandfather's study like a caged tiger. He couldn't think. Kalissa was being held by a demon. But Liam wasn't just any demon. He was more powerful than a Regal, the class of demons that were known as the meanest and cruelest of the Underworld. Mel had said she'd never felt a demon that powerful before.

"Explain to me how a human dies and becomes a demon." Ayden looked over at Noah, who was looking through some old books.

"It doesn't work that way. For a human to turn into a demon, he or she would have to have demon DNA. Liam was half demon, and for some reason, he didn't change over until his death. Usually, when a hybrid demon child is born, they go through the change within the first five years. They grow at a rapid rate, and many are fully grown by the time they are ten. Some, even younger. For some reason, I don't know why, Liam grew at a human growth rate. He must have been about to go through his change when he died." Noah continued to flip through the book in front of him. After a few more turns of the page, he said, "Ah! Here it is. Paul Loomis."

Zach looked up from his laptop. "That was the junior high football coach...and Liam's father." Zach frowned. He got up from his seat at the small, round table next to the bar and walked over to Noah to look over his shoulder. Noah was sitting in his recliner next to the sofa where Khloe was sitting.

Ayden moved to stand behind Noah's other shoulder. The book Noah was looking through was a binder with photo album sleeves. The sleeves held old newspaper clippings.

"'Jr. High Coach makes it big,'" Noah read the headline out loud. "It says here that 'the small town junior high coach traded in his football and tennis shoes for a suit and tie.' The article goes on to say that Paul was looking for a change after his son's and wife's deaths. He went to work for a large medical distribution company that moved into town." Noah looked up and shook his head. "Now how does a football coach become the director of shipping and receiving for one of the largest medical distribution companies in the U.S.?"

"You know the owner," Ayden said. 'Knowing someone' was how he'd gotten the position of sheriff. He knew Zach and most of the townspeople.

"Exactly. And who is the owner?" Everyone looked at Noah, waiting. He rolled his eyes. "Hector D. Grayson."

Ayden and Zach cursed at the same time. It was Zach who spoke. "I never made the connection before."

Demetrius was using his father's name. Ayden bet there was a lot more going on then distributing medical supplies. "I don't think Kalissa knew," Ayden said sadly. Gods, he missed her. The time apart from her was too much for him. He had to do something to bring her home. Once he had her home, he was never going to be apart from her again. "Is there an address? Maybe if we go to Paul's house, we'll find out where his son lives."

"I'll do a search. There has to be an address some-where," Khloe said softly. It was the first time she'd spoken since arriving. She'd been quietly sitting on the sofa, sipping tea and watching them. "I picked up a few things from my mother."

"Come on, then," Zach said as he went back to his laptop. Khloe got up to follow him to the table. Zach let Khloe take the driver's seat in front of the computer.

Ayden looked down at the binder his grandfather was still flipping through. Now he knew why Noah saved all that stuff. You never knew when it would come in handy. "Is there anything in there about Liam's mother's death?"

Noah nodded but stayed silent until he came to a page that held two articles. He turned the book so Ayden could read the articles. The first one was about the alleged suicide of Barbra Loomis. There was nothing out of the ordinary about the article. She had taken the death of her son very hard and had taken her own life. The second article was about Paul's new executive position at Grayson Distributions and the brand new, expensive mansion he built on the north side of Jacksonville a few weeks before his wife's suicide.

Ayden walked to Zach and Khloe at the table. Khloe tore off a Post-It note she had written on and handed it to

Ayden. "That's the address to Paul's home, or at least one that he owns," she said.

"I'm going to check out this address." Ayden held up the Post-It note.

Khloe stood up and followed. Ayden was about to say something, but Khloe held her hand up. "She's my sister. You're not shutting me out on this one. Plus, I owe the bastard a few lightning bolts up the ass."

"Wait! You can't go in there half-cocked. What if she's not there? We would spend valuable time following an empty lead or worse, a trap," Zach said with his cop hat on tight.

Ayden dropped his shoulders. "You're right. I'm not thinking straight."

"I know, cuz. There is a small coven not far from there. I can ask for someone to check it out, do some snooping," Zach said and then directed Khloe to bring up the online *magickin* social network he'd set up a couple of days ago.

"Hey, this is pretty cool," Khloe said, browsing the site. There was a chat room, and each coven had their own page with lists of residents with contact information, blogs, and news postings. Khloe was surprised by the number of active users. "What did you do to get this many covens to participate?"

"Papa has the contacts for all the U.S. Elders. I set the site up, tested it with our coven first, then emailed the site address and scope to each Elder. I also asked for it to be passed to any coven I missed, including the international ones," Zach said with a proud-of-himself grin on his face.

Khloe laughed. "It seems to have taken off."

Zach turned the computer so he could send the

Oceanway Coven a message. "You can set up your own profile and play with it later," he said.

"Can you set me up as an admin? I can help you monitor messages and emails."

Zach smiled and nodded. "Sure." He left a message for the Elder, Eleese Sanders, telling her about the situation and advising her to use extreme caution. A few seconds later, she replied, saying that she would help in any way she could and would be back in touch with him if she found out anything.

All Ayden had to do was wait. That was not going to easy.

CHAPTER TWENTY-SEVEN

After hours of Liam trying to get Kalissa to open the bedroom door—after she had sealed it with her own spell—he finally gave up and went downstairs. She didn't trust him to leave her completely alone. Slowly, she went to the door, pressed her ear to it, and listened. Nothing. She reached for the knob and cracked the door just enough to stick her head out.

Good, he wasn't waiting outside the door. But he was in the house somewhere. She could feel him. It wasn't the same way she could feel Ayden. It was the thing that allowed her to identify Liam as a demon. But he didn't feel like a regular demon. He felt more powerful somehow. Then she realized that the feeling of being watched she'd gotten from time to time lately was from him.

Stalker.

She stepped out of the space she had been placed in and listened. Liam was in the room directly below her. She focused on him and saw him at his computer in what looked like a study or a home office. Like the bedroom, the hallway had hardwood floors the color of cherry-stained oak. The flooring continued throughout the upstairs and down the staircase. The stairs were wide enough for three people to walk down side by side. She descended them, running her hand along the top of the railing to her left. The railings on either side were hand-carved, dark, cherry-stained oak that matched the floors.

Once at the base of the stairs, she wasn't sure where to go. She knew better than to try the front door. One, he would know as soon as she opened the door because of the wards he had in place. Two, he'd most likely booby-trapped all entry points of the house. She was, after all, his prisoner. She had already tried to teleport, but there was something in place to keep anyone from teleporting in or out of the house. Or maybe it was just her.

She shot a quick look at the office. The door was closed, much to her relief. She quietly walked to the living room. The first word that popped into her mind was *wow*. The living room was huge, with an oversized fireplace. Every piece of furniture matched. The sofa, loveseat, and armchair with matching ottoman were a creamy beige color. It was a nice contrast to the black marble floor. The coffee table and two end tables were black-stained wood with glass tops. Above the fireplace was a family portrait of Liam and his parents. They looked happy. Yet there was something in the young Liam's eyes. It was the same darkness she'd seen upstairs.

Something brushed against her skin. It was like the cool breeze that would come from opening a freezer door on a hot summer day. Kalissa whirled around. No one was there. She walked in the direction the force had gone, walking out of the living room. In the foyer, she saw a figure go into the kitchen. It was a woman in a white satin nightgown and matching robe. She wasn't completely solid.

Kalissa had never seen a ghost, but knew other witches who had. She'd asked her mother once about ghosts, or spirits. Her mother had told her that it was a blessing to be visited by a ghost. Most of the time, the ghost needed help or was there to deliver a message. Many of them were also sent by deceased family members as spirit guides.

She followed the spirit into the kitchen. The image of a woman hanging from a support beam in the middle of the room sent a spike of fear straight through her. Kalissa ran out of the kitchen and pressed her back to the wall beside the entrance. Her heart had fallen to her stomach and was beating ninety miles a second. *It was just a vision,* she told herself. She recognized the woman. She was the same person Kalissa had grown to love and admire when she'd dated Liam. It was his mother.

With deep breaths, she gathered her courage before pushing off the wall and entering the kitchen. This time, the woman was not hanging in the middle of the room. She was standing near the kitchen nook, looking out the window.

Kalissa slowly approached her. "Barbra?" Kalissa whispered, not wanting Liam to hear her. The woman looked at her, smiled, and nodded. "Are you stuck here?" Kalissa felt silly asking. She'd heard that some ghosts were stuck in this realm for various reasons, while others crossed over to the Afterworld.

Barbra shook her head. "No. I was sent here...for

you." Kalissa frowned, and Barbra let out a soft laugh. "Sorry, not *for* you, to bring you over, but to help you." Barbra held her hand out toward the nook, gesturing for Kalissa to take a seat. Kalissa sat, and Barbra sat across from her. "You saw how I died?" Kalissa nodded. Barbra took a sad breath. "If I knew then what I know now... anyway, what is done is done."

After a long moment of silence, Kalissa asked, "You said you are here to help me?"

"Yes. Connie asked me to come."

"Mom." It came out as a breathy whisper. Kalissa wished she could see her mother one last time. "Why can't she come?"

"Connie has fully crossed over. The time has come for her to join her *magickin* family in the Elysium Fields. I, on the other hand, still have some things that are unfinished." Barbra reached out with her ghostly, transparent hand and covered Kalissa's. Surprisingly, it wasn't cold but room temperature and soothing. "Connie says she's sorry for not protecting you. She said if she'd known about the memory spell, she would have found a way to break it." The ghost paused for a moment. "Your mother loved you and Khloe so deeply. She's happy that you found the Sinew. The demons must never possess the power it holds."

"How do you know about the Sinew?"

"I am a guardian, one of the few chosen souls that are blessed with the knowledge of all things." Barbra gave Kalissa another gentle smile. "My great-grandmother was a witch. I have *magickin* blood. I can also choose where I can cross over once my time comes: Elysium Fields with my *magickin* family or Heaven with my human family."

Kalissa let what she'd just learned sink in for a few minutes. She looked into Barbra's angelic face. A wave of sadness came over her. "You know I have to…"

"Shhh," Barbra interrupted and reached over to place a hand on Kalissa's cheek. "I know. You are at war." Barbra removed her hand and sighed. "My son and husband just happen to be on the wrong side of that war. I wish my Liam could be saved, but he has chosen his path."

"What are you doing in here, Isa?"

Kalissa jumped at Liam's question. She was so focused on Barbra that she hadn't picked up on his presence. She stood up from her seat at the nook to face him. She felt Barbra stand up behind her. "He cannot see or hear me," Barbra whispered in Kalissa's ear. "I have to leave you now." Without another word, Barbra vanished, leaving Kalissa feeling alone.

"Answer the question," Liam said. He was standing at the entrance to the kitchen. Kalissa didn't miss how his eyes flickered to where Barbra had hung herself and then back to her. He didn't like to come into the kitchen, Kalissa assumed.

"I went for a walk," she said, hating the way her voice shook. "And since I can't go outside, I was walking around the house.

"Who were you talking to?" He motioned to the nook.

"Myself. It's something I do when I'm upset," she lied. She couldn't tell him she was talking to his dead mother. It would anger him. Besides, something in Barbra's voice had made Kalissa feel as if she shouldn't tell Liam about his mother.

"Come here." It came out as a demand that made

Kalissa flinch. Liam closed his eyes and took a deep breath. He held out his hand to her and softened his voice a little. "Please." She didn't move. Liam fisted his hands at his sides. "I can come in there and drag you out," he said through clenched teeth.

He had more mood swings than a female tiger in heat.

Kalissa slowly walked toward him. She knew it wasn't a good idea to test the demon's patience, but she didn't want to be anywhere near him. This Liam scared her. He wasn't the young man she'd loved fifteen years ago. She walked a little faster to close the distance between them. She stopped at arm's length from him. "Can I ask you something?" She decided to play nice. Play his game a little to confuse him, make him think she was warming to him. He gave a short nod. "You found her?"

His gaze moved to the middle of the room and back to her face. "I did."

Kalissa knew from the pain in his face that she wasn't getting any more of an explanation than that. She remembered how much he'd loved his mother when Kalissa had dated him. It was hard not to love Barbra. Kalissa looked into Liam's midnight-blue eyes. "I'm sorry." She meant it. She knew what the loss of a mother felt like.

He waved it away. "Not your fault. My father holds that burden." He turned to walk back toward his office.

CHAPTER TWENTY-EIGHT

Khloe sat at the kitchen table, staring off into the darkness of the backyard. Her laptop lay open in front of her, providing one of two light sources in the kitchen. The second were the small, dim lights under the cabinets.

She welcomed the darkness. It fit her mood.

"You should get some sleep," Lydia said, coming into the kitchen.

"I can't sleep," Khloe quietly replied.

"Here." Lydia handed Khloe a cup of tea. "This will help you relax."

"Thanks," Khloe said. She brought the cup to her nose and breathed in deeply. It was chamomile and mint tea with a touch of honey.

She missed her sister. Ayden was in no better shape than she was. Playing this waiting game with the Oceanway Coven was wearing on all of them. She was so on board with Ayden's idea of marching into the Loomis house, full speed ahead. She wasn't stupid, and neither was

Ayden. But they knew Zach was right. They had to wait and pray to the gods that Kalissa came home alive.

Khloe looked across the table at Lydia, and a tidal wave of sadness hit her. Lydia had lost her father, husband, and brother all in a two-year span. And her mother was missing, taken from her like Kalissa had been taken from Khloe. "Have you any leads on where your mother might be?"

Lydia shot her a surprised look but then dropped her shoulders. "Not really."

"We know more now than we did before," Khloe offered.

Lydia looked at her with raised eyebrows. "How is that?"

Khloe took a sip of her tea and sighed as the cool taste of mint hit her tongue. "Well, Noah said that Demetrius owns a distribution company. Wanna bet it's a cover for other activities?"

"Oh," Lydia said, realizing where Khloe was headed. "You plan to hack into the company records?" Lydia grinned at her new friend.

"It wouldn't hurt. Zach and Ayden would want to put them on surveillance, anyway." Khloe smiled. At times, she surprised herself with her intelligence. It would also give her something to do while they waited to hear from Eleese.

"What wouldn't hurt?" Ayden's voice drifted in, followed by his body.

Khloe frowned. Ayden looked terrible. His hair stood on end more than Zach's usually did. It looked like he'd tried to pull it out. Glancing down, she noticed how he rubbed his Divinity marks. "Putting Grayson Distributions on surveillance," she answered.

"Zach's already on it," Ayden responded flatly.

"Since when?" Khloe asked in surprise.

Ayden looked down at her from where he stood, leaning against the island. "This morning."

The phone rang. She jumped up and flew to the phone, but Ayden had it to his ear before she got there. Standing on her tiptoes, she pressed her ear to the back of the phone to listen.

"Hold on," Ayden said into the receiver, pushing her slightly to back up.

She was about to snatch the phone away from him until he pushed the speaker button and held it out for everyone to hear.

"Go ahead," He prompted.

"Wrong address." Zach's voice came out of the speaker.

"What do you mean?" Khloe squeaked with fear.

"Eleese said the house is abandoned. It's up for foreclosure. No one's lived in it for years."

"Are you sure?" Panic started to set in, squeezing her chest. Her eyes filled with tears, blurring her vision.

"I checked it out myself. Ran another check on the address, and it appears the property appraiser's office had a mix-up on their website," Zach gravely stated.

"Well? What's the other address? The one it was mixed up with," she urged. There had to be something, anything.

He released a heavy sigh from the other end of the phone, sounding as tired as she felt. "It was *misplaced*."

Misplaced? Was he kidding? "How in the hell can they

misplace property records?" Anger bubbled up inside her. Lightning cracked in the sky over the house.

Ayden reached out to comfort her. She slapped away his hand. "I don't want comforting. I want my fucking sister!" She turned and ran up to her room.

KALISSA SAT CURLED up on the seat of the bay window in Liam's study. She'd asked if she could have the window opened and was surprised when he allowed it. She felt a little better sitting in front of the open window with the light summer breeze blowing inside, bringing the smells and sounds with it. There were gardenia bushes somewhere in the back yard. She smelled the fragrant flowers on the night air.

"I had forgotten your element is air."

Kalissa looked at Liam when he spoke, startled. She'd been in here with him for hours, and this was the first time he had said anything to her. He was working at his computer, not giving any information regarding what he was working on. She really didn't care, as long as it took his attention away from her.

"Did you hear me?" He was annoyed that she hadn't responded.

Good. "I heard you." She turned to look out into the dark of night. It was well past midnight.

"You should go to bed," Liam said sharply.

"I'll go to bed when I'm ready," she snapped back.

After a few moments, she looked at him and asked,

"How did you get near the cabin without Willow knowing?"

He shot her a dark look and then shrugged. "I've been to the cabin before, remember?"

Yes, she remembered. They'd all gone to the cabin for weeks at a time. She'd invited Liam to come with her when a group of the coven kids went. Now that she thought about it, Willow hadn't cared for the young Liam. She'd said he carried a darkness she didn't recognize.

"Why does your aura feel different? Why didn't you die when your heart stopped beating?" she asked, feeling very brave.

"What's with the questions?" he asked sharply.

Kalissa winced and turned back to look out the window once more. "No reason. Just feeling chatty."

After several moments of silence, Liam answered her questions. "I am half demon. My mother was half witch. My father is a full-blooded Amiddian demon. He gave me a serum that slowed the development of my demon DNA to keep me in my human state longer. He didn't realize that the serum also caused a reaction to my *magickin* half from my mother. We didn't know at the time that she carried witch DNA."

"What kind of reaction?" She had her suspicions, but she wanted to hear him say it.

He looked at her full in the face. She shivered at the shadows behind his eyes. "It mutated my DNA, making my magical side stronger. I am what my father calls a Dark Divine. I am the opposite of a Divinity. You were born a demigod. I'm a demonic witch."

Kalissa had never thought much about the Divinity

gene. She wasn't sure where it came from, but the Elders believed it was a gift from the gods. Maybe they were right. If what Liam said was true, then the Divinities were actual children of the gods like their ancestors claimed. Liam was...their dark counterpart.

"How many more are there like you?" Kalissa asked.

Before he could reply, his phone rang. He answered it, and Kalissa went back to looking out the window. She took the opportunity to make her way upstairs so she could seal the door before going to sleep.

When she reached the entry to the study, Liam said, "Where are you going?"

She stopped, closed her eyes, and answered, "To bed." She walked out of the room and ran up the stairs to Liam's bedroom. Locking and sealing the door to hopefully keep him out, she went snooping. She was looking for anything that would give a clue as to where she was. She wasn't quite sure what she'd do with the information when she found, but she had to do something. She was going stir-crazy. Looking for a way out was a good enough distraction for now.

The closet looked like a good place to start. She opened the door and gasped. It was huge. Big enough to be a nursery. *Don't even go there, Lis.* She shuddered. Peering inside the oversized closet, she frowned at the number of female items in there. He really didn't expect her to wear those clothes, did he?

His clothes were perfectly placed on the left side and hers on the right. It was creepy how he'd moved her in like she belonged there. It made her wonder how long he had been planning this. Since his death and rebirth in college?

That was almost eight years ago. Had he stalked her for eight years?

Twenty minutes later, she had gotten nowhere. Releasing a frustrated sigh, she sat down on the edge of the bed, wondering what to do now. The room was clean, too clean. She wondered if he ever slept in here. *Do demons even sleep?* she asked herself.

She knew for sure she wouldn't get much sleep. Not with *him* in the house.

There was a knock on the door. She jumped slightly and rolled her eyes as she got up and walked over to it. "What do you want?" she demanded through the door.

"Isa, let me in." It came out as a demand, which did nothing but piss her off.

"My name is Kalissa, and you're not coming in," Kalissa snapped back at him.

Liam was quiet for a few seconds before saying, "There are clothes in the closet for you." Another pause. "By the way. Your spell won't keep me out of there." He turned away from the door and walked down the hall toward the stairs.

Nope. She wouldn't sleep tonight.

CHAPTER TWENTY-NINE

Kalissa woke the next morning to the smell of coffee and bacon. For a split second, she thought she was back home with Ayden. That train of thought was quickly diminished the moment she opened her eyes. She was still at Liam's house, sleeping in his bed. Oh, gods.

She sat up, swinging her legs over the edge of the bed. She looked at the door. The spell was still in place. For that she was relieved; he had left her alone. Had he been bluffing about being able to break it?

Standing, she walked to the closet that held her borrowed clothes. There was no way she was taking any of them with her when she left. She wanted nothing that reminded her of Liam.

She opened the closet with a sigh and proceeded to search for something comfortable, yet disposable.

The smell of bacon and coffee hit her nose again, and her stomach let out a roar. She sifted through the clothes until she found a pair of jeans and a t-shirt and then headed for the shower.

The shower wasn't as long as she would have liked. The need for food overrode the need to soak in the hot sprays. She entered the kitchen, expecting to find Liam. Instead, it was empty. There was a mini buffet set up on the breakfast nook. She walked closer to the table. There was only one plate and one cup of coffee. She frowned, not knowing what to think. Yes, he'd fixed her dinner the night before, but she hadn't had the chance to eat after his tantrum. Absently, she lifted her hand to her right upper cheekbone and temple. It didn't hurt, but there was a bruise that—thanks to her incredible healing abilities— was already starting to fade.

She reached over, picked up a slice of bacon, and hesitantly brought it to her lips. She opened her mouth and bit down. The smoky, salty flavor almost made her moan. She should've never skipped out on dinner. Should have asked for something else, but that would have meant she had to apologize for being hit. Not gonna happen.

Their relationship had been aggressive. He had emotionally and mentally attacked her several times, but he'd never struck her. In the end, she would simply say she was sorry for angering him. *Gods, I was so young. And stupid.*

There was a note next to the display of food that she hadn't seen at first when arriving at the table. She narrowed her eyes at it like it would somehow jump up to bite her. Her hand hovered over it for a few hesitant seconds before she picked it up.

The food is not poisoned or spelled. Be back before noon. Stay in the house!

Short and sweet, she thought dryly. He was such an ass.

She ate her breakfast and had two cups of coffee before starting to clean up. She finished with the dishes as a scratch at the sliding glass drew her attention. Kalissa dried her hands and moved to the door. There was a yellow tabby cat sitting on the patio outside. When it saw Kalissa, it gave a soundless meow.

Without thinking, she opened the door. The cat darted off into the middle of the yard. Kalissa stepped out onto the patio, coaxing the cat to her. The cat sat down in the grass about ten feet from her and cocked its head to the side as if studying her. Kalissa slowly walked toward the cat. Before she stepped off the patio, Liam materialized in front of her.

"What are you doing?" he asked in a demanding voice.

Kalissa took a step back from him. "Testing security?" she asked in a smart-assed tone. Ayden would have smiled at her. Not Liam. He wasn't amused, so she explained. "There's a kitty." She pointed to the cat still sitting in the grass. "She looks lost and hungry."

Liam slowly turned his head to look at the cat and then looked back to Kalissa. "I told you to stay in the house."

Kalissa glared at him and crossed her arms over her breasts. She didn't like his tone. "I'm not staying cooped up in that house." She was proud of her firm resolve.

With inhuman speed, he tightly gripped her arm and pulled her back into the house, closing the door behind them with his will.

Her heart was pounding so hard it sounded like a drum inside her head as he dragged her to the office and shoved her toward the sofa. Stumbling, she fought to keep her balance and turned to look at him. His eyes were black as coal, and angry lines creased his forehead. She could almost see steam coming out of his ears.

"Why do you do it?" His tone was laced with venom that told her to shut the fuck up. "I can't go into work. I told you the windows and doors were spelled."

"I forgot," she breathed out in barely a whisper, hating her weakness. His anger pushed his power out to her in warning. Dominance rolled off him, shoving her toward submission. She tried to push back, but her magic didn't work with him. He was blocking her somehow. Like a force field that kept her from firing back. Protecting him.

As Liam stalked to her, she felt like prey about to be swallowed by the big bad wolf. Mere inches from her, he reached out. She flinched as his fingers brushed her cheek, just under where he'd hit her last night.

His power receded, and he turned to his desk. She exhaled a breath of relief and sat down on the sofa, studying him and plotting how the hell she was going to get out of there.

A KNOCK on the door brought her out of a light sleep. She watched Liam get up and walk out of the study. Standing, she followed him. There was a saying about curiosity killing the cat. Well, she couldn't help herself. It may kill her *not* to know who was on the porch.

Stopping about halfway into the foyer, she stood silently as he dropped the shields around the house and opened the door. "What the fuck do you want?" he growled at the female demon standing on the other side of the threshold.

The demoness smiled, unfazed by his rudeness. "It is wonderful to see you too, Liam." She pushed her way through the door and stopped cold when she saw Kalissa.

Kalissa instantly disliked her. The look the demoness shot back to her said the feeling was mutual. Kalissa paid no attention to the new demon as she turned around and went back to the study.

The two demons came in moments later. Liam looked annoyed as he sat behind the desk. The female hopped up on the wooden surface with an amused gaze trained on Kalissa.

After a brief moment, Kalissa asked, "Are you going to introduce me to your friend?" She could almost see smoke coming out of his ears. He didn't like the fact that she'd referred to the demoness as his friend. Interesting.

"She's leaving." He gave the female a pointed look.

The demoness just waved it off and hopped off the desk, stalking over to Kalissa with her hand outstretched in greeting. "I'm Samoan," she said sweetly.

Kalissa didn't take her hand. Instead, she looked at her straight on and noticed that Samoan was not a full demon. She was half elf. Her black and blue hair was pulled back into a ponytail, revealing her slightly pointed ears. Her beautiful, child-like face looked like it belonged on a pixie. There was no doubt in Kalissa's mind that Samoan used her looks and glamour to lure in her victims. What kind of victims and what Samoan did with them, Kalissa didn't know—nor did she care at the moment. Her concern was

Liam's mood. He was already annoyed about Kalissa going outside. His temperament had darkened further with Samoan's presence.

Samoan didn't seem to care as she moved in a little closer to Kalissa. "She's very pretty, Liam," Samoan baited him. Kalissa followed Samoan with her eyes as the she-demon circled around to the back of the sofa. Samoan stopped behind Kalissa, leaned in, and inhaled deeply. "She smells nice."

Kalissa flicked a glance at Liam. His eyes had darkened with anger. "Samoan." It came out as a deep growl. It was a warning. From demonology classes at the coven, Kalissa knew that demons were highly territorial. Samoan was invading Liam's territory. *She* was the territory.

Kalissa flinched when the heat of Samoan's mouth touched her cheek. "You should let me break her for you. I'd do it for free." Kalissa didn't need to see Samoan's face to know there was a smile there.

Then she was gone. Kalissa turned her head. Samoan had been thrown against the wall behind her, leaving a nice indentation of her body. Liam loomed over the other demon like a bull ready to charge. Kalissa stood up to face them. Liam's skin took on a silvery grey appearance. He went full demon. It didn't matter how many she had seen or fought in the past week, fear still sparked inside her.

Liam looked at Kalissa. She took a step back, gasping. Liam's eyes were completely black. "Go upstairs, Isa," he growled.

Kalissa swallowed her heart back down into her chest where it belonged. "Are you...going to kill her?" She wasn't sure why she cared. She didn't like Samoan. The bitch was evil, but she didn't want Liam to kill her. At least, not with Kalissa in the house.

Liam stared at her in silence for several minutes before speaking. "Just do as I asked." It was said in a lower tone as if he were trying to redirect his rage from her. Kalissa darted out of the study. But instead of going upstairs, she went to the door. Reaching out with her hand, she smiled. He didn't replace the spell.

Freedom!

She opened the front door and stepped outside, then waited a few seconds. The sounds of breaking glass indicated that the demons were too preoccupied to notice her. She took off to the heavily wooded area adjacent to the house. If she could make it off his property line and past the wards, she could teleport home. The mere thought of home, of Ayden and Khloe, made her cry out with glee.

CHAPTER THIRTY

Kalissa had been gone for six hours. Ayden was a mess. After Khloe's emotional blowup last night, he'd gone to the station to get some paperwork done, hoping that he could calm some of his anxiety. It didn't work. He hadn't slept at all. The only semi-rest he'd gotten was when he'd dozed off in his chair, searching public and nonpublic records for clues.

"Man, you need some sleep," Zach said, entering Ayden's office.

"Yeah. Easier said than done." Ayden raked his hand through his hair. "Heard anything?"

"Nothing yet," Zach said with a heavy sigh, sitting down in a chair across the desk from Ayden. "I just checked email."

Ayden let out a curse. Eleese had said she would keep looking and let them know if she found out anything. He was grateful for the Elder's help but too tired to express it.

The intercom buzzed on his desk phone. He picked up the receiver. "Yeah."

It was the receptionist. "You have a visitor, Sheriff."

Thank the gods. "Thanks, Amy. Send her in." He hung up the phone before Amy could question how he knew it was a woman. His connection to Kalissa allowed him to use her seer gift. Right then, it was the only thing he clung to.

A few seconds later, Amy brought in a woman who looked to be in her early thirties. Ayden thanked Amy and asked her to shut the door to his office. Zach stood so the woman could sit down and then walked around to lean against the wall behind Ayden. Ayden had a sinking feeling. It couldn't be good that Eleese had shown in person.

Eleese spoke in hushed tones. "I couldn't find the words to write down." She dropped her shoulders. Her sorrow and worry wrapped around Ayden, increasing his own. She laid a piece of paper on the desk in front of him. "She is there." She pointed at the address written on the scrap. "The house is heavily guarded with spells and wards. You won't be able to teleport in."

"How do you know?" Ayden asked, picking up the note.

"I saw her." His head snapped up, eyes meeting hers. Taking a deep breath, she continued. "My Divine gift is shapeshifting. I scrambled the house number of the original address around and searched the properties until I found one with wards."

"I didn't think about that." Damn, what was wrong with him? He was a cop. It was his job to solve crimes.

"Even if you had and went in, you would've alerted the demons. Like I said, the wards around the property are set to keep people out...and in," Eleese pointed out. "I only got close enough in cat form."

"She responded to me as I had hoped, but he showed up, angry that she had opened the door. That's when I noticed that the house was spelled to keep her inside," Eleese added.

Ayden cursed under his breath. *Liam is so going to pay.* "Thank you for your help. If there is anything you need..."

Eleese held up her hand to stop him. "I am behind the Divinities a hundred percent. I want the demons defeated and banned from this realm. You have my support in any way I can give it."

Ayden stood to walk Eleese out. "We appreciate it."

"What will you do now?" Eleese asked before Ayden opened the door.

Ayden looked her in the eyes. "I'm going to bring my magical partner home and complete the bond. No one will ever tear her away from me again."

Eleese smiled widely. "Good."

"Thank you again for your help." Ayden opened the office door, and the three of them walked out to Eleese's car.

After Eleese had driven off, Ayden said, "Let's go get Khloe and pay the demon a visit."

Zach looked over at his cousin. "You getting the same feeling I am?"

Ayden nodded. "There's something not right." Ayden could feel it. He couldn't explain it, but he felt it. Then, there it was. A brief glimpse of a vision. It was so short-lived that it looked like someone had flashed a photograph in front of his face. It didn't make sense to him, but he knew he needed to get to Kalissa soon.

In the vision, two people were surrounded by fire. He couldn't make out whom they were, but his instincts told him to get Kalissa the hell out of that house.

SHE STOPPED RUNNING SO she could catch her breath. "You should really work out more with Lo," she uttered. Her muscles burned, and she wondered how much farther until she was off Liam's land.

The snap of a twig jacked her heart rate up. Darting out of sight behind a fallen tree trunk, she waited, hoping it was just an animal of some kind. A small animal, not the large mean one she was running from.

"I know you're there, Kalissa. I can feel you." Liam's voice filtered through the trees and underbrush.

She gathered strength from the air around her and darted in the opposite direction. Running as fast as her legs could carry her, she prayed she'd make it to the perimeter before he caught her. She grasped on to the hope and need to see her family again.

There! About five yards ahead was the edge; she could see the transparent walls of the wards. She pushed herself forward with victory in sight. When she reached the energy wall, someone grabbed her by the waist and everything around her dissolved.

When clarity reached her again, Liam stood in front of her. They were back in the house, standing in the living room. She wanted to cry, lash out, vent her frustrations, but most of all, she wanted Liam dead.

Never in her life had she ever wished death on anyone. Until now.

"You've left me no choice," he informed her in a calm tone. "Once we are mated, you will not run again." He glided forward.

She took a step back, then another. He moved when she did and continued to walk her backwards until her back was pressed against the wall that separated the kitchen from the living room. He pressed his body against hers, keeping her from escaping. He leaned further in to kiss her. Kalissa turned her head to avoid his lips. "I've missed you," he whispered into her ear. "I should've done this years ago."

"Done what?" Kalissa asked in a whisper. Something told her she wasn't going to like the answer.

"Mate with you."

Yep, she was right. She didn't like it. She pressed her hands flat against his chest and pushed, but she couldn't move him. He pressed into her more and nuzzled her cheek with his. Panic soared through her veins. She couldn't use her magic. She was powerless and helpless against him. "Let me go. You can't make me mate you." The firmness of her tone surprised her and made her proud she hadn't lost her backbone.

He chuckled as he kissed her face down to her neck. "I can, and I will."

A tear escaped her eye and rolled down her cheek as realization settled in. She wished she'd had more time to show Ayden how much she loved him. She wouldn't get the chance now.

Liam pulled out a knife from his back pocket and held it in front of her face. "Through a blood bond, you will forever be mine."

Panic and fear overtook her. She did the only thing she could in that moment. She screamed.

AYDEN JERKED his Jeep into the quarter-mile-long driveway of Paul's oversized mansion. Ayden's anxiety spiked when he turned the corner and got a visual of the house. He could feel Kalissa's panic stronger now that they were at the house.

He pressed hard on the brakes, making the Jeep slide on the gravel driveway in front of the door. He stepped out of the Jeep just as a scream came from inside the house.

Kalissa!

His heart stopped beating as Kalissa screamed for her life. He cursed and ran to the door. Zach and Khloe were right on his heels. He didn't bother with the doorknob. He used his magic to blow the door off its hinges and blast through the wards. The door landed inside the entryway with a loud thud. He reached the middle of the foyer and froze.

Liam had Kalissa pressed against the wall with a knife in his hand. Ayden met Kalissa's red, tear-filled eyes, her gaze holding a mix of fear and relief. He felt Khloe and Zach come up to stand next to him, one on each side. "It's over, Liam. Let her go," Ayden demanded.

Liam looked at them, took a half step away from Kalissa, and smiled. "Look, Isa. It's a family reunion." Liam took Kalissa by the arm and pulled her away from the wall to hold her back against his chest. He held the knife to her throat as he faced Adyen and the others.

"You're outnumbered," Khloe said as she formed a fireball about ten inches in diameter in her palm.

"Think again, witch." A female demon appeared beside Liam with four other demons that formed a semi-circle behind them.

Khloe smiled. "Ayd, I think we officially have a party."

Samoan gave a nod, and the four demons charged at Ayden, Khloe, and Zach. Ayden stepped up to meet the first demon head-on. The demon swung at him, using magic to intensify the blow. Ayden quickly ducked and punched the demon in the stomach, putting a little of his magic behind it. The demon staggered back a few steps, shook it off, and thrust his hands outward, releasing a bolt. The ball of energy hit Ayden's side when he twisted, trying to avoid it.

"You all right?" Zach's voice filtered in through Ayden's mental screams.

Nodding, he hissed out, "You?"

"Can't shield."

Ayden flicked Zach a concerned look. "What do you mean?"

Shaking his head, he ducked, swinging his leg up and out behind him, kicking the demon in the chest. Ayden had always been impressed with his cousin's reflexes. "Something about the spell on the house. It weakens my magic. I can't create energy bolts either."

Ayden looked over at Khloe, who was toying with a demon by flicking small fireballs at him. "Why are you affected and not the rest of us?" he said, looking back at Zach.

Zach moved again, dodging another attack. This time, it was a bolt. Ayden waved his hand, forming a small shield to block it. "Not sure, but you're not at full power either."

"I noticed," he said sorely, noting that his adaptability gift was a lot weaker than normal. He'd actually felt the zap from the bolt. "You think it has something to do with my and Kalissa's bond?"

"That, and your gift." Zach nodded to Khloe. "She seems almost completely unaffected. Could be a twin thing."

"Stay close," he called out to Zach and was glad when the man listened, falling back a little as another demon charged them. When the energy ball flew at them, Ayden smirked and braced himself for the impact.

The magical ball hit him square in the chest. Ayden gasped at the impact and heard Kalissa scream his name. He absorbed the power, and it ran through him with electrifying force, making him fall to his knees—though more for effect than from pain. The power of the blast filled every nook and cranny of his body until it started to build. This was when a normal person, be it human, witch, or demon, would die a horrific death. For Ayden, it was when his power of adaptability intensified the power.

Ayden looked up through the hair that had fallen in front of his face. Zach was engaged in hand-to-hand combat with another demon. Khloe was toying with two others, laughing evilly. He would have to have a talk with Kalissa about her twin later. The woman wasn't quite right.

He reached out to Khloe and Zach. The demons could mind-link to one another, at least the ones in the room could. Ayden used that to link with Khloe and Zach. "*Get down*," he demanded in their minds. They didn't ask why; instead, backed off from their demons just enough. Ayden took the power that had built up inside of him and thrust it out toward the three demons. The power wave hit them with enough force to dissolve them into a pile of dust particles on the floor.

Ayden stood up slowly, staggering a little before regaining his balance. He flicked a glance to Kalissa. She was struggling to get out of Liam's hold. He looked around and noticed that the female demon was gone. "Give it up, Liam," Ayden said, still trying to catch his breath from the energy ball.

Liam glared at them. "Never. She's mine." He whirled around and headed toward the back door with his arms wrapped around Kalissa's waist.

Ayden panicked. He feared he would never see Kalissa again if Liam made it out of the house. He knew from his connection to Kalissa that Liam used most of his strength to keep her from using her magic against him. Liam didn't have the energy to teleport with Kalissa so close to her twin and magical partner. He was trying to get her away from them so he could take her to the gods knew where.

Reacting on instinct, and pulling from his love for her, he conjured a large fireball and winged it into Liam's back. As soon as it hit, Liam released Kalissa. But she didn't come to Ayden right away. Instead, she stood in front of

Liam, grabbed his arms, and intensified the flames to engulf him fully.

"Kalissa, no!" Khloe shouted. But it was too late. Kalissa was already controlling the fire, increasing its temperature and intensity.

"Kalissa," Ayden pleaded. Kalissa looked at him, then back at Liam, and let go. Liam fell in a pile of charred body parts. Kalissa turned to face Ayden and then drifted to the floor.

Ayden crossed the room to Kalissa, gathered her up in his arms, walked out of the house, and climbed into the passenger seat of his Jeep. All he could do was hold her to his chest as tightly as he could without hurting her.

Zach and Khloe came out a few seconds later. Khloe climbed into the backseat while Zach took the wheel, pulled out of the driveway, and headed home.

CHAPTER THIRTY-ONE

Kalissa woke up scared and confused. It took her several moments before she realized where she was. She was sandwiched between two people. She inhaled slowly and relaxed. She opened her eyes and saw a mound of blond curls. Kalissa smiled. She'd thought she would never see her sister again.

Khloe rolled over to face her and smiled. "Hi."

"Hi," Kalissa choked out. Her throat was raw. She lifted her hand to touch Khloe and frowned at the bandages that covered it.

Khloe sat up on the bed, tucked her legs underneath her, and faced Kalissa. "Your hands suffered the worst of it, thank the gods. Your eyes may be sensitive to light for a few more days."

Ayden tightened his arms around her and kissed her on the top of her head. "Promise to never leave again," he whispered.

Kalissa closed her eyes and folded her arms over his around her waist. After a few moments, she took his arm that had their marks and extended hers so that they were side by side. She was so happy to see the double roses on their arms. She brought his palm to her chest. "I don't plan on it."

"I will leave you two alone now," Khloe said and bent down to kiss her sister on the cheek. She got off the bed and left the room, shutting the door behind her.

Kalissa rolled over to bury her head in Ayden's chest. She breathed deeply, taking in his earthy sandalwood scent. "I thought that I would never…"

"Shh. It's okay. You're safe," Ayden whispered and tightened his arms around her. "You do know I'll never let you out of my sight from now on, right?"

Kalissa laughed. "I wouldn't have it any other way." She lifted her head from his chest to look into those baby blue eyes she remembered falling in love with fifteen years ago and had learned to love anew. "I love you."

They lay in each other's arms for several minutes before Kalissa broke the silence. "Ayden?"

"Uh-huh?"

"Let's complete the bond."

Ayden pulled back enough to look in her eyes. "Kalissa, are you asking me to marry you?" he asked with a large smile.

Kalissa returned his smile with a little seduction mixed in. "I guess I am." She climbed farther up his chest to place a kiss to his lips. She made a tiny squeal when he flipped her onto her back and then invaded her mouth with his tongue. He pulled out of the kiss and reached over to the end table beside the bed. Kalissa tried to see what he was doing but had no luck. Ayden had complete control over her, and for the first time in years, she welcomed that possession.

Ayden laid his head on her pillow next to hers. He brought a small box into her line of sight. "I was going to wait for the right time. Try to be romantic and all that. But you beat me to it." He laughed and opened the box. "Yes, Kalissa. I will be your magical partner, eternal lover, and companion for the rest of our existence. I give you my mother's ring as a token of my love."

Kalissa gasped. The ring was the largest purple diamond she'd ever seen—it had to be at least five carats. The band was white gold with a rose vine etched around it to make the diamond look like it grew out of a stem like a fully blossomed violet rose.

She raised her hand, only to frown that her hands were covered with bandages. She shook them in the air. "Take these off." Ayden immediately unwrapped the bandages. When he'd finished, she examined her pink, slightly swollen hands, flipping them from front to back to front again. They were still raw and tender from the burns.

"Lydia said it would take longer to heal burns that severe. I'm afraid you won't be able to wear the ring until they're completely healed." He sat up and moved to get up from the bed. He walked around to Kalissa's side and helped her sit up, tucking her pillows behind her for support. He sat down on the edge of the mattress to face her and picked up a bowl from the end table.

Kalissa noticed it was a cream of some kind. "Wait. Can I hold it…before you put that on my hands?"

Ayden touched her cheek and pressed a kiss to her lips. He picked up the box, took the ring out, and placed it in her palm. Very carefully, she picked up the ring. The skin on her fingers began to tighten from being exposed to the air. She handed the ring back to Ayden. "I love you and accept your mother's ring as a symbol of our union." She leaned forward and kissed him. Out of reflex, she reached up to touch his face and hissed as the pain reminded her of her burned palms.

Ayden gently took her hands and placed them in cream and herb mixture in the bowl. He set the bowl in her lap with her hands inside. "I'm going to go get the salve Mel mixed up and some clean bandages."

Kalissa stared down at her submerged hands. She wouldn't change a thing. No matter how much pain she was in at this moment, she also knew that it could have been a lot worse. She was not bitter for not having Ayden the last fifteen years. They were together now and would be for the rest of their long existences. They had centuries together to make up the lost time.

That last thought brought a smile to her lips.

The bedroom door opened to Lydia peeking around the door. Smiling at Kalissa, she walked into the room and sat down on the edge of the bed. She pulled one of Kalissa's hands out of the bowl and gently dried it with a hand towel she'd brought in with her. "The burns look better today. A few more days and I can speed the healing a little."

Kalissa looked at Lydia and asked, "How long have I been asleep?"

"About three days."

"Three days?" Kalissa asked.

Lydia nodded and took Kalissa's other hand out of the bowl and dried it. "Yes. You were exhausted, and dehydrated. I am guessing you didn't eat, drink, or sleep much in the eighteen hours you were being held."

Kalissa raised her eyebrows. "Do you blame me?"

"No. I would have done the same. Then you used all your magical strength to dispose of Liam. It wiped you out," Lydia finished as Ayden walked back into the room with Khloe and Melaina behind him. Ayden handed Lydia a small container with a thick salve, picked up the bowl of cream, and set it on the end table. "Thanks," Lydia said then went to work coating Kalissa's hands with the salve.

Ayden came around the bed to sit next to Kalissa. Kalissa laid her head on his shoulder.

"I'm going to leave your fingers and thumbs out since the worst is on your palms and the backs of your hands. That way, you can have a little use of your hands." She gave Kalissa a sly smile and gave Ayden a pointed look.

Kalissa could feel her cheeks start to blush.

Khloe spoke up with a question for Ayden. "Have you asked her?"

Ayden chuckled. "She beat me to it."

"That sounds like my sister. Always in charge." Khloe picked up the ring box and dodged Kalissa's foot as it swung out at her. Lydia finished wrapping her hands and moved to sit at the foot of the bed.

"He said the vows first, though." Kalissa pressed her lips to Ayden's and then laid her head on his chest.

"So, when's the binding ritual?" Khloe said with the eagerness of a five-year-old.

"Not sure. I want to wait until my hands are healed enough to wear the ring." Kalissa looked at Lydia.

"Another week, at least. I don't want to rush the growth of new skin cells."

Khloe clapped her hands together. "Great! Let's make it for two weeks from today. I'll take care of the catering. Oh. And I can guarantee no rain."

Ayden went to say something, but Kalissa stopped him. "Don't bother. She's unstoppable now." Ayden wrapped her in his arms and kissed the top of her head. "What about Demetrius?"

Melaina broke her silence from the chair by the window. "He's been quiet. We took care of the Etchens. He didn't have a backup plan. Apparently, Liam was his spy. That's how he was able to stay a step ahead of us. Now, I think he is regrouping and thinking of another strategy. I'm sure we haven't heard the last of him."

"We have to build up our resources."

"Zach has done an awesome job with the network. We call it the Enchanted Engagement. I thought of the name and put it to a vote. It is truly a work of art. Zach and I are admins. I set everyone up with a login. Your temporary passwords should be in your email accounts." Khloe beamed as she bragged about Zach's design.

Lydia stood up and said goodnight. Melaina followed suit. Khloe, on the other hand, was a little more reluctant to leave her sister's room. Kalissa cleared her throat. Khloe looked at her and smiled. "Okay. I can take a hint." Khloe grabbed Kalissa in a tight embrace. "I love you," she whispered in Kalissa's ear.

Kalissa kissed her sister on her cheek. "Love you, too." Khloe released her and left the room.

"She was worried about you."

Kalissa shivered with chills that came from Ayden's husky voice in her ear. "I know."

"So was I." He rolled her to her back and kissed his way down her cheek to her jawline and then down her neck to her breast. "I've missed every inch of you."

"Have you?" she asked. He nodded as he kissed his way down her stomach. "Show me every day for the rest of our lives."

He came back up her body to look in her violet eyes. "Multiple times a day, if needed."

Kalissa cupped his face with her bandaged hands and kissed him deeply, only breaking to say, "I'll love you forever."

Ayden smiled. "And I you."

EPILOGUE

The day had finally come. In just a few hours, Ayden and Kalissa would complete the ritual that would bind them to each other until one or both of them died. Kalissa looked at herself in the full-length mirror for one last check before walking down the aisle. Her elegant, form-fitting, lavender satin dress barely touched the floor and had a slit running up her right leg to mid-thigh. The spaghetti strap top was embroidered with roses in a slightly darker shade of purple than the dress. Her newly cut hair fell two inches below her shoulders and was left to flow loosely around them. There was no makeup, no shoes, no jewelry, and no nail polish on fingers or toes. Everything was left natural. It was the only rule they had for their rituals.

"You are breathtaking as always." Khloe's face came into view in the mirror. She also sported the natural look, and looked completely identical to Kalissa except for her eyes. "Are you ready?" she whispered, her teal eyes glossy.

Kalissa nodded nervously, picking a couple of tissues out of the box to hold in her clammy hands.

A little while later, Noah came in. "If you will let me, I would like to give you away."

Tears threatened to spill over Kalissa's lids, wishing her father could be there. "That would be nice." She gave him a puzzled look before asking, "Aren't you performing the ritual?"

He smiled at her. "Someone else has stepped in to do the honors."

By his tone, and the look in his eyes, she knew better than ask who. Noah was the most secretive man she knew. There was no getting any information out of him. She took a deep breath. "I'm ready." She looped her arm in his and let him lead her to the backyard.

The area had been converted into a wedding scene fit for a fantasy. The guest's seats were arranged in a half circle in front of the altar. This wedding was different because it was the union between two Divinities. The other Divinities took their places along the edge of the circle at the four points of direction: North, East, South, and West.

Glass globes strung along the pathway from the house to the circle held fireflies and glowed a soft, pale lavender with the aid of pixie dust. A bonfire in the middle of the circle blazed with radiant orange and blue behind the altar. Ayden stood next to an unfamiliar woman with power emanating from her. Kalissa possessed a strong urge to bow to her. Was it really her? She tightened her grip on Noah's arm. "Is that…?"

He nodded. "It is. Hecate. She insisted on performing

the ritual. She is of higher power. Who am I to argue?" he said with a grin.

Kalissa was more nervous now than before. She had never met the goddess before. She had only heard about her from her mother. She fixed her eyes on Ayden as she walked across the yard toward the circle. He gave her a smile that made her want to run to him. When they reached the inside of the circle, Noah placed Kalissa's hands in Ayden's and kissed her on the forehead. It was something her father would have done if he had been there to give her away. Noah walked around to stand on Hecate's right.

Hecate turned to Noah. "Where is your other grandson?" Her tone was soothing but firm.

Before Noah could answer, Zach came across the yard, buttoning his white dress shirt. "So sorry, Goddess. There was a shooting in Jacksonville that spilled over to Maxville. The humans just don't have the sense to take a vacation from killing one another." He stopped in front of her and went down on one knee.

Kalissa swore she saw a half smile form on the goddess's lips before she caught herself and forced a straight and firm face. "You may stand and take your place."

Zach stood, sent Kalissa a grin, and took his place on the opposite side of Hecate from Noah.

"We are here on this beautiful night to unite two *magickin* together. But these are not your ordinary witches. Ayden Daniels and Kalissa Bradenton are Divinities. They have pledged their love for one another, and wish to be bound together, body, mind, and spirit." Hecate held her hand out toward Noah. He placed a medium-sized dagger in her palm. She held her other hand out to Zach, who handed her a small ceramic bowl from the altar table behind her. Hecate offered the knife to Kalissa and instructed her to prick her finger on the tip of the blade and let her blood drop into the bowl. Kalissa did what she was told and gave the boline to Ayden, who repeated the act before giving the bowl and dagger to Noah. Noah disappeared behind Hecate.

Hecate took Ayden's and Kalissa's linked hands in hers. "I bind this couple together as magical partners to protect, love, and cherish one another until death parts them."

Kalissa gasped as she felt energy come from Ayden into her, return to Ayden, and then back to her again. Their magic mixed together and wrapped around them both. She felt a tingle on her arm where her marks lay. She looked down, and Ayden's rose was as vivid as hers. The vine grew to coil up and around her arm. Ayden took her left hand and slipped the exquisite purple diamond onto her ring finger. Then he grabbed her by the waist and pulled her into a deep, passionate kiss. They were fully bonded. Her awareness of him was incredible.

She leaned into him, loving the wholeness she felt. He really did complete her in every way.

Lydia carried the bowl back to the center of the circle, diverting Kalissa's attention from Ayden and transferring it to Zach. Taking it, Zach added his blood to the mix and handed it to Hecate.

Hecate pricked her own finger, adding a few drops of her blood. "With my blood and the blood of the Divinities, I bind this group together to protect humanity from the evils of Khan and his followers." She lit the contents of the bowl on fire. The fire flared brightly and then was gone in a puff of smoke. The smoke swirled in the air and around each Divinity, binding them as one.

"The bond is strong. You can merge together as one and become an unbeatable force. Your new mark is your link to me," Hecate said and went to speak to Noah.

Kalissa looked at her arm. Etched on the inside of her wrist was a replica of the Sinew—a multi-colored sphere encased in Hecate's Wheel. She smiled and hugged Ayden tightly. For the first time in her life, she had a mission, and she was going to be sure to do her best to succeed. As she looked around at the rest of the Divinities who now lived with her and Khloe, she knew she wouldn't have to fight this battle alone.

∼

Get updates on releases via Lia's newsletter
https://www.subscribepage.com/authorliadavis

ABOUT LIA DAVIS

USA Today bestselling author Lia Davis spends most of her time writing racy romance and witty women's fiction, the majority of which takes place in fantasy worlds full of magic and mayhem. She prides herself on her ability to craft strong and sassy heroines, emotionally intelligent alpha heroes, and rich, expansive universes that readers want to visit again and again.

She is the mastermind behind the bestselling Ashwood Falls Series and the co-author of the beloved Witching After Forty Series.

She currently resides in Florida where she's working on her very own happily-ever-after with her supportive husband and spends her free time doting on a pack of feisty felines and her loving family.

Find all of Lia's online hangouts here:
https://solo.to/authorliadavis

Check out the official Davis Raynes Merch Etsy Store:
https://www.etsy.com/shop/davisraynesmerch

ALSO BY LIA DAVIS

Paranormal Women's Fiction

Witching After Forty (Co-written with L.A. Boruff)

Fanged After Forty (Co-written with L.A. Boruff)

Shifting Through Midlife (Co-written with L.A. Boruff and Lacey Carter)

Packless in Seattle

Paranormal Romance Series

Shifters of Ashwood Falls

Bears of Blackrock

Dragons of Ares

Gods and Dragons

Dark Scales Division (Co-written with Kerry Adrienne)

Shifting Magick Trilogy

The Divinities

Witches of Rose Lake

Coven's End (Co-written with L.A. Boruff)

Academy's Rise (Co-written with L.A. Boruff)

Wolf Ranch

Singles Titles

First Contact (MM co-written with Kerry Adrienne)

Ghost in the Bottle (co-written with Kerry Adrienne)

Dragon's Web

Royal Enchantment

Marked by Darkness

His Big Bad Wolf (MM)

Their Royal Ash

Tempting the Wolf

Hexed with Sass (part of the Milly Taiden Sassy Ever After World)

Claiming Her Dragons (Part of the Milly Taiden Paranormal Dating Agency)

Rogue Alliance (Part of the Wolves of Chaos Valley Shared World)

Rune of Passing (Part of the Immortal Keepers Shared World)

Contemporaries

Pleasures of the Heart Series

Single Titles

His Guarded Heart (MM)